The List

Other books by
Tymira Mack

The List. Work-It-Out Book

Love and the Affair

Daughters of Integrity Virtue And Spirituality
One Year Keepsake Journal

The List

Tymira Mack

ISBN 978- 0-9769104-4-2

Cover design by Wendy_Graphics (UK)
Cover image by Still AB/Shutterstock.com

Visit Amazon Author Profile: amazon.com/author/tymiramack
Visit Ty's Website: www.tymackmotivates.com

Your reading this book is not by accident; so it's dedicated to you. May it achieve its inspired purpose, for His glory.

⊰ ⊱

If only one person needs to know...

Introspection

Checking it twice. *Are you kidding me? How hard can this freaking be? And why the hell am I even doing this in the first place? What's the point?* I thought as I scribbled indiscriminately through the names in my journal while vigorously rubbing my left temple in tiny circles. The realization that my temple massage was woefully ineffective hit me at about the same time that I realized, *Oh crap, you just swiped off all of your left eyebrow filler. Dang it and there's at least 100 feet of grande expresso crackheads crammed in between this freaking café table and the nearest ladies room mirror.*

Geez Dr. Spock, just focus and get this over with, I told myself as I reluctantly turned my attention back to the open page in my journal. I was so overwhelmed by what had started out as a mindless doodle but quickly morphed into a diagram whose arrows and scribbles resembled a complicated athletic playbook, that I unwittingly reached up and completely smeared the coco-colored, penciled-in filler on my other fiercely shaped eyebrow.

So there I sat, with only a quarter of a brow, completely dumbfounded that it had taken me the better part of an hour to list all the sexual partners of my past. It took so long 'cause I was trying to recall the exact order that each of our paths had crossed. But the frustration of that task soon gave way to my desperate attempt to go back and fill in the last names of ten of the guys on the list. *Damnnnn that's almost a quarter of the list.* Never mind I only knew two of those bastard ten by their nicknames or criminal aliases. *How da hell could you sleep with two somebodies and you ain't even know their government names?*

vii

But I didn't dwell on that too long once I eyeballed the word 'Twin' which stuck out like a dislocated bone in the closet of my throbbing mind. Yep Twin, that's all I could scribble 'cause I was never quite sure which one it was that I hooked up with in the backseat of the car that one night at Haulover Beach. *Humph, all I know is their names rhymed.* And finally, there was the one guy that for the life of me I honestly couldn't remember if I ever even slept with him at all?

Dang forty? Forty? For real? FORTY? Ok home girl you never were good at math, maybe you double or triple counted somebody? I thought as I flipped my pencil over and used the eraser to count the list for the third time.

But how is that even possible? I'm barely 24? I wondered as I created my own word problem:

Q: *If Tammy is 24 years old and she started having sex at age 14 (yup that's right 14) AND she's already hooked up with 40 guys; then, how long did it take her to amass such an extensive list?*

Even though I'm no mathematician, it took me only a few pencil strokes to figure out the answer:

A: *24 years old – 14 years old = 10. Ten, the answer is 10 years!*

I was pretty proud of how quickly I figured out the answer until the reality of that number actually sunk in. *Ooooh that would equate to about one guy every three months...unless you take into account the fact that I had three monogamous relationships during about 2 ½ years of that time.*

I sighed deeply, rolled my neck side-to-side to help relive the mounting tension and then aimlessly fixed my gaze on the LED lights adorning the cafés dark ceiling tiles. *Geeez, forty guys in eight years? That would mean that I had even less time to rack up this freaking list,* I thought as I continued staring upwards desperately hoping the harsh reality I'd just uncovered would somehow disappear into the blackness beyond the ceiling.

It's so wild how life has a way of eventually smacking you in the face. Before walking into the coffee shop, I've never really considered myself to be a 'hoe'; *I mean it's not like I've been out just sleeping around with any and everybody.* But as I gazed back down at my journal, I just couldn't help trying to come up with any possible way to justify that stupid list.

Heck, most of these guys were my 'boyfriend' at some point or another. Right? But before I could answer myself mama's voice popped into the forefront of my mind; her frequent warning ringing so loudly inside my head, my brain actually rattled. *"You change boyfriends more often than you change your drawers."*

I use to think mama's country sayings were old-fashioned and over-dramatic; but by the looks of things, it seems there really was a time in my life when clean underwear and new 'boyfriends' were running neck and neck.

Resigned that it was way too late to put the kitty back in the cage, I began wondering, *well where do I go from here? I know, since I can't remember everybody in exact order, why don't I just categorize them*? I adjusted my journal a few inches to the right and spent the next few minutes reshuffling the names into groups on the backside of the facing page; and, chuckling as I cleverly nicknamed each group. *Let's see there were the thugs, the scrubs, the sort-of loves and the just be-causes.*

After reshuffling the list of names into their respective categories, I was once again astounded. All my life I've characterized myself as having an affinity for bad boys and thugs. You know the type. They sold a little something-something. Or smoked or snorted a little something-something. Or stole a little something-something. Or 'caught a case' for a little something-something. But low and behold, according to the list, there were only five true thugs in the whole bunch.

Ok, maybe in hindsight I now realize that some of those brothers that as a teen I considered to be bad boys were in all actuality scrubs perpetrating like thugs. Scrubs. You know, the 'between brothers.' Between high-school graduation and G.E.D's.

Between jobs. Between cars. Between having their own apartments and living with their mamas. Between baby mammas and child support payments. Between being locked up and being off probation. Between lady luck, bad luck, hard luck or some other sob story. There were nine scrubs in all.

Then there were the sort-of loves. These were the four guys in my past that left a favorable mark in my memories. In their own ways, they each made me feel special, if only for a season. One represented my first true crush who for years kept creeping in and out of my life; the second represented someone who tried to convince me that I was worth far more than the way that I was acting and the friends that I'd chosen to hang around; the third had the most vibrant personality I've ever met and proved to be one of the biggest challenges I'd ever faced; and, the last literally started out as a sick game that I was trying to run on a younger guy, and by the time the script-got flipped I was already emotionally caught up.

Hummm how odd is it that when I look back over my sexual history, the list of names that I associate with love turns out to be the shortest list of all?

And last, but by no means least, were the twenty-two just be-causes. Just because I could. Just because he was fine. Just because I was bored or lonely. Just because he was chocolate and fine. Just because I was a virgin when we dated and I decided to backtrack for just one night. Just because he was sexy and fine. Just because he looked a lot like the finest guy on campus who'd I'd lusted after for over a year. Just because he had a gorgeous smile and was fine. Just because he was a highly acclaimed college football player who might one day go pro. Just because he was slim and tall and fine. Just because he was a challenge. Just because he was fine.

Ah hello, do we see a pattern here? Truth is, although my definition of fine was adjustable at times, considering the fact that I stand almost six feet tall and have silky chocolate skin myself, you can put money on the fact that any Mr. Flexibly Fine that would turn my head would have to have three specific assets, at a minimum. The brotha had to be tall. *Duh!* He needed to be brown-skinned or darker. And, finally he had to have a warm, yet sly, smile.

As I sat reminiscing, I sadly concluded that not a single one of the just because's meant much of anything to me. Truth be told, one or two were simply personal conquests. A couple were just plain old fine; and, more than a couple were fun to hang out with….for just a minute. But for the most part, after our brief liaisons ended, the only real reason that I can come up with for having slept with all those guys is simply just be-DAMN-cause.

I licked my finger to capture the remaining crumbs inside my pastry bag, closed my journal and scooped up my empty coffee cup; pausing briefly to recall my first love. He wasn't what many would consider gorgeous, but he set a standard that was tough for anyone to follow. Although he was more than twice my age, I absolutely loved hanging out with him. We had so much in common and we spent all of our free time together. It seemed as if there was nothing he wouldn't do for me. He loved to spend money on me and often showered me with gifts. And, I could even talk to him about anything.

Undoubtedly my first love was my father. Although I don't believe in the whole "it's my parents' fault that I'm so screwed up thing," I do believe that our parents leave an unforgettable mark on our lives. Unlike many of my girlfriends, I didn't run into the arms of the freaky forty because I was trying desperately to fill the void of an absentee father. Quite the contrary 'cause up until the past couple of years, I didn't really place a high value on any guy. *Humph, the only thing I needed those dudes for was sex 'cause daddy provided me with everything else that I could possibly need.* But boy was I wrong. I had the right facts, but I was worshipping the wrong father.

☙ ❧

Every girl has a story
she must someday be woman enough to tell

Part 0:
Undefiled Underclassman

1

Black Butterfly

Outcast. I remember being about eleven or twelve years old, sitting meekly on the church steps with a group of popular girls waiting for our monthly Youth Group meeting to start one Saturday afternoon. Seemingly out of nowhere, a group of pre-teen boys whizzed by recklessly on their bikes. As they passed by, they began yelling a bunch of hey baby's, pssssst's and other cat calls in our general direction.

Since one of the boys was a member of my church, some of the girls' yelled smart remarks back at him and the rest of the boys as they rode off. Although the girls pretended to be outraged, they also giggled and mumbled to each other about which of the boys were 'rebels', which ones were 'cute' and which ones were 'fine.'

Being a rather chubby, buck-toothed and self-conscious seventh grader, I hadn't really discovered boys yet, but I was interested in finding out what the popular girls considered to be appealing in the opposite sex. At about that same time, the boys circled back around and begun positioning themselves on their bikes in the middle of the roadway in front of the church steps.

As I looked up to see what was causing all the girls to gasp, I stared directly into the cutest young boy's face that I'd ever seen in my life. I was immediately captivated by the round-faced, brown-skinned fellow with the long eyelashes and phenomenal

3

smile sitting on the bike directly in front of me. I just couldn't take my seventh grade eyes off him.

But just as quickly as they had come, cutie pie and the other guys had turned and gone, and I was left trying to make sense of the tingling sensation I was feeling in the pit of my stomach. Somehow I managed to get up enough courage to ask the popular girls the name of that boy who had just made my hands sweat and my tummy tingle.

Mickey? As in Mouse? To me, Mickey's smile lit up heaven and earth. For months after that incident, I would sit on my porch or stare out of my bedroom window, hoping to catch a quick glance of him as he rode by on his bike. Pretty soon though, as happens with most crushes, my interest in him faded and I forgot all about that cute chubby faced young fellow. Well at least for the time being, 'cause that tingly feeling in my stomach had definitely started something.

The remainder of my middle school years were pretty uneventful. Other than being groped occasionally by the hormone-crazed boys that roamed the school hallways, I really didn't get much play because I wasn't a part of the in crowd. But, thanks to my mother's rigid diet of fruit, fruit and more fruit; the dominant tall genes in my family; and, a talented orthodontist, by the end of my eighth grade year, I had shed those extra pounds, grown long legs and was developing a pretty smile.

Yup I'm definitely emerging from my cocoon - How ya'll like me now?

Part 1:
High School Heresy

‖‖ ‖‖ ‖‖

୫୦ ୦୫

There's more to sex than mere skin on skin. Sex is as much spiritual mystery as physical fact. As written in Scripture, "The two become one." Since we want to become spiritually one with the Master, we must not pursue the kind of sex that avoids commitment and intimacy, leaving us more lonely than ever—the kind of sex that can never "become one."
1 Corinthians 6:16-17 MSG

2
Big Pimpin'

Freshmeat, picnic's & chocolate kisses. Even though I'd managed to blossom the summer before ninth grade, I still rolled into high school very green and naive. High school was such new territory for me and I was immediately overwhelmed. I went from being one of the big dawgs on campus in eighth grade to being an insignificant freshman all over again.

At my high school, most of the black juniors and seniors would hang out before school, after-school and during lunch in an area nick-named Neg-ga Square. From the Square, the juniors and seniors took great pride in ruthlessly harassing us underclassmen. As a freshman I lived in constant fear because I just never knew when it would be my turn to be the recipient of their ruthless jokes and evil mind games.

To make matters worse, the Square sat smack dab in the middle of the school campus; between the math building, the business building, the gym, the cafeteria and the school busses. It was simple: if you wanted to get to class on time, you had to pass through the Square.

Although I'd shed the baby fat and was now rather tall and slim, I still had none of the assets that attracted black guys. I had my fair share of boobs; but I had no booty, nada, zippo, none. So I knew that it was only a matter of time before my flat butt would be noticed by the neg-gas in the square.

7

Tymira Mack

My second greatest challenge as a freshman was that many high school classes were a mixture of grade levels; and because I was smart, I often had advanced academic classes with upper classmen. Even worse, I had electives like P.E. with them too.

It was in my mixed grade P.E. class at the beginning of the school year that I first encountered the smoothest Negro on planet earth. He reminded me so much of that sexy swagalicious guy from the music videos that I secretly nickname him Puffy.

In a lot of ways even as a senior in high school this brotha was a Baller. He was extremely confident. His pockets always seemed to be fat. He had a popular car. He was one of the captains of the basketball team. He was tall and almost chocolate; but since he was so smooth it was easy to overlook that tiny flaw. In short he was just big pimping.

Is it any wonder that a lot of the girls in our class were sweating him? And although he was still in high school, his game was so smooth that he was able to make each of us feel like we were the only female in whole freaking gym that he was interested in. Like the consummate player, Puffy worked the crowd and narrowed us down one-by one until he found the perfect victim.

Fortunately, or unfortunately for me, I wasn't giving it up yet, so he opted for a chick who wasn't a rookie in the sex game. She was so darn talkative and flirtatious that I jealously nicknamed her Tweety. *Yeah Tweety, that sounds wayyyy better than all the other names I really wanna call her.* Tweety was new to our school and she'd started hanging out with some of the girls from my extended crew.

I can't lie, it hurt my heart a bit when I found out that she was Puffy's 'chosen one;' but I knew that I wasn't ready to play in the major leagues; not yet anyway. After all, I hadn't even been to first base yet.

CR SO

8

The List.

Even though I wasn't a real big fan of Tweety's, one day I let her talk me into going off campus for a late lunch with her and Puffy and another sexy senior boy. As they were driving us to this secluded looking spot, the guys simply told us that we were going on a picnic. Although I'd been attending that school for over eight years I had no clue there was a lake just behind the wooded area across the street.

Now if my game had been at the All Star MVP level that it reached at the peak of my career, I would have instinctively known from the jump start that these brothers regularly brought young unsuspecting females to this spot for lunch picnics. Thankfully though, even as a freshman, I was savvy enough to quickly figure out that my lunch date was really a wolf in grandmama's clothing. And fortunately he didn't have a very forceful personality, because I managed to get my little-GREEN-riding hood butt out of that situation with my dignity and my virginity still intact.

But as for Puffy and Tweety, well they did their thang. And no sooner than the brother had gotten his fill, it was time out for Tweety 'cause the picnic was over.

Just to show you how smooth and double-dog dirty Puffy was, when we got back to the school campus, he had the nerve to wink at me and whisper into my ear, "baby girl, whenever you're ready, I can help you fatten up that A–."

Well you best believe there were no more big pimpin' picnics for me. No-sir-ee. I ate lunch in the cafeteria for a couple of months after that close call.

☙ ❧

One Monday morning, not too long after my little lunch in the woods incident, there was a big scene going on in the Square. It seems that one of the seniors had thrown a party at his house over the weekend. Although he'd invited mostly juniors and seniors,

9

one of my fellow freshman sisters happened to be at the party because her boyfriend was a senior.

According to the buzz spreading through the Square, during the party homegirl and her boyfriend had gone into a bedroom to get busy, when a group of other guys busted in. Although her boyfriend didn't allow the guys to run a train on her, he couldn't stop them from taking some of her clothes.

So they brought her panties and bra to school, bright and early, and hung them up in the middle of the Square. I didn't realize it at the time, but that one single incident ruined her reputation for the rest of our high school years. And, from that day on she was referred to as a hoe.

Well all-righty-then.

After the panties and bra incident in the Square, I decided that it would be a good idea to only kick it with the freshman and sophomores who were more my own speed. And, I pretty much stuck to this rule until I began to notice a chocolate fellow with gorgeous brown eyes and a fierce jheri-curl. He was soooo cute and he even had braces just like mine.

Even though he was a junior, I was so intrigued by the chocolate that I broke my own rule. Not long afterward, sexy-chocolate soon became the first boy I'd ever kissed. I was super excited 'cause I figured that my first kiss was going to be this really passionate and exciting event like they showed in the movies and described in books; but the truth of the matter is that the darn thing just wasn't that eventful. *Is that all? Where are the fireworks and stuff like in the movies?*

Probably the best part of the whole kiss was being close enough to look into his gorgeous brown eyes and the fact that our braces didn't lock as so many of my girlfriends had warned.

Too bad I'd broken my own rule and got involved with a junior, because as quickly as he came, he had to go. It turns out that Mr. Dreamy Eyes was meeting me after my fourth period lunch to walk me to my honors English class and then going off to spend his fifth period lunch with a girl who'd I'd been friends with since elementary

The List.

school. And, since I'd never had to share my goodies before, I wasn't about to start by sharing my chocolate kisses.

Sorry Dreamy, but I've awakened and you've got to go!

3
Mr. Big

Two tear drops. Ok, so screw the boyfriend thing. Right? Wrong! A couple of weeks after breaking up with Dreamy Eyes I was scheduled to finally get my braces off. I'd left school early that Friday and was planning to meet up with my girlfriend at the basketball game later on to show off my new smile.

Well that night was the first time that Lloyd noticed me. He was a junior and he was on the basketball team, so I kind of knew who he was. Although he was slim and tall and chocolate, I hadn't really paid a lot of attention to him; that is, until he paid attention to me.

Lloyd was one of the first people I saw when I got to the game that night. He must have noticed by my huge smile that I'd gotten my braces off because he stopped to give me a compliment.

Gee, I didn't know he even knew who I was. Well who says flattery gets you nowhere, because that next week Lloyd became my first real boyfriend.

Since he lived in Ft. Lauderdale and I lived in Hollywood and wasn't allowed to date, we really only saw each other at school. We had different schedules and different lunch periods, so when we could, we would steal a kiss between afternoon classes near the lockers behind the Science Building. And that was precisely what we were doing when one of the Deans caught us. The worst

12

part is that the Dean was one of my father's close friends and weekend fishing buddies.

As fate would have it, this was a game night and after sending Lloyd to class, the Dean gave me an ultimatum. "Either you tell your father when you get home, or I'll tell him tonight at the game."

That was just about the longest afternoon of my life; and, even though the Dean had given me an ultimatum, I simply couldn't bring myself to tell my daddy that I got caught kissing in the hallway. Lucky for me the Dean didn't tell my dad either; but, he did warn me that if he ever caught me smooching in the halls again, he would tell everything he knew.

Whew, another close call!

ଔ ଛ

Even after that close call, I kept taking chances. The rule in my house was, you had to be sixteen to have a boyfriend. Therein lay the problem. I really liked the idea of being Lloyd's girlfriend; but I was only thirteen.

So since I was horribly spoiled and accustomed to getting exactly what I wanted, when I wanted it, I figured that having a relationship with Lloyd was no different. *Yep, having Lloyd as my boyfriend is simply gonna have to be an exception to their stupid, old-fashioned rule.*

From that day on, I simply told my parents I was staying after school to watch the basketball games with my girlfriends, when in actuality I was really spending time with Lloyd. That decision marked my first official foray into the world of dating and deception.

ଔ ଛ

On one particular game day, Lloyd had gone to the local burger joint to get something to eat; and, while I waited for him to come back, I went up in the bleachers and sat in front of his best friend and Puffy. At some point during our rather generic conversation, Puffy reached down and pulled me back by the shoulders, resting my body in between his legs. Then he started spitting mad game to me.

"Baby Girl you're cute you know that, with your slim chocolate self?" He whispered smoothly in my ear.

"You know I like 'em slim don't ya baby girl?"

Baby girl this and baby girl that. Yadda, yadda, yadda. That brother was blowing so much hot air up my butt that he had my whole head in a fog.

I was so into Puffy and his lies that I even had the nerve to make myself comfortable all up in between his legs. In fact, I was so caught up in what Puffy was saying, I didn't see Lloyd when he entered into the gym. But no doubt, Lloyd saw me leaning back in Puffy's lap and he quickly called me to come over to him.

"Why you disrespecting me?"

"What?" I asked wondering, *how come he all pissed off?* "How you figure?"

"Cause you up in here sitting all up under Puffy, that's how!"

Maybe it was my youthful naivety, but I just blew him off because in my mind, it wasn't even like that. "Lloyd what you trippin' for? I'm your girl."

Nevertheless, he wasn't having it. "Look, just sit down and shut up."

"Say what?" But, it didn't really matter that I'd tried to mount a weak protest 'cause Lloyd had already begun watching the game with his boys and was basically ignoring me.

Having studied the situation, and being the ultimate player, Puffy waited for the perfect opportunity to motion for me to come back over to him. And, since there was something that was just so alluring and irresistible about Puffy, just like a hypnotized zombie, I took my butt right back over and sat with him.

Immediately, he picked up where he'd left off and continued gassing my head up.

The List.

"Baby girl how you gone just let that nig control you and order you around like you're his property?"

"I' own know?"

"Baby girl that was real rude how you just up and left to go see what Lloyd wanted, right in the middle of our conversation."

"Oh, I'm sorry," I said feeling real guilty that I'd disrespected Puffy.

"Look Baby Girl, don't let him man-handle you. Next time tell that nig two tear drops in a bucket."

"Huh, two what?"

"Just tell him two teardrops in a bucket."

"Huh?" *What in the world is he talking about?*

"It's like this shorty, tell that neg-ga Lloyd, two tear drops in a bucket. Mother F-it!"

Ooooh Puffy just rhymed. He's so smooth, I thought still totally mesmerized by this slick mouthed brother.

I was so smitten with Puffy that I was too green to realize I was being set-up like a 5 gallon bucket in the midst of a pissing contest. Both Lloyd and Puffy had something to prove to each other and I was just an unsuspecting pawn in their game.

So when Lloyd all but ordered me to come and sit with him, I gave him the big dis' and stayed with Puffy to save myself some cool points. About five minutes later I headed out of the gym to go to the concession stand, figuring when I came back inside I'd just go and sit with Lloyd without looking stupid.

But, Lloyd's ego had other plans because before I could get out of the gym and turn the corner to go to the concession stand, I felt a strong hand on my arm pulling me toward the dark pool area behind the gym. For a minute I feared I was about to be mugged or raped. In fact, I think I probably would have preferred for that to have been the case. Instead, with the quickness, Lloyd asked me "why you back up there with Puffy? Didn't I tell you to stay away from that neg-ga?"

Figuring I'd be sassy, I flipped one of Puffy's lines at him, "two tear drops in a bucket Lloyd."

"What?" He said looking at me like I was straight stupid.

15

Tymira Mack

"Yeah neg-ga. Two, tear drops in a bucket. Mother F-it," I clucked while turning to go back into the gym.

Before I could take two solid steps, Lloyd had spun me around, slapped me in my face and was holding me tightly by both arms. "What the F' is wrong with you disrespecting me like that?"

Who do he think he is, Mr. Big Stuff?

As I struggled to regain my composure and respond, I saw Pops, the old janitor that all us student's relentlessly teased. Fortunately for me Pops didn't hold grudges cause that night he came to my rescue, "hey look'a here boy, you betta t'rn that gu'l loose."

With Pops words still looming in the air, Lloyd angrily turned me loose, ordering me to "come on."

Although I didn't dare say a word to him, I'd hoped that Pops could read the sincerity in my eyes. *Ooooh, thank-you Pop's I owe you one and I ain't never gonna tease you no more;* I thought as I followed Lloyd back into the gym.

I spent the rest of the game sitting in-between Lloyd's legs, not daring to even look Puffy's way again for the rest of the night. Somehow in my immature mind, that little physical altercation convinced me that Lloyd really cared for me. And, from that point on, our relationship (or should I say I thought that our relationship) got serious.

ༀ ༄

Since my parents didn't let me date, but my childhood friend's mom did, I had my first real date while spending the night at her house. It was a double date with Lloyd and one of his friends who my girl was seeing. My friend Aayden lived about as far west as you could go in Ft. Lauderdale back in those days. I mean you literally had to pack a lunch to get to her house.

You'd think that I'd remember where I went on my first date. I'm not really all that sure; but I think we went to the drive-in movies at the Swap-Shop that night. What I do remember clearly

The List.

is that by the end of the date, we ended up on the opposite side of town, all the way east on Ft. Lauderdale Beach.

I'm a big girl now. Here I am on a date, walking along the beach at night with my boyfriend. It's so romantic, just like the movies. Right?

Wrong. The breeze off the ocean was cold as heck that night. Lucky for us Lloyd and his friend just happened to have blankets in the trunk of the car.

I don't really remember how it happened that Aayden and her date disappeared down the beach with the blankets; but in the meantime, Lloyd and I warmed each other up in the backseat of the car. Although I was feeling all grown up. And, I really liked Lloyd. And I was really, really enjoying the way that he kissed and rubbed various parts of my body. I still wasn't ready to go ALL the way. Fortunately for me Aayden's date knocked on the foggy car window just in the nick of time.

"Yo man, if we don't leave right now, we'll never make it all the way out west before their midnight curfew."

ଔ ଓ

During the remainder of that year, Lloyd and I had a couple more touchy-feely-kissy events that mostly occurred when we got out of school early for semester exams. Ironically, on a couple of those days, we even caught a ride to Lloyd's friend's house with Puffy.

Before long though, my whole relationship with Lloyd came crashing down around me when I was confronted by an upper class girl in the locker room after P.E. one day. Ms. Thang was a cheerleader and a stank, cocky little witch.

"Hey LITTLE GIRL."

I was looking around to see who she was talking to because I didn't even know the chick.

"Don't you hear me talking to you?"

"Oh? Who me?" I asked pointing to myself while I finished pulling my bra strap onto my shoulder. I was standing there basically stupefied wondering, *what the heck can she possibly want with me?*

"Yeah you," she confirmed as all my friends made a pathway for her to approach me. "You call yourself messing with Lloyd?"

Although I'd heard her clearly, the words just weren't registering in my brain. Besides that, all the oooooo–ing that my so called friends were doing in the background was only adding to my state of utter confusion.

"Yeah 'um I go with Lloyd. Why?"

"Oh you DO? Well check this out LITTLE girl, Lloyd is MY man."

"What! Come again?"

"Yup that's right, Lloyd is my man. Newsflash, you're just his silly little freshman TRICK." She insisted as she got right up in my face.

Ok witch, I don't know who you are, and I don't care if you're a junior, a cheerleader or whatever, but you got 5 seconds to back the F' up off me.

Before I could fix my mouth to get fly with homegirl, she'd rolled her eyes, turned and snapped her neck. "If you know what's good for you LITTLE GIRL, you'll just step the hell off."

With that Oscar winning scene in the can, homegirl made an abrupt departure in grand style, leaving me standing there half naked, humiliated and fuming mad.

I don't know who I was madder at? Lloyd for obviously playing me all this time; myself, for not realizing something like this was going on; or Ms. Rah-Rah for making such a big scene and embarrassing me in the locker room.

Needless to say, once the smoke cleared, later that day I did decide to step the hell off. Not because sister-girl had intimidated me, because once I had a chance to think about that thing, I ain't have no fear in my heart. Instead, I decided to get to stepping because I wasn't trying to play seconds to no-one.

The List.

Thank GOD the school year is almost over, 'cause this piece of freshmeat has truly been seasoned, and I sho-nuff need some time out to marinate!

4
Tricks are for Kids

Bamboozled. Bert was my first. Ironically his smile, his build, even the shape of his head, sort of reminded me of one of those puppet characters of my youth.

Bert's bio read like that of a scrub. He was nineteen or twenty-something (or so he said). He didn't live near me, but everyday he'd leave his mama's house and catch a ride, or the City bus, to our neighborhood. He split his days in between hanging out at his baby's mama's house and hanging out with the fellas on the hill at the entrance to the local community center.

I wasn't allowed to hang out at the community center, so I'd only seen Bert a couple of times. All I knew was that he was a friend of the two guys my best friend and I liked.

ରେ ଔ

My girlfriend just happened to live next door to one of the more popular guys in our neighborhood. And, one sunny afternoon during the summer between my ninth and tenth grade year, Bert and one of his partners that my girl was sweating just happened to drop by to see ole dude next door. On their way out, they stopped and kicked it with us for a minute or two before inviting us down the street to chill out over Black's house.

The List.

I really wasn't down for going to Black's house, 'cause I didn't know him like that; but, my friend liked Black so much that she begged me to go over there with her. In the end, I figured it wouldn't be that big a deal for me to go with her since I wasn't trying to mess with neither Black nor Bert.

CR SO

Black's mama's house was quite clean and they had real nice furniture. At first the whole situation seemed pretty cool.

Here we are, all grown, hanging out with the popular guys in the neighborhood, I remember thinking as we watched a little TV.

"Ya'll want some Private Stock," Bert asked.

"Unn– Unn," we both replied in unison.

Both the guys seemed cool with our decision not to drink beer and didn't push the issue. In fact, they were acting like the perfect gentlemen?

But these guy's game was so much more advanced than ours, 'cause somehow, they managed to make us feel comfortable enough to where they were eventually able to divide and conquer. While my girl pretended to be reluctant as Black ushered her back to his bedroom, I was left making small talk in the family room with Bert.

That particular day I was dressed in a brand new little summer white mini-dress that had a ruffled hemline. And, I remember Bert commenting on how nice I looked.

"Dang slim, you looking real nice in that dress," he grinned as he reached out and smoothed down the ruffled hemline of my dress and felt on my thighs in the process.

"Thank you," I responded timidly as I jerked to move my leg from under his hand.

"What's wrong, you ain't never had a man touch you like that before?" He asked with this sly grin on his face.

"Unh-uh," I admitted getting real nervous.

"It's cool slim let me show you something," he said as he slid my hand onto his lap to feel his excited private parts.

I tried to snatch my hand back, but he held it there. "You know what that is?"

I mumbled "Unn - Uh," 'cause truth be told I'd never seen one of those things before in my life.

"Well come on let me show you," he insisted as he pulled me into a bedroom that had a set of bunk beds and a bunch of football trophies in it.

I was so scared; I had no idea what to do as he touched all over me, lifted my mini-skirt up around my waist, and tried to pull down my panties.

At that point I pushed him away. "Un-Unn," I groaned as I squirmed, desperately trying to get up.

But he reassured me "It's ok;" so I relaxed thinking that I was out of the woods.

But I wasn't.

A lot of what happened next is truly a blur. I was pretty sure a lawyer couldn't have gotten a rape conviction for what went down that day – after all I had voluntarily gone somewhere that I had no business being and I'd gotten more than I bargained for.

I wouldn't exactly say that I was raped.

Raped???? I didn't think so 'cause the term date rape wasn't really popular back then. *But Tricked?* Hell Yeah!

Because even though I was fourteen, I had no idea that you could have sex while your panties were still on!

To make matters worse, when we finally got outside I found out that my friend and Black didn't even do "it" – so she was still a virgin.

Un-freakin-believable. Coming over here was all her idea, but I'm the one who just got played!

5
Call Me Big Papa

Who's ya daddy? I spent the next couple of weeks angry, embarrassed, and scared. Angry when I found out that all the information my girlfriend had told me about sex was from what she'd snuck and read in some of her mother's kinky books; not from actual experience like she'd led me to believe.

Embarrassed because I'd had sex; unintentionally; and, with someone I didn't even love. And, scared that I might run into Bert again, or worse; be pregnant.

After all, if a guy already made one baby, he'll probably make one every time he does it. Right?

Anyway, I managed to avoid Bert for a while. He didn't dare call or come by my house 'cause he knew my parents were strict and they would easily pick up on the fact that he was way too old for me, even if I hadn't figured it out. Plus, I was still mad at my only real friend in the neighborhood. So it was easy for me to keep a low profile.

Aside from the anger, I was also really confused. *Since me and Bert did 'it' don't that technically mean that I kinda have to 'go with' him now? But, how in the world can I 'go-with' someone who I'm scared to see again face-to-face? After all, he's tricked me once, so what else does he have up his slimy sleeves?*

ॐ ☙

Tymira Mack

A couple of days before I was scheduled to go to spend the last two weeks of the summer in New York with my grandma, my friend called and asked if she could come over.

"Hello."

"What-cha doing?" She asked.

"Nothing much, just bored."

"You still sore down there?" She questioned seeming concerned about what'd happened a couple of weeks earlier.

"Nope not anymore," I groaned, hating she'd even brought up the subject.

"I'm bored too," she mumbled, trying to change the subject. "You care if I come over?"

"No I don't care." I thought out loud, 'cause I really missed my friend.

"Ok, I'll be there in five minutes." Click.

Within ten minutes after she'd first called, we were sitting outside on my porch and right back to being best buddies. As fate would have it, while we were sitting outside, Bert and Black rode by on a bicycle and politely invited themselves and their 6-pack of Old English or Private Stock or some other cheap piss-tasting beer inside my house. I felt pretty safe though, because this time we were on my home turf. Besides my grandfather would be coming home from the Senior Center within the hour.

Well who knew an hour would be just enough time for my girlfriend to hook up with Black just so she could keep score with me?

How dumb was that?

During the whole time that she and Black were over there doing their thing, Bert was begging me to have sex with him.

"What's up slim? You gone show a Neg-ga your bedroom or what?"

"Nope!" I said with as much conviction as I could muster.

"Why?" He begged, seemingly crushed.

"Cause," was all I could come up with to say.

The List.

"Cause what?" He pressed me for an answer; obviously looking for any opening he could find to trick me again.

But I wasn't with that program. So after I'd refused him about a dozen times, the Negro actually cried. Yup, he cried a real tear.

"Girl you know I'm in love with you?"

Yeah right, he love me? Even though I definitely wasn't that experienced in the love and romance department, I knew what he'd just said didn't even sound half way right.

"Slim can I please make love to you again? I'own want you running up there to the Big Apple and falling all in love with one of them City Neg-ga's."

"Nope."

"Check it. If you worried 'bout getting pregnant, it's cool, I got you covered."

"Nope."

Although I wasn't falling for all the crap Bert was feeding me, I was totally confused by the tears. On the one hand I thought that maybe his tears showed that he really was in love with me. But on the other hand, I knew it was considered punkish for a dude to cry.

All's I know is 'um just glad I wasn't wearing a mini-skirt; because he wasn't able to trick me into getting none!

ର ଛ

Turned out that Bert was absolutely right about two things; when I came back from New York I wasn't pregnant and I certainly didn't have no love for his simple butt! Instead, I stayed busy by getting my gear and my ride correct for tenth grade.

Even though I was technically only fourteen, my sister had just bought a brand new car, and by default I became the proud new owner of her old Chevy Malibu. We called it Puff the Magic Dragon 'cause when you started it up, it spit out a cloud of smoke and fumes. But gosh darn-it, I was a sophomore and I was riding. No more catching a crowded school bus every day or walking off campus to lunch.

Tymira Mack

Ya girl is da bomb!

During the first half of my sophomore year I really didn't get into dudes all that much. But in order to drive at age fourteen, I had to have a licensed driver in the car with me. So, one of my licensed homeboys from the neighborhood, his cousin, and their bag of Sensi would ride with me and my girl to school every day. And thanks to them, I found a new pastime – WEED! Oh, I didn't make a habit of smoking and driving, I was too scared to do that. Instead, we'd get high in the parking lot before school at least once or twice a week.

After a couple of tokes of the herb, I was usually good to go, just in time for first period. My class had stadium/theatre style seating and luckily my seat was on the top row. Most days I'd just float into class and try to remain inconspicuous until my high wore off. But one of my classmates, a long tall dude nicknamed Chubby, made it his personal mission to tease me every freaking day.

"Hey reefer-head. Got the munchies? Want some chips?"

And if enduring his crap wasn't bad enough, then my teacher, Coach What's His Name, would invariably call me outside, point to the same stinking crack in the sidewalk, and bark, "Williams, walk this line."

"Quit tripping Coach," I'd always whine, "can I please just go inside and sit down?"

Since I was an A student in his class, most days he'd just leave me alone, after making it clear I wasn't fooling him.

Dang, how come they always know when I be high? Maaaan, I put, 'um, I put eye drops, yeah that's it, eye drops – that little watery stuff in that little bottle. Yup, I put that in my eyes.

Hummm, I wonder if they can smell the weed in my hair? Gotta get me some perfume for that. Hummm. Dang look-a-this hole in my shirt. How I, ohhhh that's right, I did burn a hole in my what-cha call it from when that seed popped? Dang, um-ma have to hide this shirt when I get home.

Shoot I forgot. Now what I was fixin'na do? Oh yeah go back inside and sit down. Hummm, maybe reefer does kill brain cells after all?

The List.

After a solid month of being teased and called a reefer-head by Chubby (which at our school was just one step above being a chicken-head) I decided to chill with the weed. And, not long after I started going to class sober, I came to appreciate Chubby's keen sense of humor, especially now that it wasn't directed at me.

By the end of the semester, Chubby and I had gotten to be such good buddies I even gave him a ride home from school after our social studies exam. Remember I told you that Chubby was tall; I forgot to tell you that he was also chocolate. And, well you guessed it, somehow my buddy-ole-pal Chubby and I got busy, just that once.

Afterward, I felt really awkward, because although I liked Chubby as a great friend, I wasn't interested in him as a boyfriend. It's a good thing that at the end of the week school was out for the holidays, because I don't think I could have looked my friend in the face again so soon after having hooked up with him.

 లు ఎం

Somehow or another I ended up spending the first weekend of Christmas break at my God sisters house in Ft. Lauderdale. We were just hanging out, doing our usual gossiping and sitting out on the porch, when her new guy friend called. As it turns out I knew him because he'd graduated from my high school the year before; and he was also one of Puffy's partners.

As fate would have it, Puffy was home from college on winter break and was hanging out with dude when he called my God sister. Well next thing you know, in less than an hour I was once again standing toe-to-toe with Puffy. But this time, ya girl was all grown up and I could hold my own?

Back then, I really use to believe the myth that you could look at young girls' hips and determine whether they were sexually active. So when Puffy took one look at me and whispered "Baby girl, I can tell that someone has been fattening up that A–," I was dumbfounded. After all at that point, I'd only had sex twice in my whole life.

Oh geeeez, if he can tell just by looking at me, does that mean that the rest of the world – including my mama – can tell also?

I'm sure now that Puffy made that comment in an effort to figure out if I was giving it up yet; but back then, the worried look on my face must have given him just the information he needed to kick his game into high gear. And as I later found out, the brother had come prepared with all the stuff he needed to execute his plan.

Just as soon as my God sister's mom left for her date, Puffy swooped out to his car and brought in some weed, some Hennessey and some coke (–a–cola, that is). Eager to show the Don Dadda that I wasn't a little girl anymore, I happily sampled all of his goodies.

A couple of strong drinks; a few tokes of the herb; and, badda-bing it was on. I was Puffy's prey and thanks to the effects of the Hennessey & Coke and the weed, he had me just where he wanted me.

Although I was high and tipsy I can clearly remember thinking, *this time the whole sexual experience is finally going to be different. My first time with Bert was unintentional, and the second time with Chubby was uneventful. But this time with Puffy it's going to be special. After all, we've both liked each other for over a year?*

And boy was I right. After I had sex with Puffy, unlike the other two before him, we were (or should I say I was) in LOVE. And, just about every day during the remainder of the Christmas holiday break, I enjoyed having sex with him and fantasizing about the fact that I had indeed become Puff Daddy's baby girl.

You the man Da-Da!

6
Just Get Here If You Can

You can reach me by... Unfortunately, where there is a badda-bing, there will usually be a badda-boom. One month after the Don Dadda had gone back to school, I began getting tired, sick and achy all over. But, worst of all, I was late.

It soon became apparent to me that I might be pregnant. To top it all off, I hadn't heard from Puffy since he left to go back to college for his spring semester. So I began frantically calling and writing him. But his phone had been disconnected. And, he didn't return my letters.

When Puffy didn't respond to my desperate attempts to contact him, I decided to tell his brother that I was pregnant. Since they were very close, I figured that his brother could get the message through to him for me. But in the meantime, I couldn't hide the situation any longer because one First Sunday morning after fainting at the altar in church during Holy Communion, I had to confess everything to my parents.

That scene turned out to be so ugly that for years I found it very hard to happily commemorate Christ's death and resurrection every month. Instead, First Sunday's reminded me of the death of my relationship with my mother. And, I seriously doubted it could ever be resurrected.

Tymira Mack

All I kept remembering was how my very religious mother ranted and raved.

"You're running around out here like a slut, a 'b–word' and a whore."

"Do you realize that you have embarrassed not only yourself but the family too?"

"What do you think the neighbors and the people up at the church are gonna think?"

"Do your friends know about this? Do they think this is cute?"

"I just can't understand this. I mean, nice girls in my day just didn't do such despicable and nasty things."

She went on and on and on for what felt like hours. Essentially, she left me feeling like I was the scum of the earth.

To make matters worse, she made an appointment for me to see her gynecologist to get a pregnancy test the first thing that next Tuesday morning. Unfortunately, this would be my first ever visit to a gynecologist and no one had prepared me for what to expect. In fact, not only didn't she tell me about what would happen during the doctor's visit; she hadn't even spoken one single word to me since I'd dropped the whole pregnancy bomb on her.

❧ ☙

There I was naked from the waist down, sitting on a cold examination table with a sheet draped over my lap, when in comes this sixty-something-year-old looking white man with this long iron funnel in his hand. Without as much as saying hello, he looked at me with a disapproving frown and proceeded to turn on this bright metal headlight.

Then he nonchalantly told me "lay down, scoot to the end of the table and spread your legs."

Wooooah......buddy! I thought that I would just pee in a cup and then you'd call us in a few days and tell us if the rabbit died, just like they did on the stories. What do you mean lie down and open my legs? Shoot all the lights are still on. Ain't nobody ever seen me naked in the

The List.

light and I sure don't want some Santa Claus looking dude with a spotlight looking at me down there. And by the way, exactly what are you planning to do with that big iron funnel?

Needless to say that was probably one of the most embarrassing and uncomfortable physical examinations I had ever experienced. And after having been (what felt like) physically violated by this old geezer, I had to put my clothes back on and go into his office to hear the results.

There he sat behind his big fancy desk adorned by all his snooty family pictures, college diplomas and medical certificates. And there my mother sat in one of the two chairs directly in front of his desk, with her head hung in embarrassment. But I was told to sit in the chair next to the door, as if I didn't even exist.

In fact, the doctor and my mother proceeded to talk as if I weren't even in the room. I felt like I was having an out of body experience; just sitting on the sidelines kinda watching the whole situation play itself out.

I don't remember a lot of their conversation 'cause I was still mad at the dude for violating me, but I do remember the moment when the nurse came in and handed the old geezer my pregnancy test results.

"Well she's definitely pregnant," the doctor informed my mom, "so now then, what are 'we' (meaning him and her, minus me) going to do about it?"

I'm not sure what happened next, I just remembered my mother crying and mumbling a whole bunch of incoherent sentences that began and ended with "Jesus have mercy."

In an effort to calm my mother down, the doctor began to tell her about our (not my but our) options.

"Well let's see. There's Plan A. She can complete the pregnancy and you" he paused and looked directly at my mom for emphasis "can either raise the baby yourself; OR," he stressed, "you can consider putting it up for adoption."

"Humph, since she's about eight or nine weeks pregnant, she'll be able to finish out the school year in relative 'secrecy,' but the baby would be due in September, so she probably wouldn't be able to start her 11ᵗʰ grade year."

But mama's face pretty much told him that she wasn't real happy about Plan A. So he switched gears and moved on to Plan B, "Of course there's always the big A."

The Big A?

"Abortion." He said nonchalantly just like he was saying applesauce or something.

Oh, abortion? Abortion, what's that?

"You know you can opt to terminate her pregnancy."

Oh, terminate my pregnancy, whatever that means?

"It's a relatively quick and safe procedure these days; but at this stage in her pregnancy, if you choose abortion you don't have very much time to waste," he warned with a sense of urgency in his voice. "Yes-sir-eee, pretty soon abortion won't be a viable option."

The reality of it all seemed to be sinking in as my mother just kind of sat there in a catatonic state of shock. Then she shrugged her shoulders and nodded in my general direction. "Well it's ultimately her decision to make."

Well what do you know? Someone finally wants to include me in all of this.

So acknowledging my existence for the first time since he violated me, Grandpa looked up and asked me sternly "Well young lady, it looks like we've got ourselves a little problem. Now what are we going to do about it?"

I felt so overwhelmed and I remember thinking, *wow, would I really not be able to go back to school next year? How fat will I get? I wonder if it's a boy or a girl? Either way, I bet it will be cute just like me and Puffy. When Puffy graduates from college, maybe me and him and the baby could just live happily ever after? Shoot, why do they want me to make such a BIG decision all by myself? Couldn't it wait a couple of weeks? Surely by then Puffy will have called me and he'd know what 'we' should do about 'our' baby?*

The List.

I was so confused. But sensing the urgency in the doctor's cold stare and the dazed look on my mother's face, I knew I had to say something.

So figuring it was what they all wanted to hear anyway, "I guess I'll have an abortion."

Well you would have thought he'd hit the lotto the way that doctor jumped up all excited and ran to the door to call his nurse.

"Can you please schedule a procedure to have this little lady's little problem taken care of as soon as possible?"

A few minutes later the nurse returned, "Doctor, the usual place only 'takes care of problems' on Wednesdays and Saturdays, so I'm afraid that it's too late to get her an appointment for tomorrow morning."

"Oh don't worry, Saturday won't be too late," the doctor reassured us. "Besides, a Saturday appointment will be better anyway because it would give her enough time to recuperate and return to school on that following Monday."

So my mother and I left the gynecologist's office with an appointment for an abortion on that upcoming Saturday; and, the doctor's assurance that everything was going to be ok now.

Well if that's the case, why does mama still look so sad and why do I feel like my whole world is being turned upside down?

ᘓ ᘔ

On the way home, my mother warned me not to breathe a word of my condition to anyone. "Not to your friends, not to your sister, not your grandma, NOT ANYONE."

Other than that specific warning, my mom didn't say one single word to me for the next four days. When she wasn't at work, she was in her room either crying, praying or having a closed door discussion with my dad.

I know ya'll in there talking about me.

All the while I was desperately hoping that either Puffy would call me – or better yet come home – to help me figure everything out before it was too late. Or, that my daddy would talk my mother out of making me go through with the abortion.

But neither happened. Puffy didn't call and my father told me "I support your mother's and your decision about having the abortion."

My mother's and my decision, my foot! As far as I'm concerned, it was never really my decision to make.

Besides all she's worried about is what the church people are going to think. Yeah getting pregnant is a sin, but having an abortion is specifically breaking one of the Ten Commandments. How hypocritical is that? Mama already thinks that I'm a slut and a whore, now she also wants me to become a murderer?

I hate her!

7

The Chronic

Roll it up. My parents handled the whole pregnancy termination as if it were some super top secret military operation. It seemed like everyone was walking around the house on egg shells for four days. During the whole time, we never openly talked about the issue; it was only discussed once or twice in this sort of secret code.

I guess my parents felt there was less of a chance of running into anyone we knew if we had my little problem taken care of in another city; so my abortion procedure was done at a covert, upscale corporate office looking building somewhere in Miami. But the fancy office building we went to, turned out to be nothing more than a bustling baby killing factory.

Ya'll trying to be all secret. Did ya'll ever once stop to think that if we ran into anyone familiar who even knew what really went on inside this beautifully adorned building, then they must have done business here before themselves?

Anyway, the place was jammed packed with people of all ages and colors. No wonder this place was in a Trump Plaza looking corporate office building because by the looks of the number of people in the waiting room, it sure seemed 'taking care of problems' was a big business.

35

Tymira Mack

One by one we were called up to a desk to fill out some papers and to pay our $200 (which was a lot of money back then). But when the 'taking care of problems' people realized I was only fourteen, my parents had to sign some extra papers.

Afterward, I was ushered from the outer waiting room into the inner waiting room; and, my parents were instructed to leave, go get some breakfast and come back around lunchtime.

Oh great, I haven't been allowed to eat or drink or even brush my freaking teeth since midnight while I wait for some stranger to stick a hanger or something up my privates and yank out my kid; meanwhile you guys get to go to breakfast? Where is the justice in that?

ର ଛ

Once the 'taking care of problems' people got me inside, they closed the door behind me, shoved a hospital gown in my hands, and pointed towards a row of poorly built closets.

Then the nurse lady told me, "go in there and undress completely from the waist down."

"Huh?"

"Take off your jeans and panties and put them in this bag," she replied like I was a retard or something. Then she handed me a brown paper bag with my initials and some secret code number written on it in magic marker.

The fifteen foot walk from the inner waiting room door to the dressing rooms seemed like the longest walk of my life; and I don't remember a time when I'd ever felt so all alone. As I stood in the dressing room mechanically taking off my jeans and my underwear and balling them up in that grocery bag I remember helplessly wondering *where's mama and daddy??? Why hasn't Puffy called yet?* And even, *oh shucks, I'm gonna miss my favorite cartoons.*

I was thinking about everything except the reality that I was all alone and about to have an abortion procedure no one had even bothered to explain to me.

The List.

Luckily, a nurse knocked on my dressing room door and interrupted my thoughts before the fear of the whole situation had a chance to totally overtake me. When I cracked the door open a bit, she reached in and handed me two huge horse pills and a Dixie cup of water.

"What's this for?"

"They're tranquilizers," she advised, sounding like she really wanted to add "stupid" to the end of her statement. But instead she instructed me, "Once you're done come out and have a seat in the inner waiting room."

"Ok." I simply replied as I scooped the pills out of the palm of her hand because I was too afraid to tell her I'd never swallowed a pill before in my life.

After all, mama had always bought me the children's chewables or the liquid medicines. Where are you mama? I cain't swallow these pills. I don't know what to do. I neeeeed you mommy.

I tried so hard to swallow those pills, but I just couldn't seem to get them to go down. Meanwhile the time had come for my problem to be taken care of; but when she couldn't find me in the waiting area, the nurse came looking for me.

Pointing to a row of chairs, "you're supposed to be sitting out there."

"Yes, but you told me to go and sit out there after I'd swallowed those pills. But I couldn't swallow them," I admitted embarrassingly.

I could tell by the way she huffed over to the desk in the corner of the room that she was frustrated with me. "Unbelievable, we've got a schedule to keep, and her *'I can't swallow no pills'* behind is about to throw the whole morning off."

As she scrounged around in the drawers of that ratty looking old desk I could hear her mumbling, "…and I'm not trying to have my lunch cut short two days in a row either." After about a minute of searching, she came up with a pack of stale looking soda crackers and headed back over to my dressing room. "Here, chew these up, put the pills in your mouth, and swallow all of it together at one time."

While I struggled to follow her instructions, she walked off shaking her head. "Her big ole' butt grown enough to get pregnant but she can't even swallow no pills. It's a damn shame."

Lease' I don't kill babies for a living, I thought as I overheard what she'd said about me.

After umpteen tries, I was finally able to swallow one of the pills while chewing the crackers, but I still couldn't swallow the other one. So when the evil old nurse came back for me the second time, I lied and said I'd swallowed both the tranquillizers; when in reality I'd stuffed the second pill down inside the grocery bag along with my pants and my Saturday embroidered underwear.

Since I was only half tranquillized, the details of the remainder of the procedure are somewhat fuzzy. I remember being taken into an examination room, being placed on another cold table and having yet another one of those huge, bright headlights shone directly into my private area. And, I remember hearing the doctor and nurses make rude comments about my age and my ethnicity.

I also remember thinking about how they had it all wrong. *I wasn't poor, or immoral or 'typical' by any means. Just the opposite. I was middle class. I lived in a five bedroom, three bathroom home. I had my own room, my own stereo and TV, and even my own car. I had a 3.5 GPA and I was the Junior Superintendent of my Church's Sunday School. My parents were still together, they were both well educated, and my mother was a Sunday School teacher. And NO, some guy didn't just knock me up. My BOYFRIEND loved me. Only he couldn't be here today because he's away in college bettering himself!*

But before I could tell them all of these wonderful facts about my life, I was cut off by the sound of this awful machine humming in the background.

I remember thinking *wow how cool, my body is vibrating to the exact rhythm of that humming machine.* And then every so often, it would get quiet just before the machine took a quick break to spit.

To spit? I thought to myself as I looked around.

The List.

Machines don't spit. But as I floated around the room checking out the whole scene from above, the machine was indeed spitting this gooey wet stuff into a big jar.

Wow that jar and its gooey contents kind of resemble the jars my biology teacher stores those petrified frogs and rats in to keep them from rotting on the shelf.

And, that's when it dawned on me, *oh my goodness, that gooey wet stuff going into that jar is MY BABY.*

At that point I didn't need that second tranquilizer because I'm sure I blacked out. The next thing I recall is being shaken vigorously by a nurse, and waking up in this recovery room packed with about six other moaning and groaning women lying on army–like cots. I remember being really afraid and asking for my mama. But the nurse told me that I couldn't see my mama or go home until I stayed wide awake for at least thirty minutes.

ଓ ଧ

Thank goodness, my thirty minutes were finally up and I could go home. I was so happy to see my parents, but aside from asking me if I was ok, neither one of them could really look me in my eyes. Other than for my mother warning me again "you had better not tell a soul," it was silent all the way home. And, except for my follow-up gynecologist visit two weeks later, to this very day, my mother and I have never spoken of the incident again.

However, just like the post-traumatic stress syndrome often associated with war, the abortion and recovery room scene replayed itself in my mind over a million times for many, many, many years. And, just like lots of soldiers traumatized by war, I turned to marijuana to numb the pain.

It's all about the CHRONIC baby!

8
Go DJ

Dr. Jared & Mr. Hakeem. After the whole pregnancy incident, my mom kept both me and my car on lock down. This was actually kinda funny to me, 'cause if I really wanted to, I could have had sex anytime and anywhere I pleased. But while she was still stuck on the whole 'slutty whore' thing, she had no clue that sex and boys were truly the last things on my mind.

Rather I spent most of my time wondering why I still hadn't heard from Puffy and basically getting high every day to erase the pain. I used the weed to kill the pain of the realization that Puffy didn't give a fart about me and to dull the memory of that awful abortion and recovery room scene.

My mom would sometimes make passing comments about my eyes always being red, but I think after the whole pregnancy thing, she just couldn't bear the thought that not only was I a fornicator – and by default a murderer – but now I'd become a drug addict too.

Since I'd lost my driving privileges, without a car I could no longer hook my homeboys up with a ride to school; so they stopped hooking me up with weed. Thus, I had to adjust to life back on the school bus and life without weed. At first it seemed like it wouldn't be any fun facing life sober, but I managed to make the best of it. And while walking to the bus stop every day,

The List.

I even ended up making friends with this freshman who was new to our school.

She was slightly handicapped due to an extremely serious car accident; and I'm embarrassed to admit because of her disability, I'd never really paid much attention to her around school before my mom took away the keys to Puff the Magic Dragon. As it turns out she was really cool and we got to be good friends.

We had a lot in common, including the fact that both our moms kept us on a tight leash. So we'd spend our afternoons on her front porch or mine, watching everybody come and go from the community center until it was time for our curfews at dark. Mostly we liked hanging out on her porch since the parking lot of her apartment complex was regularly used as a shortcut to the community center.

Since she'd gone to school in our neighborhood all her life, she knew a whole lot more people around our hood than I did. So as we would sit out on the second floor stoop of the public housing complex where she lived, she would fill me in on the neighborhood gossip about all the people that passed by.

◌ ◌

And then one day it happened. I could hardly believe my eyes. There he was in the flesh. That round-faced, brown-skinned, long eye-lashed, gorgeous smile fellow I hadn't seen since the seventh grade.

As he walked by with some girl, he flashed us a smile and said "hello".

Oh my goodness. I must be dreaming? There was something even more spectacular about his smile than I'd remembered from the past. This time it wasn't just gorgeous, but it was dazzling. And, that's when it dawned on me, the brother had gotten some gold caps.

Ooooh-la-la!

41

Tymira Mack

I guess my friend noticed me drooling as I watched him disappear out of sight.

"You know DJ?" She asked, referring to him by his nickname.

That's not the name I remember. Humph, maybe he's not my Mickey after all?

"No, I don't think so."

"Oh well anyway, his name is Mickey, but everybody just call him by his nickname DJ, cause he's a DJ."

"Oh yeah, for real?" I mumbled as the realization that this was indeed my Mickey began to sink in.

"Yeah. DJ's pretty cool. "

"Oh? Well who's that girl who was with him?"

"She's SUPPOSED to be his girlfriend, but…" she paused for emphasis, "she's basically the neighborhood slut and DJ's probably just going with her cause everybody knows she's giving it up to any and everybody."

Humph, slut. There's that word again. Is that what my mama thought about me when she used that word? That I was giving it up to any and everybody?

ര ഇ

For the next few weeks, I made a point of my girlfriend and me hanging out on her porch, just so I could catch another glimpse of Mickey. Evidentially my girlfriend's mom had been sitting in the living room window listening to all our conversations 'cause one afternoon she came outside and announced "I think um'ma throw an end of the year party."

"For real ma?"

"Yup, for real. Look do me a favor, the next time ya'll see Mickey stop him and tell him I need to talk to him."

Oh my goodness was I hearing her right? Stop Mickey? Indeed!

As fate would have it, later that afternoon while we were still hanging out on the stoop, Mickey and some of his boys walked by. "DJ hold up; my mama wanna speak to you."

42

The List.

So there he was down below, staring up at us on the stoop. I just couldn't take my eyes off him and by his smile it was obvious that he knew I was sweating him.

How romantic. It's like he's my Romeo and I'm his Juliet.

Anyway, back to reality. My friend's mom came out and told him, "DJ, I'm thinking about throwing an end of the year thing-a-ma-jig for my kids and I was wondering if you would do the party."

"Alright, just let me know when."

"OK, well 'um just leave your telephone number and I'll have one of them call you with all the details," she said pointing to me and my friend.

Well I was so busy smiling about the thought of getting to call DJ about anything, that I didn't even hear her as she called me. "Tammy. Tammy!"

"Huh?" I said snapping out of my trance.

"Run in the house and get a pen and a piece of paper off the table so you can write DJ's number down for me."

Shoot, write it down? You best believe I'm gonna memorize that mam-a-jamma!

"All right then DJ, just give the girls your number and we'll call you. Oh yeah you can bring a couple of your buddies and your girlfriend to the party if you want to."

His girlfriend? Ahhhh HELLO? What the heck is she thinking? Don't she know I'm seriously vibing on DJ?

"Alright thanks. I'll probably bring a couple of friends to help me with the equipment," he paused, "but I don't have a girl-friend anymore."

I was so excited about the breakup news I almost pee'd on myself. H*ummm, they broke up huh? Awwww that's too bad!*

Not missing a beat, my friend's mom lit her cigarette and jumped right back into the conversation, "oh well I can't really say I'm sorry to hear that ya'll broke up, 'cause she wasn't really the right kinda girl for you. You know what I mean?"

Tymira Mack

Taking a quick drag off her cigarette, "well any-who I'm sure you'll find some little birdie to take her place. Ain't that right little birdie," she grinned and winked at me as she turned and headed back inside to roost on her favorite easy chair next to the living room window.

DJ had turned at the same time and begun to walk off too. "Alright just call me."

But after how my homegirl's mom had just played me, I was too embarrassed to even look up, let alone say good-bye. And then he was gone.

Seeing DJ, talking to him in the flesh and then fantasizing about the upcoming party was enough to make me hop off the ledge of the stoop and do the happy dance, until I remembered I still had one colossal problem standing in my way. My mama had me on lockdown, and there was no way in hell she trusted me enough to let me go to a party.

"Dang girl, I know you like DJ and all, but why you looking like your mama just died? You'll see him again tomorrow."

"No," I twisted the truth a bit. "It's not DJ, it's just that well, you know my mama's all strict and she ain't going to let me go to no party."

"Hold on, don't worry," my friend encouraged as she ran inside the house.

A couple of minutes later, her mom came out. "Don't worry birdie, I'll call your mama and ask her if you can come to the party. And, I'll let her know that I'll personally be keeping my eyes on you."

"Ooooh, thank-you, thank-you, thank-you," I screamed as I leaped down off the ledge of the balcony and gave her a great big hug.

CR SO

Amazingly my mom agreed to let me go to the party. Maybe she said ok because my friend's mom had personally called and asked her. Or, maybe it was because the party was going to be

The List.

held right across the street from my house and she figured she could still keep an eye on me herself. But, I truly believe the real reason she said ok is because my father pushed her into letting me go, 'cause he knew that in reality there was little anybody could do to stop me from doing 'it' again if I really wanted to.

ଓ ଅ

My friend's mom had conveniently assigned me the task of calling Mickey to provide him with the details of the party. And even though I happily accepted the assignment, it took every ounce of courage I had to dial his number.

This was my first real crush since Puffy had knocked me up and left me to face the music alone; so I distrusted guys and was truly terrified about the thought of getting back into the whole boy – girl dating thing. In fact, I was so afraid that I had my girl dial Mickey up on three-way and initiate the conversation for me.

When he answered the phone, it was as if I could hear his radiant smile come right through the line with every word. Even so, he seemed quite bashful and laidback. He wasn't at all smooth and slick at the mouth like Puff-Puff. There was just something so calm and reassuring about his mild manner that I immediately felt like he was someone who was safe and could be trusted? *Right?*

I made up reasons to call him up a couple of more times before the night of the party; but since he wasn't the talkative type, the conversations never really lasted long. Every single time I hung up with him I always wondered, *is he even interested in me at all?*

ଓ ଅ

Nevertheless, the night of the party couldn't come soon enough; and, when it finally came, I rushed and got dressed early. Yup, I put on my cutest and tightest jean outfit and headed over to the community room in the building next to my girlfriend's house so I could help set up for the party.

Tymira Mack

While I was across the room taping newspaper to the windows and fantasizing about kicking it with Mickey later on that evening, a voice startled me.

"Hey slim, where do they want us to set up?"

As I turned to see who the freak was calling me "hey slim," I saw Mickey bringing in his DJ equipment.

Surely mild-mannered Mickey didn't just call me 'Hey Slim'?

But there was no one else in the room. In that instant I sensed that something about him...his walk...his mannerisms... even his smile... were different. He had a harder edge to him than I'd ever seen before. But when he realized that I was looking at him crazy and trying to figure out this alter ego of his, he broke into that easy-going, intriguing, be-dazzling smile.

Later that night as the party got crunk and he got on the mic, I got another glimpse of Mickey's alter ego. It seems that when he got behind the turntables and the mic – just like Superman in the telephone booth – mild mannered Mickey disappeared and his alter ego Mr. DJ came out. Well at that point I was gone because as my stats would eventually show, I was a big sucker for a sexy brother with a slick mouth. Plus he was kind and polite; he had a job; he had an edgy side to his personality; and he was chocolate, with a pretty smile.

Oh my goodness, it just doesn't get any better than this.
Puff who?

9

Hey Shorty, It's Ya Birthday!

looking for the perfect beat. I spent the summer between my tenth and eleventh grade year romanticizing the relationship that was developing between Mickey and me. Although we didn't get to spend very much time together – he spent his days helping with his step-fathers business and his evenings either working at a local fast-food joint or DJ-ing – it was still better that what I almost had to do; stay inside trying to hide an unintentional pregnancy from the world.

Mickey's passion was music so he usually spent most of his free time with his stinking DJ equipment. Thus, there were lots of afternoons when I would have to settle for sitting in his garage while he fooled around with all that stuff. It really didn't bother me though, because I was hooked on the bass. Besides, watching his alter ego Mr. DJ, really turned me on.

And yup you guessed absolutely right; it didn't take very long before Mickey and I got into this routine of taking short intermissions from his DJ-ing to sneak back to his bedroom. We'd simply sneak back there; turn off the lights; pull down the window shades; undress from the waist down; do our thing; and in a matter of minutes be right back in the garage listening to music.

CR BO

Usually when you sow a seed, you reap a bush. Once I allowed myself to give in to that one temptation – the sex game – it wasn't long before I began to pick up my other bad habits again. The fact that I had turned fifteen, had gotten a job making my own money, and had earned back the right to use Puff the Magic Dragon again probably made matters worse. And if all of that wasn't bad enough, I'd also started hanging out with my friend's cousin – who was ten times slicker and had a zillion times more freedom.

I don't know if it was because I'd started back smoking weed; or because I'd begun hanging with a wilder crew; or because I'd told Mickey about the whole Puffy incident; or because Mickey had already hit the pu-nanny; or because he'd seen that real sexy chocolate guy from the rival neighborhood sneaking out my side door the weekend my mama was out of town; but whatever the reason, Mickey basically called me up one night and told me that "we could just be friends."

Even though my outward response was "well whatever playa," I was truly crushed because I really, really, really liked Mickey.

Unbelievably, my mom noticed I was closed up in my room early on a Friday night and she came in to check on me.

I didn't even know you knew that I still existed, I thought to myself as she entered my room.

Instinctively she knew something was wrong. "What's the matter?"

"Nothing," I lied. *There's no way I'm about to talk to you about NO boy problems!*

But she sat down on my bed, grabbed a pillow, lay my head in her lap, brushed my hair back and encouraged me to tell her what was wrong.

48

The List.

So I confided, "Mickey just called me up and broke up with me." And then out popped the tears. I don't know if the tears were for Mickey or for the fact that my mom had actually seemed as if she cared about my life.

"It's gonna be ok," she reassured as she continued to stroke my hair. "You'll see, hundreds of boys will come and go before you find Mr. Right. So stop being in a rush to kiss so many toads, you've got a long time before you should be worried about finding Prince Charming."

I thought, *Kissing Toads? Prince Charming? This is not the Stone Ages and my life is not a fairy tale? She has no clue what it's like to be a teenager these days.*

But even so, this was probably the first sign of affection I'd gotten from my mom in more than six months, and it couldn't have come at a better time.

Even though I thought she was way out of touch with my reality, that night her tender touch was just what I needed to cope with the loss of Mickey.

If only the whole Puffy incident could have gone down so well.

చ ఐ

There were about three main DJ groups in or around our community and at any given time during the summer, one of them would crank up the music and a block party would jump off. At other times, they would all battle each other in the parking lot of the local community center.

Well it just so happened that two of my new friends were kicking it with guys from a rival DJ group from across town. And, one Friday night not long after Mickey and I broke up, this other group had come to our neighborhood to battle Mickey's DJ group.

Still not appreciating the fact that homeboy had cut me loose so easily with no real explanation, I felt like I had something to prove. And after going to the park and seeing Mr. DJ with another female all up in his face, I was pi-zzzz-sed.

49

Tymira Mack

So when my girls introduced me to this dude with a seriously booming car from the other hood, it was on. And, even though the fellow was a little on the short side for my taste, at least he was chocolate and he had a cute smile. Plus once I peeped his car, as far as I was concerned, his banging ride was enough to compensate for what he lacked in height.

After making a point of flirting with dude all up in Mickey's face for a couple of hours, I exchanged numbers with Shorty and headed home to beat my nine o'clock curfew.

I must admit, I was a bit surprised when Shorty called me before noon the next day. And, since he was a lot more talkative than Mickey, we spent quite a bit of time on the phone together over the remainder of the summer.

ॐ ॐ

Because he was small in stature and had a kid like face, I was stunned when Shorty told me that he had just celebrated his twenty-first birthday. Likewise, I think he was shocked to know that my tall, slim, filled-out, flirty young butt was barely even fifteen years old.

In my youthful naivety I found it appealing to be kicking it with a dude who was twenty-one. For some reason, I felt it signified the fact that my game had been elevated to the next level.

Dang, my rap game is through the roof, I even got this old A– dude sweating me!

It never once dawned on me that in reality there was something seriously wrong with a grown man who spent the bulk of his time on the phone trying to hit on a fifteen year old girl.

That was until the afternoon the brother had the nerve to pull his pimped out ride up in my driveway, get out and ring my doorbell, thinking my peeps was gonna let him come in to see me.

Wrong! My parents took one look at this dude in his jean shorts and combat boots; sporting a pager, a huge gold medallion and a pimped out ride; and, in less than ten seconds my daddy had dismissed him. I was so embarrassed. As soon as he got in his car and turned the corner I paged him 911 to call me back.

"Ohhhh, I'm so shame. I'm sooooo sorry my Daddy dissed you like that."

But much to my surprise, he was cool about it. "Tam, I understand. Chill out. Your Daddy just wants the best for you. Besides, if I had a daughter, I'd probably be the same way."

ʘ ɶ

Later that night when we met up at the secret spot where he always picked me up to ride out with him for a little while, he spent a lot of time talking to me about my behavior and the friends I was hanging out with.

By now he and I had been intimate with each other probably one or two times, because of course that's all I knew to do in a relationship. But he actually spent far more time discouraging my fake, wanna-be hood rat routine, and encouraging me to live up to my full potential; than he did trying to get into my panties.

He also encouraged me to examine the character of the friends I was hanging around. And, he ordered me point blank to stop smoking weed. But what really pissed me off was his insistence that I stop trying to fight the fact that I was "a smart, gifted and talented young lady."

"Look at where you come from Tammy. Look at what your parents have accomplished……Why you trying to just throw away all their hard work? Out here perpetrating like you all hood?"

The whole time he was lecturing me, I was tripping off the fact that he'd pause after every question, waiting for me to answer him like I was his child or something.

Pretty soon it got to the point that every time we were together, Shorty would lecture me on my behavior, or my friends, or my clothes. And finally I started thinking there was something really wrong with the brother. After all, he wasn't all about getting some cooch and he constantly made a point of focusing on the potential that he said he saw in me.

Obviously this brother doesn't know my past, 'cause if he did, he certainly wouldn't use words like potential and privilege. Nope, he'd probably call me a slut and a 'b-word' just like my mama did.

But to my surprise, even when I told him the whole Puffy story, Shorty didn't disappear like Mickey did. Instead, his advice to me was "count it as a life lesson and try not to make the same mistake twice."

Ok are you for real? You're a nice guy. You drive a nice car. And it's been nice to know ya. But you are seriously killing my high. And since I ain't into the soft sensitive type of brotha's, let's just be friends. C-Ya!

That was basically the last time I spent hanging out with Shorty. However, over the next two years, it seemed like his positive comments would haunt me just as often as my mother's negative comments would. Thankfully, some of the things he'd spoken to me eventually sunk in because by the beginning of my junior year, I'd slowly begun to change my friends and was trying to let go of the weed thing.

Thanks Shorty!

10
If Only for One Night?

Stuck on stupid. Even though Mickey and I were no longer going together, we had an undeniable attraction to each other and still hooked up occasionally. That was until his new girlfriend moved in with him.

She moved in? Seriously? Uggghhh, how freakin' scandalous!

Once again, Mickey had managed to leave me utterly dumbfounded. I couldn't, for the life of me, figure out how his mama would let some girl live with him while he was still a senior in high school? So after that complete shocker, I decided it was time to re-group and change up my game.

Since it seemed like 95% of the girls in my neighborhood hated me, even though the majority of them didn't even know me, I decided to stop hanging out in my hood and I started kicking it in Ft. Lauderdale a whole lot more.

By this time, I'd cut back on the weed and I wasn't dating anyone in specific. I'd also started back hanging out with Aayden and some of her clique. You see, back in the tenth grade, Aayden and I had gone our separate ways. She had become a cheerleader and had begun hanging out with the sophisticated, but still hoochie, clique, and I'd opted to keep it real with a more roughneck acting crowd.

Tymira Mack

But having been friends since meeting on the playground on the first day of kindergarten, through the years, our friendship always managed to drift back together.

ᑫ ᔕ

Now Aayden's mom traveled out of town on business a lot when we were in high school. So Aayden quickly developed quite an underground rep for throwing hell-a parties. Since my girl lived way out in the boonies with chez–whitey, in order to attend one of her parties you had to have a car and a personal invitation.

I remember being at one particular party where there was quite an eclectic mix of people. The dudes at the party that night were these fly-by-night Ft. Lauderdale DJ's that were evidentially popular up that way, but to me they couldn't hold a candle to the DJ's from down my way.

Anyhow, as weird as they may have seemed, they certainly had all the paraphernalia necessary to get the party started. They had the DJ equipment, the records, the weed and the coke(aine). *Cocaine?*

Over the past two years, I had become a lot of things but I certainly wasn't no true dope fiend, and neither were the other four girls at the party. So we opted to simply sit on the sidelines and watch as the fellas sliced – diced – cut – spread and snorted.

Realizing that we weren't down with the coke, but not wanting us to feel left out, the dudes pulled out this bag of about 10 neatly rolled joints. Figuring that this was more my speed, I took one out and fired it up.

But once again I learned the hard way that I was way outta my league. Not only did these brothers introduce me to the fine art of the 'shot-gun'; but, they also taught me a lesson about smoking stuff that I didn't see get rolled.

At first, I thought that it was the shotguns that gave me the most incredible weed high I'd ever had; but as it turns out, those joints were laced with coke or angel dust or something.

The List.

That was real foul of these clowns. Weed is one thing, but I have my limits, and it definitely doesn't include being F'd-up with the powder.

In the midst of all the madness one of the guys got several 9-1-1 pages from his sister. And when he called her back he found out that his step-dad was on a rampage and beating the hell out of his mom.

Before my F'd-up brain could make sense of what was going on, all of the guys had jumped up, one of them put a gun up in his waist, and within a matter of seconds they'd hollered "Let's ride."

When I knew anything, us five girls were across town, in front of dude's mama's house, crouched down in the back of a pick-up truck, in the rain, hearing gunfire.

Was that gunshots? What-tha-freak have I gotten myself into? Dang I gotta leave that weed alone!

Next thing I know, somebody yelled something about the Police being called.

Well there goes my high!

All I could do was picture myself begging the cops not to unlock the cell 'cause my mama was surely going to beat the hell out of me.

ભ્ર ૭૦

How in the heck nine black teenagers speeding back to white suburbia in a pick-up truck, managed to escape unnoticed is still a mystery to me. But since our clothes were completely soaked from riding all the way back out west in the rain, when we got back to Aayden's house, some of us decided to just jump in her pool and keep the party going.

Before the night was over, I'd hooked up in the pool with this cute, mild mannered, high-yellow, brother with freckles. As it turns out this brother had a few too many family and emotional issues – stemming from the fact that he was mixed – for my taste. So our little tryst ended up being my first of four successive one-night-stands in a three or four month period.

Tymira Mack

Not long after freckles, I had my second one-night-stand in the back seat of a car, with another high-yella fellow that I'd met at the skating ring. Truth be told, I don't even remember his name. I know he was a twin, but I'm not exactly sure which one of them I hooked up with. And then there was the one afternoon at a local park with one of the dumbest jocks on our high school football team.

By this time I really didn't care anymore. I was just out to get me, me.

Last, but not least there was the one time I backtracked and laid up with Lloyd, out of curiosity over what I'd missed out on back in the ninth grade. Unfortunately for me, this time he left a few little creepy crawly friends behind for me to remember him by.

Ewww, yuck! What the freak was I thinking? Well so much for cleaning up my image, 'cause things are definitely starting to go downhill. Why can't I just leave well enough alone?

//
Let the Mutha Burn!

Same stuff different day. By the beginning of senior year I had slowed down a lot and I definitely wasn't smoking marijuana anymore. I'd pretty much given up my double life of being an honor roll student by day and a weed smoking hoochie by night. I'd even started trying to be more personally responsible; and as always, I remained devoted to keeping my grades up 'cause in my mind college equaled FREEDOM!

Fortunately for me, I'd gotten a job at a local drugstore which also helped to slow down my Dr. Jekyll and Mrs. Hoochie lifestyle. In fact, I'd chilled out so much during the first half of the school year that I didn't really date anyone at all. I'd simply gotten tired of the whole boyfriend–girlfriend drama stuff.

I remember being pretty proud of myself around homecoming time. Once again I'd earned excellent grades; but more importantly, I'd made it three whole months and only gotten weak once when it came to having sex.

But gosh darn-it, there was this sexy chocolate brother with these juicy lips that worked at the restaurant connected to my job. Although I'd been working at the drugstore for a while, I had never noticed this guy much before I got assigned to work at the front register. However, once I started working up there, I spent

57

most of my time staring at his tight little football player tush while he leaned over busting tables all night long.

Around closing time every single night, he would come over to my register and buy a chocolate bar in order to get change to catch the bus. By the second or third week of this routine, we began vibing off of each other; kicking game; and exchanging small talk back and forth.

"Can a brother get a slim good bar?" He'd always ask.

And of course I'd always respond with, "Ooooh-la-la. One chocolate bar for Mr. Sexy Chocolate, coming right up."

On the occasional nights when the cool managers were working in both the restaurant and the drugstore, the two of us would take our breaks at the same time and stand outside and talk for a few minutes. But other than that, we didn't get a chance to kick it much because the restaurant closed one hour earlier than the drug store; and, Chocolate was usually gone by the time I'd counted out my register and blocked my assigned isles.

On one Friday night, though, the dishwashing machine or something broke causing Mr. Chocolate to leave work around the same time as I did.

Thinking he lived in one of the Negro hoods nearby, I offered Mr. Chocolate a ride home. But, to my surprise his family was a part of the large migration of Caribbean folks who were settling out in the County's southwestern suburbs. So although we worked all the way east, almost on the beach, he lived about as far west as you could go in the southern part of the County in those days.

No wonder this brother is eager for a ride home. I wouldn't wanna catch the bus way out there neither.

On the way to his house, he asked me to stop at this little row of run down looking duplexes 'cause he needed to stop and take care of some business.

Hummm, he must either know someone who lives here or he's up in there scoring some weed. Either way, I hope he hurries up because this place is dark and downright creepy. Oh good, here he comes.

The List.

But when Sexy Choc came back to the car he opened my door and told me "come on."

Looking around I thought, *Come on where?*

Unfamiliar with the area, I had no idea that this place was a No-tell–get a room by the hour–Motel. And, the clock was ticking on the two hours that he'd just bought.

He simply took me by the hand, helped me out of the car, and led me to a room.

How presumptuous of him? What made him think he had it like that? Besides, he barely even knows me? And, he sure doesn't know any of the people I know, so he couldn't have heard anything about me? Right?

Oh well, what the heck? After all he IS sexy and chocolate.

That was the first hotel room I'd ever been in with a boy. And it sure didn't come close to the Holiday Inn's that I usually stayed in when I went on church trips with my grandma.

I'm sorry buddy but this is just about the nastiest place I've ever seen, I thought.

Let's just do what we came to do, real fast, and get the heck out of here. I sure do hope they'll give you credit for partial minutes used, otherwise you just lost all your hard earned tip money, cause I gotta get out of this nasty behind place.

Yuck! If this is the best that you can do, or better yet if this is all that you feel I deserve, well it's been nice knowing you, but you've gotta to go!

ભ છ

I wish dropping that brother off at his house and never speaking to him again could have been the end of it. But it wasn't that simple. Unfortunately, when you lay and play, sometimes you end up having to pay.

This time I wasn't pregnant. No sir-ee. And I didn't have the creepy crawlies again. Nope, not that either. Instead, I had a whole 'nother problem.

Tymira Mack

After embarrassingly visiting a local health department (two towns over, of course) I was informed "I'm sorry Tracy (yup I used an alias), you have an STD."

"An STD?" I repeated confused.

"Yes a sex-U-al-LY trans-MIT-ted dis-E-ase," the public health nurse enunciated real slowly like I was retarded or something.

But that's for those nasty folks. How could I have an STD? I wondered.

"Did you and your partner use protection?"

"Did we use protection?" I repeated once again like a retard.

Protection? Oh, you mean to prevent pregnancies?

"Oh, it's ok. I'm protected." I said confidently, "I've been on the pill for over a year."

"Yes, but you do realize Ms." She paused as she looked at my chart "Ms. Will-o-suckle. Willosuckle?" She paused again obviously having lost her train of thought after reading the ridiculous alias that I'd invented. "Well anyway, 'um as I was saying, the pill only prevents pregnancies, it doesn't protect you from everything."

"Oh, yeah of course I know that the pills only prevent pregnancy and don't protect me from everything," I repeated having no idea what she meant.

Everything like what? I wondered.

"That's why I'm sorry to inform you that you've contracted Gonorrhea."

"Gono–who?" I blurted out, fully expecting that she had read my chart wrong or something.

Gonorrhea? What exactly is that and how the heck do I get rid of it?

"Gonorrhea, but its ok, just a little shot and we'll clear it right up."

"Oh just a little shot will clear it right up?" Feeling somewhat relieved, "ok, well here's my arm, shoot away."

"Oh the shot isn't meant to go in my arm?" All of a sudden I felt dumb all over again. "Turn around and do what?"

The List.

Drop my pants? Oh, you've got to put the shot in my butt? Oh, umm-hummm. You mean my hip to be more exact? Oh great, just freaking great!

ೞ ೲ

I left the health department with a sore hip, a bag full of condoms and a huge dilemma. I'd lied to the nurse and told her I hadn't had sex with anyone else, 'cause I wasn't about to have the Health Department knocking on doors in my neighborhood looking for guys who may have slept with me, like I'd heard they were doing for these two other girls who, rumor had it, were 'burning.'

But the truth was, somewhere in the mix, I'd had another encounter with Mickey; I told you we were fatally attracted to each other. Even so, I just couldn't bear the thought of telling him he needed to go to the Health Department and get checked out because I may have given him the Big G.

ೞ ೲ

Ok, I can do this. I'll just ride by his house, drop the bomb and drive off before he has an opportunity to kill me.

Oh great he would have to be standing outside with a couple of his boys. This was not how the plan was supposed to work. It's too late to turn back now, I've already turned onto his block and it would look real stupid if I just turn around. Oh well, here goes.

There's that smile, I thought as he looked over his shoulder toward the house before leaning in the car, "what's up slim?"

Oh how I love the way you call me that. Oh what's up?

"Well I really need to talk to you in private," I whispered.

"Oh yeah? Well 'um I was just about to leave for work, plus my girls inside and she might trip if she looks out here and sees your car parked all in front of the house."

Oh, you're on your way to work and your girl is in the house? Oh golly, good for her. Well partner, I sure hope she isn't burning—yet, I

61

thought to myself, angry because it had been less than a week since we'd been together and I couldn't believe that this Negro was standing here trying to blow me off.

"I'll check you later. Alright?" He said as he tapped my window frame and turned to walk off.

Oh, you'll call me later? Oh no you ain't 'bout to walk off from me? "Well, ummmm, alright partner, but you might want to make that call REAL soon because I have something VERY important to tell you." *But then again, that's on you partner, cause sooner or later, you WILL figure it out!* I thought smugly to myself as I drove the heck off.

ରେ ଓ

Mickey's boy must have overheard our brief conversation because later that night while working he'd told Mickey I sounded like I might be pregnant or something. So he convinced Mickey to call me when they went on their first break at eleven o'clock.

Negro IS you crazy? You know my mamma don't let me accept calls after 10 pm. "Do you know what time it is?" I whispered. "You better be glad I was sleeping with the phone in my bed."

"Yeah well my partner told me I better call you and see what's up cause it sounded like it was serious. Like you was pregnant or something," he half-asked nervously.

"Say what?" I was pissed his boy had been eavesdropping on our conversation in the first place; and, livid that somebody even had to convince Mickey to call me back in the second place.

Oh, so the only reason you're calling me so quick is 'cause your boy done got you all scared that you 'bout to be my baby daddy?

"You're really tripping Mickey. Like I told you before, I don't even play those kind of mind games. I'm a big girl and I definitely ain't trying for another neg-ga to leave me high and dry with no baby. Therefore, thanks to the pill, I handle mine!"

The List.

And before he could say anything, I continued, "but as for you, you might want to go get yourself checked out before you and your girl go up in flames."

"That's right playa, according to the Health Department, either you or me picked up something from somewhere, and since I take care of mine, you might want to check out who your girl been kicking it with while you're at work all night long." Click!

Burn, Mutha, Burn!

12
Merry Christmas Baby

That's just my baby daddy. For weeks I hadn't answered the phone or hung out in the hood, because I was trying to avoid Mickey, just in case he was angry with me. I figured that if I had indeed burned him, I surely would have heard something by now. And, even though I knew he wasn't the violent type, I decided to stay on the low-low, just to be on the safe side.

That's exactly what I was doing one afternoon during Christmas Break when the phone rang. As soon as I picked up, the voice on the other end of the phone made my heart sink. I could have sworn I was hearing a ghost.

"What's up baby girl?"

I was speechless and literally couldn't move.

"Merry Christmas, Daddy's home," proclaimed the mysterious voice from my past.

I remember being both excited and angry all at the same time.

What the freak do you mean daddy's home? Neg-ga did you take a wrong turn on your way to the store to get some cigarettes and milk? What? Was I just supposed to be like 'hey daddy I been thinking of you'?

"Oh what a brotha go away for a minute, you fall all in love with a DJ and forgot all about me?" Puff-Puff-Pass, the original Don Dada himself, asked.

The List.

Ok, how the hell does he know all of my business; and after all this time, how did he remember my phone number?

"I heard you're even pushing a brand new ride these days baby girl. Why don't you stop by and let a brother roll with you in your ride."

Oh my goodness, this boy must be psychic?

"Look I'm getting ready to jump in the shower baby girl, so you just be up here by one o'clock," he ordered with the utmost confidence.

"But I gotta be at school for chorus practice at one o'clock," I weakly protested.

"Alright, I guess that means you'll be up here by twelve–thirty then," he declared before hanging up the phone.

Un-BE-freaking-lievable. After almost a year and a half, this Negro just breezes back in town and expects me to drop everything and welcome him back with open arms? I remember thinking as I drove north on I-95 to go pick him up.

Oh yeah, this Negro has a lot of explaining to do!

Ok, just calm down, I'm sure he has a rational explanation for not responding to all the letters and phone calls? Maybe he never got the letters? And, his phone was turned off. Right? So maybe he didn't even know about the baby after all? Right?

Yeah right; you know darn well his brother told him what the deal was and besides how do you explain the fact that Puffy seems to know every other detail of the past eighteen months of your life?

Ok, well maybe he was just as scared as I was and he ran because he didn't know how to handle the situation?

You're really tripping now. That brother sells more dope, kicks more game and is a freaking engineering major. Get a grip. He ain't never been scared or dumb. Besides you didn't know how to handle the situation either, but did you run and hide?

ෞ ෨

65

Tymira Mack

"Damn baby girl, you all grown up and filled out and stuff, huh?" He complemented after closing the front door and taking a moment to admire my emerging curves.

That's right, I'm looking good ain't I?

"Oh you ain't got no love for me no more baby girl?" He asked while holding his arms open wide and awaiting a hug in mock surprise.

Darn stop smiling. You're supposed to be mad at his tail. But those 20 extra pounds do look nice on him; and he IS truly wearing the hell outta them jeans! All right control yourself; you can't fall for this brotha again this fast!

As I was trying to encourage myself to be strong, I heard an undeniably familiar female laugh coming from one of the back bedrooms. I guess he noticed the puzzled look on my face and he wasted no time confirming that the voice I heard was indeed my neighbor.

Oh that explains how he got my phone number and knows all of my business. Hold up one freakin' minute. Did he say my neighbor was over here? But she's only fourteen. What in the hell is she doing up here? Oh yeah that's right, he does have a little sister just about that age, maybe they're friends?

"Oh what? She's friends with your little sister?"

Shaking his head, "naw baby girl, she's friends with my sister NOW, but that ain't why she's up here."

"What's up? Don't tell me you're kicking it with her too?" I asked figuring that he was up to his normal low-down tricks.

"Naw baby girl, she's kicking it with my little brother," he informed me like it wasn't a big deal.

And that's when my whole world came crashing down around me. It was like deja-vu.

"Little brother my behind, that neg-ga is nineteen years old," I groaned as the reality of the situation left me totally speechless.

Awwww man, what have I done? During the height of my wild days, I'd taken my little neighbor under my wings as my little protégé. I loved her like a sister. Everywhere I went, she went.

The List.

Unfortunately, this meant she often had a front row seat, to witness–and obviously learn from–most of the scandalous stuff I did. And now, here she was following right in my shameful footsteps.

When we got in the car I managed to find my voice and totally unleash my frustration on Puffy. Me screwing up my life was one thing, but I couldn't stand seeing my little neighbor heading down the same destructive path. "What in the FREAK is your brother doing with that little girl?"

"Look baby girl, when I came home from school and found out about her, I tried to convince him to leave her alone, but…"

"But what?" I screamed, almost afraid to hear the answer.

"But it's too late anyhow 'cause she's already pregnant."

"She's already what!?!?" Instinctively my eyes closed tightly as I tried to block out the sheer rage that was welling up inside me. But my blood pressure had risen to such an intense boil so quickly that I believe I blacked out temporarily. I came back to myself at the same time that Puffy was jerking the steering wheel to keep us from running off the road.

෪ ෨

For the next two hours, my head was spinning at warp speed. Between the disgust I felt for what both Puffy's brother and I had done to my neighbor, and my throbbing headache, I couldn't focus on what was going on at practice.

How can I possibly sing praises, when I'm partially responsible for leading an innocent, young girl down the path of no return?

I was so glad when practice was finally over, 'cause I had a lotta stuff I had to sort out in my head.

Intuitively, Puffy sensed that I was totally bummed out. "You hungry baby girl?"

"Huh?" I said snapping out of my trance. "Yeah, I guess so."

"Tell you what, don't take me home, just head up Sunrise toward the beach."

Tymira Mack

"What are we going to the beach for Puffy?" I asked in no mood to go anywhere even remotely romantic with this brotha.

"Relax baby girl, daddy's got you covered."

Then in his signature smooth style, Puffy proceeded to calmly give me directions to one of the area's upscale malls located on the Intercostal Waterway.

Ok not the beach, but the mall? But I thought this neg-ga was supposed to be taking me to eat. Hummm maybe he's about to drop a few coins on a sista for Christmas? Yeah right.

My mind was racing a mile a minute as I parked in the underground lot, where he instructed me. Then he led me up the escalator, through the mall to Ruby Tuesdays where we sat down for lunch.

Back in those days, Ruby's was not a regular stomping ground for black folks, let alone a high school girl like me. So you couldn't tell me I wasn't the stuff right about then.

Once we were seated, Puffy proceeded to order us two cocktails; but since I looked much younger than 21, I got carded. Big deal, Puffy still let me sip on his drinks. I believe he was drinking amaretto sours or some other expensive sounding mixed liqueur drink. All I know is it wasn't no Private Stock or Wine Coolers.

Humph. This brother done gone off to school and come back all worldly. Now this is what I'm talking about. By the looks of this place, I could truly get use to Big Papa taking me out for 'lunch and cocktails' on the regular.

ℚ ℠

Since it was Christmastime, after lunch Puff and I strolled through Burdines and he helped me pick out gifts to myself with the money my parents had given me for the holidays. Lunch was the bomb and I was having just as much fun shopping, so by all accounts it was turning out to be a nice afternoon after all.

I don't know, maybe, it was the two or three amaretto sours at lunch; but by 5 pm, the initial tension and awkwardness between us had completely worn off. And once again, I'd settled back into that familiar desire to be the Don Dadda's little girl. In fact, I'd basically forgotten that neither one of us had cleared the air about our baby yet.

ଔ ଓ

On the way home from the mall, Puffy asked me if we could stop by and see one of his classmates who had been seriously injured in a tragic car accident. Since this was the same guy who was with Aayden on the night of my first ever date, I naturally said ok. But stupid me, I forgot that homeboy and Lloyd were also good friends since they lived directly across the street from each other.

What are the odds that Lloyd, his best friend, Puffy and I would all end up visiting ole' dude at the same exact time? So much for an un-tense evening. That visit turned out to be just about the longest hour I'd ever spent in my whole life.

Talk about uncomfortable? Lloyd alternated looking at Puffy like he was crazy and scowling at me like I was some evil vixen. All the while Puffy sat there with his chest all swole. It was just like living that whole high school gym pissing contest all over again.

Once we got back out to the car, Puffy made a point of asking me "how long ago you gave Lloyd some?"

"Huh?" *Dang he must be psychic for real?*

"Look baby girl, a brotha just don't get that jealous about seeing another neg-ga with a female, unless he's hit it a time or two?" he stated unequivocally.

Ooooh, you just think you know every freaking thing. I hate you so much. "Duh, me and him did use to go together," I insisted trying to cover my guilt.

"Yeah, but baby girl you told me back in the day that you ain't never gave him none."

69

"That's true; we didn't ever do it back when we was going together. I was a virgin the whole time me and Lloyd was together," I stated feeling confident I'd rather smartly avoided the issue.

"Yeah but you ain't no virgin now."

Duh, you know that for yourself.

"So you ain't never answer my question," he reiterated, obviously still waiting for an answer.

"Huh? What question?"

"I wanna know when was the last time you gave that neg-ga Lloyd some?"

I sat there for a few seconds with my nose scrunched and a completely puzzled look on my face, as I desperately searched my mind for an alternate way to avoid answering Puffy's question. At the same time I was literally amazed at how smoothly he'd managed to detour the conversation right back to the question all over again.

"Baby girl, the look on your face right now just told me all I needed to know. How many times I got to tell you that neg-ga ain't got no game?" He continued, "Never did, never will."

Game? No. Crabs? Yes, I cringed remembering the little presents Lloyd had given me the last time we'd hooked up.

Then he snapped me out of that yucky thought, "Slow up baby girl cause as soon as you cross the railroad tracks, you need to make a quick right."

Make a what? What is he talking about?

Pointing to a commercial parking lot, "just pull in right here and go around back."

Wha? Why are we...

"Close your mouth and quit trippin'," he ordered as he gently placed his index finger over my lips to quite my weak protest. "Shhhh, just get out the car and come on upstairs baby girl."

But this is the Day's Inn. Un-uh, I ain't ready to go back down that road with you again.

The List.

As if reading my mind, he reassured me "look we ain't got to do nothing. I just got the room so that we can chill out and spend some time together."

"But why can't we chill at your house?" I thought out loud.

"Because ya boy's been out on his own way too long and I need my space. Besides, my old girl's probably home from work; so come on now let's just go up and chill. You know I've missed you."

Yeah right, I'm sure you cried yourself to sleep just about every night for the first four months after you left just like I did, huh?

Ok, I've been with you since noon; so, how in the hell do you already have a key to this room and where did the fresh ice and the cold drinks come from? I knew you were good, but dang your game is through the roof now-a-days.

Before I could ask him how the heck he had gotten this all set up, the brother kissed me and I instantly melted right back into being Big Daddy's baby girl all over again.

⊰ ⊱

They say that variety is the spice of life, and after having 'lived a little' Puffy's sex game was no longer ringing my bells; a fact that no doubt didn't escape him.

But he wouldn't be the Don Dadda without an ace up his sleeve now would he? True to form, he elevated his game to the next level, making him the first guy I'd ever taken a shower with.

For a girl who–up until then–refused to be seen naked before, during or after sex, Puffy had once again managed to accomplish the impossible.

In fact, except for the five second showers we use to take in PE as freshman, I never took showers; thus, I had no idea that steam totally ruins hairdos. Once the hair reality thing set in, I concluded that the draw backs of this new sexual experience truly outweighed its benefits.

How in the heck am I going to explain what happened to my hair when I get home?

Tymira Mack

Puffy's idea was for me to just spend the night with him at the hotel, and he'd buy me a curling iron to fix my hair, before I went home in the morning.

In the morning? Is you crazy? I'm already gonna catch hell for being late for curfew as it is. And you want me to spend the night?

I ignored that Negro; got dressed as quickly as I could; did the best I could with my hair; and was just about to rush out the door when he hit me with a TKO.

"Hey, baby girl, what was it?"

"Huh? What are you talking about now?" I asked in a rush to get home before I got in serious trouble.

"The baby. What was it?"

In that instant, I felt my legs begin to buckle.

"I bet anything yours was probably a boy," he sighed like he really hated that he was gonna miss out on some father-son-bonding thing.

Reality sure is a mutha. Not only did this neg-ga know about my pregnancy all along, but I wasn't even his ONLY baby's mama.

I found the strength from somewhere to make it down those motel stairs and into my car to head home.

Well two tear drops in a gosh darn bucket. Mutha-F-it!

13

Ain't No Mountain High Enough

Free at last Even though I'd turned sixteen in March of my junior year, I'd never officially started dating, 'cause no one had been brave enough to knock on our door that whole summer. Plus, I was going through another one of my "I just wanna be by myself" phases. Puffy's surprise return home and his baby confession during the Christmas holidays only served to multiply my determination to the nth power.

It wasn't until around January or February of my senior year that I reluctantly gave into my friend's numerous attempts to hook me up with her boyfriend's brother. Although I have to admit he was cute; he wasn't exactly my type. He was yellow (yuck), with curly, 'good' hair (double yuck), and cute furry eyebrows. Even though there wasn't an ounce of chocolateness on him, what I did find appealing about him was his silly sense of humor and his partial Puerto Rican accent.

So during the second half of my senior year, Suave Rico became the first boy to come over my house and officially 'keep company with me.' Truthfully though, I don't know who he spent more of his time with, me or my mama. It seems like they became best buddies almost from the first day he ever came over to our house. And it wasn't like he was kissing up to her or anything. He was just being his normal friendly, easy-going self. And she just ate it up. So much so, I was seriously beginning to think my mamma was losing her mind.

Go figure?

To top it off, my mom didn't even trip when she found out Rico wasn't in school.

"Rico, are you a senior too?" She asked one afternoon when he was over sitting on a kitchen barstool, supposed to be visiting me.

"No ma'am," he said, as I thought *Good Answer*.

"Oh, you already graduated," she continued, obviously curious now.

"Um, no ma'am."

That's right keep your answers short and sweet, baby. Short and sweet.

"Oh I didn't know you were younger than Tammy," still probing.

"No ma'am I'm 18," he dropped his head and continued "but I'm just not in school this semester."

Oh hell you done gone and done it now. I wasn't trying for her to know that you were a high school dropout!

I could tell by the way that mama said "oh?" that his admission was the last thing she'd expected to hear.

"Ummm, well I couldn't go back to school this year 'cause my mama only had enough money to buy the girl's their school clothes."

Oh word, I ain't even know that? I thought you had just up and dropped out. Uh-oh, hold up, mama's looking kinda compassionate?

"So ummm, me and my brother just went and got jobs so we could help out instead."

And to my surprise mama didn't even trip. "I understand baby. Well I'm glad that you are at least trying to do something productive with your life."

Ok, quit playing. Who is this woman? Can somebody please tell me what happened to my real mama?

The List.

Even after his school dropout confession, mama continued to let me go out with Rico; she didn't wait up at night to see what time I got home; and she didn't really question me a lot about where I was going or who I was going to be with.

I was seriously beginning to wonder if she had some kind of terminal illness and wanted to make peace with me before she died or something?

The final straw came when she put up absolutely no resistance when I asked if two of my high school classmates and I could drive my car to Tallahassee to attend Florida A & M University's New Student Preview Weekend. Although her positive response totally threw me off, I decided to take the yes and run before she came to herself and changed her mind.

୧ ଽ

On the Thursday before my seventeenth birthday, I was allowed to drive 500 miles to a college town, stay in a hotel and be unsupervised for a whole weekend. But, never having gone to a school that was more than 20% black in my whole life, I was not prepared for FAMU. Even living smack dab in the hood all my life didn't prepare me to experience a weekend filled with five thousand of the most beautiful, intelligent, progressive young adults of every shade of black, brown, red and high yellow that I'd ever seen in my life.

The campus was alive. The people were exciting. There was just this undeniable vibe of excellence that I couldn't articulate; but, I was loving every second of it. From that moment on, no one could ever try to convince me that black people were not meant for greatness.

Fortunately, one of my classmate's cousins was a member of the infamous FAMU Marching 100 band and he made sure that we had what amounted to a VIP weekend. Besides attending the presentations made by the various academic colleges, we also got to watch the band practice, we went to a basketball game, we went to a Greek Fraternity and Sorority Step Show; and, we went to the After Party!

I was totally hooked. Not just on the partying but on the whole package. This was probably one of the most memorable birthday's I had ever had and there was no doubt that I would return to South Florida with a whole new perspective on life.

ɢଷ ଛ

I had already been accepted for admission to FAMU, but later that month when I received an acceptance letter from Clark College, my parents encouraged me to go up to Atlanta to check it out. I think they wanted to make sure my visit to FAMU hadn't totally prejudiced my judgments on other colleges.

I had pretty much settled on going to either FAMU or Howard University so I was reluctant about going to see Clark. That is until Aayden called me.

"Girrrrrl, I just got back from Atlanta," she chirped in her normal super-hyper cheerleader voice.

"What in the world were you doing in Atlanta?"

"Well you know what-cha-call-it who was on the cheerleading team last year?"

"Yeah," I replied, wondering what our homegirl Maria had to do with this.

"Well you know she goes to Clark now and she invited me to come up for the student preview weekend for the colleges in the AU Center."

"Oh, well how was it?" I asked remembering how much of the bomb FAMU's preview weekend had been.

And all she kept repeating was "Lawd have mercy, it should be a crime for that much fineness to be confined to one place."

Now Aayden and I often had different taste in guys. I liked them chocolate. She liked them from pee yellow to one shade shy of midnight. I liked juicy lips. She liked soup coolers. Get the picture? So I was a little hesitant about what to expect. Still, she had painted such a pretty picture of Atlanta that I just had to experience the Black Mecca for myself.

ର ଛ

After having driven all night, my parents and I arrived in Atlanta around 9 am and headed directly to the campus for our 10 am tour. As we drove through the AU center, I remember being struck by how preppy the students looked in comparison to the majority of the FAMU students, who were no doubt academic, yet still had a hint of thuggish-ness about them.

Good-googa-mooga, my girl Aayden was wrong. Lawd have mercy is definitely an understatement when it comes to how fine these guys are! Every time I blinked it seemed like two more fine brothers appeared from outta thin air.

For the remainder of the morning as my parents and I toured the campus they concentrated on the schools' academic assets, and I focused on the rest of the campus's assss–sets.

ର ଛ

Those two college tours really changed me. They actually offered me a glimpse of all the possibilities that life held in store. It was such a thrill to see young men without gold teeth or jherri-curls, dressed in leather and suede and sweaters, with texturized hair and pearly white smiles. It was nice to experience dance music that didn't pound every aspect of my being – from my eardrums to my heart. It was nice to feel and smell clean crisp, chilled spring air and see the budding flowers.

Yup, from then on I lost a huge part of my desire for rough-neck dudes sporting lumberjacks, wife beaters, Gap cords, and colored Converse. I no longer fiend for *2 Live Crew* and Miami bass. And, I'd had my fill of sunshine and palm trees.

For the next two months, I simply went through the motions of grad night and prom and my fading relationship with Rico. Instead I focused all of my energy towards college.

Tymira Mack

In the end, FAMU offered the most complete academic scholarship opportunity. So although I had to let go of the visions of the men of Hotlanta, it was only temporary, because I'd already been to the mountain top!

Ooooh Lawd, I've got to get back to the Promised Land!

Part 2:
Collegiate Carnality

||||| ||||| ||||| ||||| ||||| ||||| |||

☙ ❧

To be carnally minded is death…
Romans 8:6 NKJV

14
Ready for the World

Red, yellow & chocolate brown. Graduation night couldn't come fast enough. While it's true I was thrilled to finally take that walk across the stage which for most black folks signified the beginning of young adulthood; I was even more excited about leaving for college right after the ceremony. Yup, my bags were packed and sitting right outside in the parking lot in our family's van.

Unfortunately, leaving right after the ceremony meant I'd have to miss all the official and unofficial graduation parties at the various hotels on Ft. Lauderdale's Beach Strip; but I thought, *screw the stinking class of 85,* 'cause I knew there were bigger and better parties awaiting me in Tallahassee.

Although I couldn't wait to get away from my parent's house and from Hollywood to start a new chapter in my life, lying in the back of our van, in the dark, I cried myself to sleep as I reminisced over the heartaches of the previous chapter of my life which had finally come to a close.

ভ ৪০

It's true, joy really does come in the morning. We reached Tallahassee at around 7:00 am and my excitement and spirit of expectancy rose with each successive hill that our van climbed.

Tymira Mack

Alas, there it stood; on the tallest of seven hills in Florida's capital city. Florida Agricultural and Mechanical University. Home of the infamous Marching 100, the renowned School of Business and Industry, and the phenomenal Schools of Pharmacy, Nursing and Architecture.

Somebody pinch me, 'cause I think I've died and gone to heaven.

With my housing assignment letter in hand, my parents, both FAMU alumnus, and I made our way over to Cropper Hall and began unpacking my stuff. Seemingly out of nowhere, two big, burly guys appeared and helped my daddy move all my things up to my second floor dorm room.

They call this little bitty closet a room? I thought as I opened the door, revealed my new 10 x 11 foot space, and looked around. *And you say I've gotta share this cell with another female? Oh this is going to be real interesting!*

"Huh? Oh, my friends call me Tammy," I said to the BIG, tall and slightly pigeon toed Negro that had interrupted my thoughts while he toted my trunk up the flight of stairs.

"They call me Big Red," he grunted all proud.

Well that might be what they call you alright; but, that healthy sense of pride of yours sure ain't matching all the huffing and puffing you doing trying to make it up the stairs with my stuff.

Figuring he was a little too big for me to get sarcastic with, I opted to keep my reply cordial as I held the door so that he could squeeze his big self and my stuff inside. "Oh ok, it's nice to meet you Big Red."

But before Big Red could try to get his mack on, my Daddy slipped him a $10 bill and politely pushed him right on out of my dorm room and into the hallway.

As my parents were helping me to unpack my stuff, my roommate and her family came in. And, since our cell wasn't big enough for the two of us, let alone our families, my parents left to check into their hotel to rest from the all night drive; promising to call me later for dinner.

The List.

Big Red must have smelled my parents leave because he was knocking on my door before my dad's van had even cleared the alley.

"Hey Miss Tammy, since you're new at FAM, why don't you let me give you a tour around the campus?" He offered.

"Alright Red, if you aren't helping the young ladies move in, then you have to go because you know Cropper Hall is a female dorm, not the dating game," our Dorm Mother advised as she came up the back stairs just in time to hear Red's weak rap game.

"Yes ma'am," he responded half busted and half embarrassed.

Pushing him toward the stairs, "if you'd like to visit this young lady, I suggest you do it in the first floor lounge area, during visitation hours. Now back to work."

"These boys never give up," she sighed to herself as she continued on down the hall making her rounds.

I guess my roommate decided to use Big Red's invitation as an opportunity to bond with me because as soon as I'd closed the door, she started schooling me to the game. "You might as well get use to it."

"To what?" I asked.

"To all the guys hitting on you this week."

"Huh?"

"During freshman orientation every summer and fall, the football players and some of the frat guys make a habit of helping freshman move into the dorms."

"Oh well that's pretty nice," I responded as she schooled me.

"Yeah, but they don't help just to help," she continued.

"Oh really?" I thought as my eyebrows raised a bit 'cause I was quickly catching on.

"No they do it to earn a gang of tip money from the freshmen's parents; and also, to get first dibs on the freshman girls before all the other guys get back to campus."

While I appreciated the head's up my roommate was giving me, I'd already decided that Big Red was a wee bit TOO red and

TOO big for my taste. So it was seriously doubtful I'd have taken him up on his offer anyway.

"Oh ok. Thanks for the 4-1-1."

From that point on, my roommate and I hit it off pretty quickly and between her and my parents, I managed to get a feel for the campus over the next couple of days.

As eager as I had been for my independence, I must admit I was overwhelmingly sad when my parents got ready to leave. But in his classic fatherly, best friend, keeping it real kind of way my daddy unwittingly left me with possibly the best piece of advice he could have ever given me.

"This is your proving ground. This is what you've worked so hard for all these years. You can do this as long as you stay focused. There will be lots of temptations. Boys, parties, drugs and alcohol. But remember college is just FOUR years. If you devote all your energy to your studies, I promise you'll have the better part of the rest of your life to date and party. And remember what your mama's always taught you; never forget to pray."

I actually cried when my parents left, but I only had a half a day to wallow in my loneliness 'cause Aayden got to school later that afternoon. Within just a couple of days, Aayden and I were once again two peas in a pod. We were like a weird science experiment gone horribly wrong. You could be sure whenever you mixed her boldness with my cunning there would certainly be spontaneous combustion. She was definitely the ying to my yang.

ৎ ৯

By the end of our first full week at FAMU, we'd quickly figured out the cafeteria's summer schedule left us quite hungry by 8:00 pm. So much so that one night I finally gave into Big Red's continual quest to take me out. But I only agreed to go out with him on two conditions. One, he had to take me somewhere to eat; and, two, my home-girl had to come with me.

84

The List.

After all, I don't know you like that? This way if your big ole' butt gets stupid, between the two of us, me and my girl could probably take you out?

As it turned out, Big Red didn't even have a freaking car, so him and one of his teammates came to pick us up.

Awe shucks, now the odds aren't in our favor anymore. But homeboy is kinda nerdy looking; he can't be that much of a threat, I thought. *Besides, my stomach is growling like a mutha.*

The four of us ended up going to Pizza Hut and after downing two extra-large pizzas and 3 pitchers of soda, me and Aayden were full like a mug, happy as ticks and more than ready to go back to the dorms.

Up until then I must have been too busy grubbing to notice the big fat sour puss look that'd developed on Big Reds face. And just like a true baby, when I still didn't pay him any attention, he decided to act real juvenile.

"Dang, I thought ya'll would be like most other girls on a first date and try to be cute by not eating a lot."

Sike! Whatever player! We ain't most other females and besides this ain't no darn date!

"Hey slim, when the last time you ate, a week ago Saturday?"

Ahhhh Hello? The cafeteria closed at six o'clock and it is now ten o'clock. So yes, we're getting our grub on.

"Here, you wanna lick the pan?"

Ok you're really working my nerves.

"Shoot, a brotha could really go broke trying to feed ya'll!"

Ok, you big red pigeon you're about to piss me the heck off. Besides, it ain't like your big behind took us out for steak and lobster. I'm tryin' to hold my peace cause I'own wanna walk back to school, but one more slick comment out ya mouth and um-ma go City on yo' big A–!

"I know a brotha gone at least get a hug or some–shin after dropping $30 on ya'll?" Red said half playing and half serious

Bingo. That was the last dang on straw! "Nig-errr-O pla-eeze," I started. "It ain't like we costed you anything, 'cause the way I figure it, the $10 you pimped out of my pops last week for them

85

two little bags your big butt barely carried upstairs should cover those cheap little pizza's you bought tonight."

"Now shut up and pay the bill, my neg-ga," I concluded in my best don't F– with me voice.

"Dang, where ya'll from again?" Red asked me without the slightest hint of sarcasm in his voice for the first time that night.

"The bottom neg-ga," I said like a dude. "We s–kraight from the bottom!"

ଔ ಇ

During that summer, Aayden and I really adapted to college life. Attending the summer semester turned out to be one of the best decisions we could have made because it gave us an opportunity to get use to the pace of college courses, develop manageable study routines and, oh yes, ease into the college party scene.

And by summer's end, we'd made friends with quite a few upperclassmen. So when the fall semester rolled around, we were far more seasoned than the typical incoming college freshmen.

Even with that head start, though, we still made some typical freshman mistakes. Like the night before the first day of fall classes when we hung out at the apartment of some of the sophomore dudes we'd met over the summer. That night, we decided to play two popular drinking games, Thumper and Bulls—t. And since financial aid checks were still weeks away, we bought the cheapest wine the convenience store had, Wild Irish Rose and MD 20–20.

There are some things you only need to experience once in order to learn a lesson. And after the three day period it took for the hangover, nausea, and vomiting to go away, I vowed I would never play drinking games and get that drunk ever again.

ଔ ಇ

The List.

The Set was located smack dab in the middle of the street that ran through the eastern portion of the campus. The central portion of the Set, right in front of the freshman dorms and the Student Union, was always live. But during special occasions – like Homecoming, Fraternity and Sorority Weeks and the first week of school–the set was really popping. It would almost be elbow-to-elbow people.

So after we'd recovered from our three day hang-over, Aayden and I ventured out of our dorm room and took a seat on the stoop of the freshman dorm to see and be seen. While we were scoping out all the happenings, I could sense someone staring in our direction; and as I looked around, I noticed this slim, high yellow – darn near white–fellow motioning towards me.

Now where I'm from, yellow Negroes like him are a commodity and quite full of themselves since the sisters love to fight over them. So I turned around and looked behind me to figure out who Casper was trying to halla at. *Surely he's not trying to get with black little old me?*

As it turned out Casper was from up north where high-yella brothers came a dime a dozen, and he was indeed trying to halla at a sister. Although I wasn't wild about white chocolate, I was somewhat intrigued by the polite manner in which he stepped to me. This level of intrigue lasted long enough for me to find out he was a sophomore transfer student and he was attending FAMU on a basketball scholarship. Over the next few weeks Casper and I began developing a casual friendship.

At the outset we mutually agreed to keep our friendship on a platonic basis, and despite my normal horny self, I found this arrangement to be very easy to maintain. For one thing FAM didn't have any dorms with unrestricted visitation, so there weren't very many opportunities for us to dip and dab. And I especially wasn't trying to get busy in no vacant classrooms or in other remote campus locations like so many of my hot pants freshman sisters were doing. But I suppose the biggest reason why I was able to maintain my celibacy was simply because Casper wasn't chocolate.

Tymira Mack

While my first summer at FAM was fun, the fall semester was turning out to be hella-fun on steroids. There was always at least one party happening on or near campus every single weekend; most often two or three. And, on the rare occasion there wasn't a party going on at FAMU, we would simply ride down the hill and kick it at a Florida State party.

Even though Aayden and I were definitely doing our fair share of partying, we also maintained a demanding business school course load. Once you factored in studying and a little bit of sleep, there wasn't really anytime left for dating.

Instead, we opted to study and socialize in group settings with other people in our major. Sixty percent of the time this arrangement worked for me, but being a semi-around-the-way girl, there were lots of times when I just couldn't stomach spending one more second with the uppity business school crowd. On those days, I'd often dis Aayden and hang out with my other roommates.

ଓ ୭ଠ

Just hanging out is precisely what four of my five, yes five, roommates and I were doing the night I met Slow. That evening, my roomies and I were kicking it in the campus bowling alley when I noticed this dude blowing kisses at me. He was real slick with it too, 'cause every time I would tell my roommates to look at him, he'd abruptly stop; leaving me looking real stupid. That is, until the time they finally caught him in the act.

Although the kisses thing was strange, I couldn't help but notice he had the most beautiful dimples I'd ever seen. He was also tall. But best of all he was a luscious shade of chocolate brown. Notwithstanding his chocolateness, the whole kisses incident left me thinking that the brother was either a pervert or just plain retarded.

The List.

"That brother must be retarded or something," one of my roommates laughed.

"Yup, he's cute but he's definitely slow up in the head," I thought out loud.

And that's how he came to have the nickname Slow among me and my roommates.

"Yup he's definitely cute, and ya'll know I'm a sucker for the chocolate," I giggled. "But I don't do retarded. Let's get outta here before this brother starts flashing us or something far worse."

ෆ ෯

While standing outside the cafeteria with my roommates after dinner a few weeks later, I kept feeling something, as if someone were tapping me on the back. But every time I glanced over my shoulder, I didn't see anyone directly behind me.

Then all of a sudden, a pebble came from out of nowhere, whizzed across my shoulder and landed a few feet in front of me. As I spun around thoroughly pissed that someone had thrown a rock at me, I noticed Slow standing way across the sidewalk trying to hold in a laugh.

Oh I know this M - F'er ain't throwing rocks at me? He must really be retarded or else just plain stuck on stupid?

Before I could ask the Negro if he was touched in the head, he flashed a smile that revealed those sexy dimples and said "I'm sorry lady, but I just had to get your attention."

What? Have you ever heard of hello? Or excuse me? Or even Psssst?

"Ok so now you have my attention." I assured as I began walking toward him, getting louder and louder with every step. "After the kisses the night in the bowling alley and now the rocks, I'm really wondering if your retarded A— is incapable of talking or something? So what the hell do you want?"

Ok maybe my tone of voice and my comments were a little harsh, *but hell he is throwing rocks at me*. Even after having been cursed at in front of his boys, he remained calm and apologized once again.

And just as if he hadn't heard one evil thing I'd said to him, he simply asked me, "Lady, it would make me a real happy man if I could just walk you back to your dorm?"

Wha?

His response was so far out in left field I couldn't even be mad anymore. In fact, I couldn't do anything but laugh 'cause at that point I was definitely convinced he was retarded; but hey, he WAS chocolate with irresistible dimples. So I let him walk me back to my dorm and we sat outside on the upper deck and talked until it got dark.

From then on, when I wasn't in class or studying and he wasn't at basketball practice, which believe it or not was one of his only for–credit classes that semester, we would spend time together. Since I'd gotten a new car just before I came back to school for the fall, every afternoon after dinner we would ride to one of the popular local lakes and spend time together feeding the bread that we'd snuck out of the cafeteria to the ducks or just sitting on a blanket enjoying quiet time together.

For six or seven weeks we both got comfortable with our relationship and this routine. Then on our way back to campus one evening, he asked me to stop by the FSU football dorms so he could holler at one of his homeboys.

I really didn't care much for FSU and I especially hated the way the whole town seemed to treat the FSU football team like gods. I despised them because everywhere they went they seemed to behave like a bunch of pampered jerks. And even though Slow assured me that his homeboy was cool, I wasn't excited about meeting him.

ༀ ༁

Going over there was just as I figured. Those clowns actually had their own apartments. *Geez, compared to the FAMU football dorms, these guys are living in the Taj Mahal.* The parking lot was full

The List.

of fancy new cars that I was sure most of these guys couldn't spell, let alone pay for. And the number of half-dressed chicks–white, black and other–that were swarming all around was just plain re–damn–diculous. The place was simply unbelievable.

Once upstairs I was struck by how tall, super husky and intimidating Slow's homeboy looked. In spite of his looks, he was a very mild-mannered guy with a phenomenally warm and hospitable personality. In fact, he was so hospitable that almost as if on cue, he excused himself to go next door; locking the door behind him as he left.

That's when it dawned on me. Slow and I were indoors and all alone, for the first time in our relationship. True to his nature, Slow was the perfect gentleman as he pulled his favorite *Ready for the World* cassette tape out of his pocket, popped it into his homies boom-box and came on to me in a very respectful and deliberate manner.

"Lady," he said tenderly, "It would, make me a real happy man if I could make love to you."

Huh? I thought as a million things zoomed through my head.

How in the world did this happen? I've obviously lost my touch, I concluded as I realized I never saw this situation coming.

Although I had really strong feelings for Slow, after IT was over I wasn't excited about what had just happened. True enough it had been a long time, almost seven months, since I'd been sexually active, still he and I just didn't seem to click. In fact, that night when I went home and told Aayden about the whole event, we secretly concluded that we should add Drag to his nickname.

℀ ℁

The week right after Slow Drag and I had gotten busy, we were preparing to go home for Thanksgiving break. And out of the blue, Slow just up and told me, "Lady, I don't think I'm coming back after Thanksgiving."

"What?"

Tymira Mack

"I mean thangs just ain't working out here for me."

"Thangs, what thangs? I thought we were doing just fine?"

"Oh no not us, I meant school and all."

"So you're just gonna drop out?"

"Naw, I think um'ma go ahead and transfer to the junior college I told you about."

"You just told me they'd been calling your mama's house. You didn't tell me nothing about going down there to go to school!"

At that point I was furious. I felt like the whole sex thing at his homies apartment the other day had simply been a set up; especially if he had already made up his mind about leaving.

"Listen Lady FAMU ain't doing right by me. If I go to this other school, I'll have a better chance to play."

I was so bummed out by the bombshell Slow had dropped on me, I stayed awake during the all night Greyhound bus ride home. By the morning, I'd decided that although I felt sad and in some ways betrayed; I still wanted what would be best for him.

ᘓ ᘔ

Slow ended up coming back to Tallahassee after Thanksgiving to gather the rest of his things; then I drove him down to his new school. After briefly helping him to settle into the school's athletic house, I got back in my car and sadly made the one hour trip back to FAMU alone.

The first few days without having Slow Drag around were awkward, but at the same time it felt like an awakening. During the three months Slow and I dated, except for attending class, I'd all but dropped out of campus life. Now I was once again hanging out with Aayden, going to events on campus, and starting to wean Slow out of my system.

That was until he started calling me and telling me how lonely he felt at the little school in that no-name country town. Feeling sorry for him, I began making the one hour drive to pick him up

92

The List.

every Friday evening and turning right around and driving him back to school every Sunday afternoon.

That's also when he and I began a pattern of spending at least one night together each weekend at one of several $20 a night no-tell motels on Tennessee Street. Oh don't trip, since the whole cheap motel / STD incident back in high school, I made a point of having my own supply of condoms on hand at ALL times. But the wild part is that even though Slow Drag and I still weren't clicking in bed, our little hotel-motel-no-tell inn routine continued for the remaining weeks leading up to Christmas break.

Fortunately the time I was spending at FAMU by myself during the weekdays and the three weeks I was at home for Christmas Break went a long way towards helping me to completely get over him. About the second week after we returned from Christmas break, I decided the long distance love affair thing just wasn't for me.

Yup Slow, it's been real, but you're starting to become a drag in more ways than one. I'm really sorry but you've gotta go!

15
Nothing but the Dog in Me

Bow wow wow. The timing of me and Slow's break-up couldn't have been more perfect. It was the spring semester and springtime signals new beginnings. The sun begins to shine brightly. Flowers start to bloom. People and animals emerge from their cocoons and hibernations. And mating rituals begin.

Springtime also marks the beginning of Greek Week season at FAMU. During the spring semester each of the Pan-Hellenic Greek Sororities and Fraternities on campus got to spend a full week promoting their organization. Events during greek weeks ran the gamut from step-shows, to fashion shows and dating games, to parties; but, each week always culminated with an elaborate ball or event.

One of the most legendary FAMU Greek Week fraternity events was the infamous Omega Psi Phi (Que Dog) Marti Gras. The reputation of the FAMU Omega Marti Gras was so hellacious that it even made the national news one year.

Just like the New Orleans Marti Gras, Que Marti Gras party goers were unofficially expected to dress festively and get buck wild. Of course me and Aayden were definitely down for the cause. She'd just finished pledging a sorority and I'd just kicked Slow to the curb, so we were pumped up to hang out together for the first time in over eight weeks.

The List.

Hoping to blend in without being too wild, we decided to wear these silly shorts outfits with bikini bathing suit tops and beach cover-ups; completing our costumes with festive black masquerade masks that had red blinking lights, figuring the masks would help us to remain anonymous if we got too scandalous.

Remain anonymous, yeah right!

The party and the costumes were WILD. There was a little bit of everything from girls in bikini's; to dudes who were wearing absolutely nothing but bathrobes; and a whole lot more wild stuff in between. But by far the wildest outfit of the night was the dude who wore absolutely nothing but saran wrap.

Oh my! We're definitely not in Kansas anymore.

ભ 80

Never a good dancer, at least while sober anyway, I watched as Aayden and her sorority sisters disappeared onto the dance floor. Only after I'd gulped down two or three or maybe even four cups of Omega Oil, was I brave enough to head out onto the dance floor myself.

I was kind of just out there in the crowd dancing when I looked up and saw this dude that Aayden and I had nicknamed Slee, coming my way. We'd named him Slee because he looked just like those creatures from the old Saturday morning show *The Land of the Lost.*

According to Aayden, good old Slee had a serious crush on me. Although Slee had a few coins in his pocket, could dress his butt off and was chocolate, he was also butt ugly as hell. For once the chocolate just wasn't working in a brother's favor.

To this day, I don't know if it was the Omega Oil, which was famous for going down sweet and smooth–before the pure grain alcohol kicked you in the head; or the effects of staring at Slee's butt ugly self, but within a matter of minutes I began to get sick.

Awe Shucks!

Tymira Mack

Right before the nausea and wooziness took their full effect, I excused myself and made my way over to the Gym's bleachers, just in time to bend over and puke my guts out. At that exact moment, just like his nickname implied, Casper's high yellow butt appeared like a ghost from outta nowhere.

"Whatz-up girl, you ok?" He asked obviously feeling pretty mellow from a few cups of the Oil.

"Un-Un," I moaned. "I need-a lay down."

"You ain't lying. Girl you look toe down," he giggled, "You want me to walk you back to your room?"

"Un-huh," was all I could manage to mumble without risking puking again.

Casper helped me navigate through the crowd, but by the time we got outside the gym, it was obvious we were not going to make it up the hill, across the campus and over to my dorm room.

"Look girl, ain't no way you gonna make it all the way to your room," he contemplated.

"And a skinny little brotha like myself," he said as he patted his bear little pee yellow chest, "can't hardly carry you way over there."

"Look my room is right over there," he slurred while pointing toward the dorms across the parking lot. "You can just go and lay down in my room, see," he said once again pointing towards the boy's dorm.

I was in no condition to argue with Casper's logic, so I simply leaned on his shoulder as he led me across the parking lot to Gibbs Hall. Although Casper's dorm was one of the newest and nicest dorms on campus, it wasn't co-ed, so girls weren't allowed inside.

"How 'um gone get in?" I mumbled trying to figure how he was planning to get me past the man at the front desk.

Pointing to the first window on the first floor, "my room's right there, see?"

Even though his room was on the first floor, the window was at least five feet off the ground. *How in the hell am I gonna get in that window*, I wondered.

The List.

I guess Casper saw me staring at the window all cross-eyed because he said "Come on," just before grabbing my hand and taking me in the side door and down a half set of stairs.

His room was the first door by the stairwell, and since it was two am, it was a pretty sure bet that we'd escaped notice. Once we were inside, I started getting a little concerned that Casper might try to take advantage of the situation; me being tipsy and alone in his dorm room. But true to his word, he let me lay down, covered me with a blanket and put a garbage can beside the bed for me to puke in. And, then he locked the door as he headed back over to the party.

When Casper returned to his room at 4 am, I had already slept off most of the effects of the Omega Oil; and, I was feeling a whole lot better by the time he crawled into his twin–sized bed with me. After an hour or two of cuddling and a little touchy-feely, Casper and I did our thing just before sunrise. This left us with very little time for me to get out of his dorm room undetected. But who cares, because that night Casper and I definitely clicked.

Yippee – yo – yippee – yay! Who knew that white chocolate could be so scrumptious? Brotha you just woke this little dog up from a long hibernation; and, now I'm definitely ready to mate!

16
Quiet Storm

Thunder & lightening. That spring I also got my first opportunity to go back to Atlanta when Aayden and I decided to go visit our high school friend Maria. As fate would have it, our visit coincided with Freak-Nic, the 80's and 90's phenomenon that predated the Daytona, Virginia Beach and Galveston Black Student Beach parties. Held in the park, Freak-Nic was a chance to see and be seen. Kick it and chill. Hoe and hop. And that's what me and my girls did all afternoon long.

After spending the day at the park, Aayden and I went with Maria to visit her boyfriend at one of the rundown houses the Morehouse football players lived in just outside their campus. While looking for her boyfriend Maria happened to knock on the door of one of his friends and when he opened his door, *well, Glory-Glory-Glory!* Chocolate Thunder is just about the best description I could give that brother.

From his big eyes with those long lashes; to his juicy lips and white teeth with the small gap; to his muscular arms and broad shoulders; to his small waist and his thick behind that sat just within grasping distance of my hand, every single inch of the brotha was fine. Thunder was about 6'3 or 6'4 and deep dark chocolate all over.

The List.

While Maria busied herself inquiring about the whereabouts of her man, Chocolate Thunder and I both stood there in complete silence just drinking in the essence of each other; that is until the girl who was in his room spoke up and broke our trance.

Yup, I figured it was too good to be true. Well back to reality. Lawd knows there are about four or five hundred just like you in the two-mile radius that comprises the AU Center. So oh well, next specimen!

To my surprise, as we were turning to leave, Thunder slammed his room door, left the girl by herself, and followed us down the hall. But since this Negro had a female all up in his room, I kept walking because I really wasn't trying to hear what he had to say. However, while Aayden and I were waiting outside, he begged Maria to tell him where we were headed.

As fate would have it, all of us eventually ended up at the same party spot. The real crazy part is I wound up spending most of the night standing in the middle of the dance floor, literally mesmerized and somewhat embarrassed, as Chocolate Thunder danced seductively around me for hours.

Whew LAWD!

The brother truly had it going on; and, by the end of the night, he had become totally irresistible to me.

ᘓ ᘔ

That night I stayed with Thunder and he rocked my world. He did things to me that I didn't even know Black guys did, took my mind to places it had never been before, and left me feeling like I'd been STRUCK BY LIGHTENING. The brother was so smooth that for a brief minute I even thought about giving up my full scholarship at FAMU and transferring to Clark ASAP.

But just like all sexual experiences outside of a committed relationship, our brief moment of pleasure was simply that; a brief moment. A few hours later, Aayden and I were packing up for the 4 hour ride back to Tallahassee.

Tymira Mack

As much as I hate to admit it sista-girl, you may have finally met your match!

17

Homies, Lovers and Friends

Bros in multiple area codes. Believe it or not, Thunder and I actually did keep in touch; so, the rest of that spring my calling card was sprinkled with calls to Metro Atlanta. Through our dealings, I quickly figured out that Thunder was a typical New York–New Jersey boy who had a lot of street smarts; was quick witted; and, thought real fast on his feet. If that wasn't bad enough, since he was only a sophomore in college, he was also very much into partying hard, drinking hard and yes, hoe-ing hard.

Fortunately my relationship with Slow taught me that long distance love affairs with mild-mannered guys were difficult enough to manage; so I definitely decided to be extra cautious about maintaining contact with Thunder. Other than phenomenal sex, when it came to dealing with him, I had absolutely no expectations. Besides, even though the semester was about to end soon, things between Casper and I had started heating up a bit more.

❦ ❧

Summertime was quickly approaching and since my first summer at FAMU was off the chain, I just couldn't imagine going home. So, me, Aayden and one of our other roommates decided to remain in Tallahassee for summer school, and agreed to share an apartment together. The problem was, my parents were dead set against me living off campus.

With a little ingenuity, Aayden and I were able to convince my parents that I'd be living with her in their sorority house located a couple of blocks from campus. Of course they fell for it hook line and sinker. Meanwhile I was kicking it across town in my very own crib for the first time.

All we could afford was a two bedroom, two bath apartment, so my roommate and I agreed to share the bedroom with the attached bath; allowing Aayden, who had a man and who also loved to sleep in all her naked glory, to have her own room by herself. Besides, Casper was going away for a summer internship in Chicago so I wasn't expecting to have any overnight company anyway.

ଔ ଛ

A couple of weeks after we'd settled into our apartment, Aayden and I decided to take a road trip to Atlanta. But the day before the trip, Aayden had to cancel. I was totally bummed out because I was really looking forward to seeing Thunder again.

At the last minute, mother nature stepped in and convinced my other roommate to volunteer to take Aayden's place. Always down for an adventure, it seems that this time my roomie wanted to see for herself if all the hype we'd given Atlanta and its Negroes was really true.

I figured my girl would get all she bargained for and a whole lot more because Thunder and some of his fellow football homies had gotten summer jobs at an Atlanta nightclub. Nope, they weren't bartenders, or bouncers or even waiters. They were strippers. And judging by the hell-a performance Thunder had put on me the first night I met him, there was no doubt in my mind that he was cut out for the job.

I made sure we rolled into Atlanta on one of Thunder's work nights; 'cause I'd never been to a male strip show before, and I was itching to see what one was all about. I don't remember if he

102

The List.

was working at the Phoenix or at Excelsior Mills that night, but I do know for sure that it was Ladies Night.

Hummm there sure seems to be a lot more hood rats than college girls up in here I thought as I scanned the crowd. Oh well, these hoochies can't be all that bad?

But I soon found out, this definitely wasn't no tuxedo wearing, white boy, non-rhythm having strip show. No sir, those fellas were absolutely mind boggling. And the hoochies were truly out of the box. Girls were flashing $1's and $5's and $10's and $20's left and right. Things were heating up so much, it started getting hard to tell exactly who the strippers were and who the audience was.

If that wasn't bad enough, then the tricks started feeling the guys up as they stuffed their tip money way down inside what little costumes the dudes were still wearing. It was just wild. But I think what really took the cake was when this woman that was about eight months pregnant paid the guys to lap dance all up on her belly.

Ewww Yuck! Ok I have just seen it all!

After Thunder and his boy had gone into the dressing room and put back on their clothes, I was ready to go. I could handle the regular freaks all over him during the show, because hey, that was his job. But I was truly irked when he and his boy actually freaked the pregnant chick. It just seemed so disrespectful and disgusting to me.

That was until we got outside.

"Those freaks up in there are a real trip," I was still whining when we reached the car. "I can't believe how they let ya'll dance with your stank pricks all up on them and in their faces," I continued in disgust.

"Tammy, I warned you that it was wild," Thunder reminded me, obviously tickled that I was so perturbed by the whole scene.

"I know, but a pregnant girl, Thunder?" I groaned, looking at him like he was straight crazy. "How in the world could ya'll freak a pregnant girl?"

103

Tymira Mack

"Look Tam, I told you it's just a job. It covers all the expenses my measly little scholarship doesn't pick-up," he said as he handed me his tip money. "Here count this for me."

Ooooh. Not bad. Not bad indeed for only 2 ½ hours of work, I thought as I was reaching the $150 dollar mark, and still counting.

"Shoot I' own care if they're 8 to 80, blind, cripple or crazy, you better go'ne shake that thang boy! Do you need an agent?" I giggled.

ଔ ଋ

Thunder was a real take charge kind of guy and I enjoyed the fact that I didn't have to communicate my desires to him. Instinctively after he'd finished his set, he'd insisted on us leaving so that we could maximize our time together; and, I was all too happy to blow the joint because the chicks up in there were ruthless. They saw the brother was chilling with me after the show and yet they still were trying to get all up in his face.

On the way home Thunder asked "So what did you think about the show?"

"Honestly, those girls at the club were so wild I really couldn't get close enough to see most of your act," I sadly admitted. Not to worry though 'cause when we got back to his place, Thunder gave me my very own, up close and personal VIP dance.

Ohhhh, but unlike those other hoochies, I don't have to tip 'cause mine's on the house!

ଔ ଋ

The next morning, Thunder had to get up early and go to a Football meeting or something; leaving me all alone in his room for a couple of hours. I'm sure he probably thought that I would be asleep; but I took full advantage of that time to snoop through his room.

Being ultra-sneaky myself, I knew that when it came to relationships you could only believe one-half of what you saw and one-quarter of what you heard. And, even though Thunder

The List.

and I had clearly established we could each do our own thing, as long as we made sure no one would be disrespected when it was our time in town together, I still needed to know some thangs in order to keep the upper hand.

Now I wasn't fool enough to think that fine ole' Chocolate Thunder was in Hot–lanta all alone during those weeks when I was in Tallahassee; and he didn't fool himself into thinking I was living lonely in Tally either. In fact, Thunder had candidly told me about some of his female friends in Atlanta, and in my arrogance I just didn't give a flip.

How in the heck can their man spend a whole weekend in town without seeing them? Not counting the weeks that I blow into town on a Wednesday or Thursday night. Worse yet, when I am in town, he takes me to all the hot spots, so somebody has to have seen us together. Shoot them other tricks can't be much comp. Yup, they're either real weak or real stupid.

To tell you the truth, although they were all very attractive, I wasn't worried about the Atlanta-based chicks. But mindful of the fond spot that Mickey still had in my heart, I did set my sights on finding out whether the brother still had ties to any first loves back home. Yup, I knew all too well how strong of a pull first loves could have. Even though Thunder was a wild boy, I was certain that somewhere along the line, someone had once stolen, or still had, a piece of his heart.

BINGO just as I thought. Way down inside his foot locker I found two framed pictures and newspaper clippings of some girl who ran track at a college in another state. The detective in me spied the name under the picture in the article and determined right away that it wasn't his sister. As I read a little farther I realized she had attended a high school in his hometown.

Yup! She's definitely the one. Hummm. She's cute but she looks a little tom-boyish. Ok, so I'm still not feeling the competition. But just to be on the safe side, I better file all her vital stats in my little memory bank. I'm sure the info will come in handy sooner or later.

Tymira Mack

Ooooh and while I'm at it, why don't I just put her pictures back on the dresser where they probably were just before I came to visit? Men are so predictable and so stupid. If his game was really on point, he would have put this stuff in one of his boy's room for safe keeping during my visit.

When Thunder came back from his meeting, he found me pretending to be asleep in his bed just where he'd left me. However, when he went to put his shoes in his closet, he noticed that the two pictures were sitting back on top of his chest of drawers.

All the brother could do was giggle and say "Dang you're good."

"I thought you knew bro," I said confidently. "Now come on over here and let me give you a few more reasons to forget all about Ms. Flo-Jo."

CR SO

The rest of our weekend was a blast and I left Atlanta still madly in like with Thunder. At the same time though, I was in a bit of a hurry to get back to Tallahassee to see Casper because he'd been assigned to an eight week internship in Chicago.

I made it back to Tally just in time to spend a couple of intimate days with Casper and then he was gone; and, back to classes it was for me.

CR SO

The summer went by pretty fast. I'd gone back to Atlanta to kick it with Thunder at least 2 or 3 more times and I also managed to keep in contact with Casper. In fact in July, somewhere around *Taste of Chicago* time, Casper even invited me up to see him.

I'd never been to Chicago before so I figured, *what the heck I'm down*. That was until I got to Tallahassee's rinky-dinky little airport and boarded a six seater crop duster airplane. *Surely you don't expect me to fly all the way to Chicago in this tiny little bucket?*

The List.

As it turns out it was a commuter flight which would take me to either Jacksonville or Atlanta, I can't remember now, where I would board a jet to Chi–cago, Chi–cago.

Casper met me at O'Hare Airport with this big ole' greasy grin and a bear hug. He truly seemed happier to see me than I'd expected. And the hug really caught me off guard, because outside of the bed, Casper wasn't a real touchy-feely, affectionate type of guy, at least not with me anyway.

Ok who are you and what have you done with the real Casper?

His internship had hooked him up with a room at a downtown Chicago-area College, so we caught the train downtown and walked the couple of blocks to his dorm. Since he was staying at a white college, his dorm was unisex and I was allowed to go upstairs (unlike most historically black colleges).

The fact that Casper didn't have a roommate also worked in our favor; leaving us free to chill together however we pleased.

Later on that evening, one of Casper's mutual internship friends came over to hang out with us.

"Tam this is Quentin" Casper informed me. "But I just call him Q or M & M."

As I extended my hand out to Q, I was stuck by how familiar he looked. "It's nice to meet you."

Then I turned to Casper, "What's with all the initials, 'Q' and 'M & M'?"

"Cause every time you turn around he's like 'a Morehouse Man this' and 'a Morehouse Man that'," Casper laughed obviously dogging Q.

Morehouse? Did you say Morehouse? I thought as I looked a little closer at Q this time and kind of jerked my hand out of his.

As it turned out Q was a student at Morehouse College. *Yup, that's right, Thunder's school.*

Oh boy! What are the freaking odds? Ok quit staring at me and chill with all the questions. I promise that I DON'T look familiar to you!

Fortunately after a couple of beers, Q began to mellow out enough to subscribe to my theory that I must have had a long lost

107

twin in Atlanta. With that little problem out of the way, I was free to relax and enjoy all of the Chicago landmarks they took me to see over the weekend.

∝ ∾

Since I only had classes on Tuesday's and Thursday's I wasn't scheduled to leave Chicago until Monday afternoon. So while Casper went to work on Monday morning I went shopping at Marshall Fields. Before he left for work, Casper told me he'd call if he could meet me for lunch; thus, after some quick shopping I'd hurried to get back to his room by noon.

When the phone rang, I just instinctively picked it up, thinking it was him calling, "Hello." *Hello, is anyone there?*

"Hello?" Click. *Umm, I guess it was a wrong number?* I thought to myself.

Then the phone rang right back.

"Hello," I answered eagerly.

"Hello?" replied the obviously surprised female voice on the other end of the phone. "Is Casper there?"

Oh she sounds too young to be his mom, so it must be his sister.

"No I'm sorry he's at work," I chirped in my 'wanna make your family like me' voice, "but I'll be meeting him for lunch, can I give him a message?"

"Yes, YOU can tell him that his GIRLFRIEND Samantha called!" She insisted angrily.

His girlfriend Samantha? Ok think fast. I don't know anyone named Samantha at FAMU, so she can't be a chick on the side at school. And, if he had already picked up some trick in Chicago, surely she would know that he was at work. So let's just get to the bottom of this. If I get her area code I can figure out just where Ms. Thang is calling from.

"Ok Samantha, if you give me a number where he can reach you, I'll be sure to give him the message," I said hoping to narrow down just where this heifer lived.

"He knows the number," she said snottily.

Ok, so she's smarter than I thought.

The List.

"Alright, ok then, not a problem. I'll tell him that you called," I hissed politely through gritted teeth. I was more than ready to hang up with Miss-Missy cause I was unsure how much longer I could be nice. But she wouldn't let it go. "Who is this?"

Oh now wouldn't you love to know who I am you little witch? I said to myself as I got more irritated. "Ooooh, I'm just a friend that he flew up from Florida to spend the weekend," I declared hoping to piss her off.

Well actually him and my Financial Aid check paid for the plane fare; but anyway, did I forget to mention that I've been screwing his brains out all weekend? I mumbled to myself.

Since my beef wasn't with this female, I decided to take the high road and deal with the whole stinking issue at its slithering roots. "Samantha, I'll be sure to give him your message, just as soon as he gets in. Ok hon? Good-bye." Click!

Girlfriend Samantha? So Mr. Casper, you've got yourself a girlfriend, huh? Well all right ya piss yella punk. You've got games? So let's just see what we can find on Ms. Samantha.

As I scanned the room trying to decide the best place to start snooping, it all of a sudden dawned on me. Sitting on his desk the whole weekend were these two pictures mounted separately in the same double frame. One was no doubt his mom, and naturally I figured the other high yellow heifer to be his sister.

Not so fast. The Sherlock Holmes in me tells me that something literally ain't quite right with that picture.

And low and behold, when I opened up the frame and looked at the back of the picture, it read something like, "To Casper, I miss you a lot, Love Samantha."

Well you sly old puppy. You almost got one over on me. But you gotta eat a little more Mutt Chow before you're big and bad enough to dog me out.

ଔ ଓ

A little bit later, Casper and I indeed met and had a wonderful lunch; his treat of course. After lunch, he gave me cab

109

fare to the airport; and as we prepared to part, we hugged and shared a brief kiss.

"Have a safe trip back home Tam, and call me to let me know you got in ok."

"Oh yeah, I almost forgot," I called out after him as he turned to go back to work. "Your girlfriend Samantha called. She said you had the number."

You would think that it would be impossible for a half–white black guy to get any paler, but the sound of my words stopped him dead in his tracks and he immediately turned two shades lighter than transparent.

Before he could start with the lies, I cut him off. "No need to explain partner, 'cause we're just friends remember? By the looks of her pictures, Samantha's real cute. And, please tell her I said I had a lovely time talking with her. I'll see you when you get back to Tally."

Now don't lose no freaking sleep trying figure out what all I told her. Peace and I'm out.

CR SO

I never really believed in luck, but what are the odds the sexy chocolate brother who was good friends with my newly adopted Tallahassee family would be working at the airport when my flight got in.

Well what a fitting welcome back to Tally!

This brother was tall, dark and most certainly handsome; and, both he and I knew it.

Mental note to self, you WILL get with Mr. Chocolate Pudding Pop.

CR SO

When I returned from Chicago there were only a couple of weeks left in the summer school term. Since I wasn't feeling Thunder or Casper at the time, besides going to class, I occupied

The List.

my spare time by hanging out with my roommates and just plain old having fun.

By summer's end, we learned that Aayden was being assigned to an internship up North for the whole fall semester; and since we knew we couldn't swing the rent alone, my other roommate and I reluctantly decided to move out as well.

The really screwed up part was the fact that FAMU still hadn't finished renovating the dorms most of the business school students preferred to live in; so there was an on campus housing shortage. *Oh bummer!* And by the time I tried to get a room on campus, there were none to be found. *Awwww shucks!*

Thankfully, my grades for the entire freshman year were the bomb so the combination of my good grades and the on-campus housing shortage really helped sway my parents toward giving me permission to move off campus. Ok, go ahead and laugh 'cause you know that's funny.

As it turns out, the joke really was on me, because there was very little decent off campus housing near FAMU; and affordable housing near FSU filled up fast.

So there I was, Little Ms. Slick Pants, with no freaking where to live. But just like a cat with multiple lives, I once again managed to land with my feet planted firmly on the ground, when my new Tallahassee family took me in for a few weeks until I could find my own place.

Look at luck. Not only do I have a place to crash for a while, but I also get a chance to see Mr. Chocolate Pudding Pop on the regular since he's like a son to my new family. Man that's like giving a diabetic a 2nd slice of pecan pie with whipped cream and caramel on top.

Don't get me wrong, even though being that close to Pudding on a regular basis, and not being able to touch him, was like coming off of heroine cold turkey, I totally respected their house. But my goodness, by the time my apartment was ready to move into, me and Mr. Pudding Pop were more than hyped to play horizontal twister.

Tymira Mack

Once I moved, Pudding and I managed to keep our little tryst on the "hush." In actuality though, we only hooked up a couple of times because I began feeling like I was betraying the trust of a family I'd grown very close to. Caring about the feelings of others was definitely a new and uncharacteristic trait for me; and since my passion for all things Chocolate was still a whole lot stronger than my consideration for the feelings of others, it was lucky for me that I had to redirect my focus to the start of the new school semester.

Time out for yummy deserts. At least not for now.........

18
Don't Push Me 'Cause

Snap, crackle, pop. Even though the fall semester had gotten into full swing, I'd once again found myself feeling kind of lonely. Other than the time that I spent on campus in class, I really didn't have an opportunity to interact much with anyone. My ace-boon-coon Aayden was away interning and I was living by myself in an apartment above this strange hippy couple's garage, in an area where there weren't a lot of college students.

If that wasn't bad enough, although he was back in town, Casper had started being missing in action on a regular basis; and I was getting fed up with all of his excuses. "I gotta study for this." Or "me and my boys are planning to do that." Blasé – blasé. Yadda, Yadda, Yadda.

Ok you should know by now not to play me for boo-boo the fool. Do you honestly expect me to believe that your yellow A– is studying or hanging out with a bunch of dudes at 1 and 2 am on weeknights?

Although I was somewhat suspicious and a lot pissed with his nonchalant attitude, I really didn't have a lot of time to devote to figuring out what the heck Casper was up to. Instead, I was busy trying to get my own hustle on.

Hanging out with Aayden and her sorority sisters had given me a sideline taste of the Greek-life and all its perks. I was definitely vibing on how the frats and sororities seemed to run

113

things around campus. And truth be told, I got caught up in the whole power and mystique thing they held.

As with all my endeavors, except relationships, I was always one for thoroughly doing my homework. So for about four or five months, I'd secretly been peeping out the various sorority options at FAMU. In the end, I set my sights on one of the two most popular sororities on campus.

While I'm sure my final selection came as a shock to some people, because I didn't decide to try to pledge the sorority Aayden had joined; it's like I told you before, she was ying, down for acting cute and conceited, and I was yang, cute but one snap short of crazy.

ෙ ෩

Within one hour of entering into the unofficial pledge period, I realized I had indeed chosen the right sorority. With names like 'Big Sister Psycho the Psychotic Witch' there was no doubt that a whole lot of these heifers were one snap short of crazy, just like me.

Over the next eight weeks, I handled the little mind games; I endured the public humiliation of dressing in identical homely outfits and not being allowed to wear makeup; and, I even adapted to walking everywhere in a straight line with my head held down. I learned to deal with the constant sleep deprivation; and, even survived living with 32 other females in a three bedroom, two bathroom apartment for six weeks.

Ohhhh, but the day came when one of those 5'2" little 'Big Sister' heifers stood on her tiny little tippy toes and screamed all up in my 5'11" face, just one time too freaking many.

Oh, Snap!

Fortunately for the both of us, that little chi-wa-wa came to her senses and backed the heck up. 'Cause she was about one second shy of getting the taste pimp slapped out of her, and I was about one second from being permanently kicked off line. That would have been a waste of 10 whole weeks of my time and over $1,000 of my money.

The List.

❧ ❧

Somehow I managed to make it through all the drama of the pledge period and emerged a proud sorority sista. It felt good. Nope great! I was on top of the world. And guess what else? As it turns out, Casper hadn't given me the big dis after all. Just like me, he had been trying to survive the Greek pledging process himself.

As for all those days (and nights) that I thought he'd gone AWOL, it turns out that he was actually involved in pre-pledging activities. What's even funnier is that he and I ended up pledging organizations that were unofficially considered brothers and sisters.

After spending a couple of months on total lockdown, most pledgee's ended their pledge periods totally stressed out, with only three things on their minds. One was to celebrate being officially inducted in to their fraternity or sorority by stepping on 'the Set' with their fellow line brothers or line sisters. The second was to get sexed. And, the third was to get some sleep. In that exact order. And, Casper and I were no exception to this rule.

A few days after having completed steps one through three, I was no longer stressed out, and I was ready to party. Lucky for me, the end of our pledge period coincided with the beginning of the annual FAMU – Bethune Cookman College Thanksgiving Classic Football Weekend. Even better yet, Aayden's internship had ended and she was headed home for the holidays. The timing couldn't have been more perfect.

It's about to be on and poppin'.

19
Fire & Desire

Creep, creep, creep, creep. The funny thing about pledging is that when you're first inducted into the organization, you're totally on fire. On fire to hang out with your fellow fraternity and sorority members. On fire to party. Even on fire to do community service, which ironically is the true purpose for the existence of fraternities and sororities.

For most people, during the first few months right after you join the frat or sorority, your level of commitment rages like a hellacious towering inferno. Then it gradually cools down and becomes a lifetime simmering flame.

There are also the rare bunch whose fires never die down. Every time you see them, they are stepping and shouting their organization's call 24/7. They are the first ones to get to every party, they stay on the dance floor all night, and they are the last to go home. They hoe and hop; and, hop and hoe, like rabbits in heat. They do everything on campus, except study, with such extreme fervor that eventually they self-destruct.

I guess I was somewhere in between both extremes. I was on fire for my sorority while I was in college; going to all the parties and availing myself of all the membership perks of these elite campus

The List.

organizations. But just as soon as I graduated, it seems I all but forgot that my pledge was supposed to be a lifetime commitment.

Ooops!

ભ જ

Albeit short lived, my period of true commitment toward my sorority began when I returned to school from Thanksgiving break. For those couple of weeks between the Thanksgiving and Christmas breaks, I was consumed with sorority life. I went to all the parties. I participated in community service activities, and I even spent all of my free time hanging out with a small group of my sorority sisters.

Except for trying to repair my GPA – which went from a 3.0 before I pledged, to a 2.3 the semester I pledged – all I did was eat, sleep and drink sorority life and all of its many perks. And I wasn't alone. Almost all of the major Greek organizations on campus had inducted pledge lines that semester. So by December of 1986, our campus was filled with about 75 new sorority girls and fraternity guys.

With the distraction of all the new Greeks on campus, plus our own selfish desires to live our new frat and sorority lifestyles to the fullest, Casper and I didn't really put much effort into rekindling what was left of our fading relationship. And since, I was having so much fun enjoying sorority life I really wasn't fazed; that was until the dirty dog had the nerve to start dating one of my sorority sisters.

It's bad enough that you're dating one of my soror's you little weasel; but out of all the chicks in my sorority your punk A– got the nerve to pick one of my line sisters?

I didn't fault my sorority sister for hooking up with him though, because she had no way of knowing about the secret relationship that Casper and I had been having for over a year. But as for him, I really wanted to yank his freaking chain!

ભ જ

117

Tymira Mack

As hurtful as it was to my ego, not my heart, the situation with Casper dating my line sister really opened my eyes to something I hadn't even paid attention to before; the fact that the members of the Greek organizations on campus had a bad habit of dating and hooking up with each other.

It was almost like a collegiate swingers club. Boy in Frat A dates Girl in Sorority A today; next week he hooks up with Girl in Sorority B; all the while maintaining a secret relationship with another girl in Sorority A. *Ohhhh, and let's not forget his fetish for making secret video tapes of all his girls.*

Now by no coincidence, almost 75% of all fraternity and sorority members on campus were either attractive or popular or both. And of course, since my definition of attractive included some measure of chocolate-ness, it goes without saying that the campus fraternities were virtual storehouses for the types of Negroes that appealed to me. Thankfully though, the whole Casper hooking up with my soror incident happened as I was just beginning to get caught up in the whole frat/sorority lifestyle.

Yup, I see I'm gonna have to step outside the campus fraternity arena to hunt for my next Chocolate Kiss.

20
Secret Lovers

A mirror to his soul. After going home for Thanksgiving and seeing the level of stress my mom was dealing with while trying to work and care for my ailing grandfather, I requested an internship assignment at home for the next semester. Although I wasn't excited about missing my first full semester on campus as a sorority girl, I knew that physically and emotionally my mother really needed some help.

My college major was accounting, so I was assigned to intern at a major bank located in downtown Miami. Although this was an opportunity a lot of students would have killed for, I was less than enthusiastic.

I hated wearing the corporate, banker's blue suits and crisp white shirts every day. I hated the daily two hour roundtrip commute in heavy traffic. I hated the griminess of downtown Miami and the daily harassment from all the homeless people. And most of all, I hated having to brown-nose and pretend like I enjoyed working in the corporate world every day.

To make matters worse, Mickey, my hometown hook-up, had left town and joined the military. But, since I worked 8 to 5 during the day and spent alternating nights caring for my grandfather, I really didn't have time for much of a social life anyhow.

Tymira Mack

Even though I wasn't seeing anyone in town, Thunder was calling me from Atlanta regularly and sweating me for a more exclusive type of relationship. Fortunately all the attention I was getting from him went a long way toward satisfying most of my desires for male companionship.

CR SO

Now don't get me wrong, I did manage to do a little partying here and there in Miami; and, I managed to take time off from work to go back to Tallahassee to catch the last half of my sorority's Greek week. Although I was mostly going to Tally to kick it for sorority week, I was also a sister on a mission.

It seems while hanging out with fellow classmates one day, Aayden learned that a guy from one of our freshman classes secretly had a crush on me. Although he and I had flirted a bit during our freshman year, he was a little on the Caucasian acting, non-thuggish side, and he simply took too long to halla at a sister. In the meantime I'd hooked up with Slow and he'd hooked up with his current girlfriend.

Naturally after he confided the truth about this crush to Aayden, my girl felt compelled to reveal, quite to his surprise, that I'd had a crush on him as well.

But she didn't stop there. Nope, being ever the matchmaker, Aayden made a point of getting the two of us communicating while I was still in Miami on internship.

So although I was technically in Tally for my sorority week, I was also looking forward to discussing this mutual attraction with Greg in person.

Once I got to town, I found it a little difficult for Greg and me to hook-up. He had baseball practice just about every afternoon; and well, all my evenings were reserved for hanging out at sorority parties.

The List.

It's too bad he can't hang out at the parties with me, I remember debating with myself; *but, hey what do you expect, you know he has a girlfriend?*

❧ ☙

Since I hadn't been in town in over 3 months, and since being seen with Greg in public was not an option, *yet?*, I ended up going to my sorority ball alone. The ball was fantastic, the music was hot and the alcohol flowed all night. But still, by the end of the night I was a little lonely and ready for some male companionship.

Greg lived alone in an apartment near FSU and by the time I reached his place, I was still buzzing from the alcohol I'd been drinking all night. Of course, this made me bolder and more courageous than I would normally have been when I was totally sober.

Greg was a really intelligent guy and he was giving me all these polite, white-boyish compliments from the moment I entered his apartment in my strapless party dress. I don't know if I was still tipsy, or just plain old horny since I'd been involuntarily celibate for the past four months; but all the while we sat there talking, each time he smiled, he seemed to get cuter and cuter and cuter.

Ok, I gotta be buzzing because your proper butt is really turning me on!

We just sat there in his living room hanging out, watching videos and chit-chatting about all sorts of stuff for over two hours, until we both felt comfortable enough to talk about our mutual attraction.

Of course, I couldn't help but ask him about his girlfriend, "So what's up with you and Aneesa?"

"What do you mean?" He asked in his proper white boyish way.

"I mean like, what's up with ya'lls relationship?"

"Oh well, nothing's up," he said. "I mean we're still together."

"No stupid," I said getting frustrated with his cute proper self. "I mean how do you feel about her and stuff?"

"Oh, I mean I love her," he proudly proclaimed with this stupid grin on his face.

You love her? Yeah right, you love your girlfriend? So then why am I here? "Ok if you say so," I said not really buying his last statement about loving her.

Then I couldn't leave well enough alone. I just had to know what it was that he saw in her. After all, he was a cute, semi-chocolate fellow from the Atlanta suburbs. And, she was literally two shades shy of midnight, which wasn't so bad except that she also wore thick glasses, had really ashy lips, a bad perm and mounds of dandruff , and she was from deep in the hood.

She is nice and all, but what in the world could he possibly see in her?

"Well for one thing," he said smiling, "from the first time that I saw her I was attracted to her long legs."

Attracted to her freaking long legs? What kind of answer is that? Beep. Beep. Beep. FREAK ALERT. Watch out this brother may be a serial killer?

"What?" I asked partially dumbfounded. "I've known brothers to be attracted to a lot of things, but long legs?"

"Yeah," he said quite seductively, "long legs just like yours."

For some reason, his lips looked oh so sexy when he said that. And they were getting sexier and sexier by the minute.

"Greg, you've really got to explain the legs thing to me, 'cause I just don't get it."

And that's when the brother in him finally kicked in. He leaned over, kissed me, grabbed my hand, led me to his bedroom and told me "I can show you why I love long legs better than I can tell you."

Wow! They must put something in the water up there in Atlanta? He's wasting his time in college. He should really look into a career in pro wrestling!

CR SO

122

The List.

Afterward, we stayed up for a long time talking about all sorts of life stuff. I'd never really slept with anyone who appealed to the intelligent side of me before, so I was really enjoying talking about "deep" stuff with Greg.

Somehow though, we got on the subject of God. Boy, why did I want to do that? It seemed like the brother's whole body literally turned as cold as ice, and I immediately sensed that something was wrong.

So I asked, "You do believe in God, don't you?"

And the brother quickly and firmly said "NO."

Whoa – hold up now.

"Ok, considering the fact that I'm laying naked in your bed, you know that I'm a LONG way from being Mother Theresa, but how can you say .you don't believe in God?" I asked while I strained to look at his face because the room was perfectly dark except for the lighted numbers on his clock-radio.

And, I will never forget what happened next for as long as I live! When the brother turned toward me to respond to my question, both of his eyes glowed an indescribably intense shade of red, and he said "I believe that there is a higher power in this world, I just don't happen to believe that it's God."

Awe shucks. I done did it now. I done slept with the son of Satan himself. Father God, please forgive me and PLEASE get me out of here alive. I PROMISE, no… I SWEAR, I won't creep no more!

21

No More Drama

This is only a test Since I was an accounting major, in order to graduate I was required to complete my third internship during tax season. But because I'd been going through school at such an accelerated pace, in order to properly align my third internship with tax season, I would have to complete my second internship back to back with the first one.

To make a long story short, I ended up having to go directly from my spring internship assignment in Miami to a summer internship assignment at a major international appliance manufacturing company in Louisville, Kentucky. I wasn't thrilled about this internship, though 'cause I didn't think that there were any Black people living in Kentucky. And besides, this would mean that I would be away from school, my friends and my sorority for another whole semester.

Oh well. I gotta do what I gotta do. At least I'm only gonna miss a summer term this time!

❧ ❧

Although I'd made numerous road trips between home and Tallahassee and between Tallahassee and Atlanta, I'd never driven really far before; especially not by myself. So I decided to make a bunch of pit stops on my way up to Kentucky.

The List.

First, I stopped in Tallahassee and stayed with my adopted family for a couple of days. This gave me a chance to hang out on the Hill and catch up on all the school gossip I'd missed out on the previous semester.

I probably would have stayed a few more days in Tallahassee if Thunder hadn't been blowing up my phone. During the whole time I was interning in Miami, he'd been calling me quite a bit, and constantly asking me the same question. "Why do you keep refusing to believe I'm serious about the two of us taking this thing to the next level?"

The two of us? Don't you mean all of us – me and you, plus your girls and my men?

"The next level?" I joked. "I think we've taken each other to more than the next level quite a few times."

"Get serious Tammy, I'm for real. I'm ready to do this," he'd always say with as much sincere conviction as a true player could manage to cough up.

"Come on Thunder, our friendship has always worked out fine this way. Why would you want to commit to something that you, well we, aren't ready for?" I'd always reply.

Duhhh. Although I often fantasize about a fairy tale happily ever after ending with you, I'm realistic enough to know that you aren't ready, or even capable of committing all of yourself to me. Not now, and considering the way we started this little love affair; probably not ever.

"So I just prefer to keep things the way they are, that way you never have a reason to feel compelled to lie to me about what you're doing," I'd rationalize.

ଔ ഌ

Thunder was still at work when I first rolled into Atlanta, so I made my way over to Maria's apartment, planning to meet up with him later that night. Coincidentally, another one of my high school classmates was also in town visiting Maria for the weekend.

125

Tymira Mack

When I got to the apartment, my homegirls mentioned they'd called a couple of the fellas that we went to high school with to come over since they lived in Atlanta also.

That's cool, I can just kill the time reminiscing with my homies until Thunder gets off work, I thought as I plopped down in the chair next to the front door.

I'd noticed that my visiting home girl was rushing around, primping her hair and fixing her clothes and make-up, so I joked her, "I wonder who these Negro's are that's got you still vibing on them after over three years?"

And my homie Maria piped in, "Oh girl, not them. HIM. She only got love for one Negro, and they make a point of seeing each other every time she comes to town. I sometimes wonder who she really comes up here to see."

Just about the time my curiosity was starting to get the best of me—*hmmm, who did she use to mess with in school?*—there was a knock at the door. Since I was the closest, I got up and answered it, only to find myself face to face with Puffy.

It had been more than two years since our last face to face encounter at the Day's Inn in Ft. Lauderdale and neither one of us was prepared for this situation. I tried to play it cool and snap out of the flashback I was having, remembering how hurt I was to find out that Puffy had intentionally ignored my pregnancy; and, play it cool. And for once, even Mr. GQ smooth was short on words.

I've gotta do something before everyone picks up on our negative vibes, I thought as it was becoming obvious there was quite a bit of unspoken tension between Puffy and I. So I completely swallowed my pride and greeted Puffy and my other homeboy with a weak hug before politely excusing myself to go lay down in the bedroom and rest.

Now Maria knew it wasn't like me to come to Atlanta and waste valuable hanging-out time, so she came back to the room to check on me.

"Girl what is wrong with you?" she asked. "Puffy and what-ya-call-it brought over some Hennessey & Coke, and some

The List.

Bacardi and we're about to make some daiquiri's. I know you ain't gonna stay locked up in this room until Thunder comes home?"

Humph I see the neg-ga still rolls with a stash of Hennessey and Coke in the trunk of his car. I guess some things never change.

"Naw I'm cool," I said, "I don't want to be a fifth wheel to ya'lls party."

"Oh don't worry, her and Puffy will be gone in less than five minutes," she assured me. "I told you, she don't come to Atlanta to see me."

Just as I was wondering to myself, *Hmmm, I wonder how far back their relationship goes,* she continued, "Girl she's been in love with Puffy ever since he got her pregnant and her mamma made her have an abortion back in the eleventh grade."

Oh my gosh, she's the one!

Now that I had the final clue to the age old mystery, I just had to go back out into the living room to witness this little love affair for myself. But, by the time we got back out there, Puffy and ya girl had already crept out and left. It seems the only thing Puffy had left behind was his boy, his Bacardi and his bag of sensi.

At that point I hadn't smoked anything since my freshman year at FAMU when my roommates and I drove over to Frenchtown and bought some local weed. To this day I have no idea what we bought. It didn't look like no other weed I'd ever seen before. In fact, it looked and smelled a lot like oregano. But once we rolled it in some zig-zags, smoked it, and followed it with a couple of Jakarta cigars, our butts were in the parking lot of the football stadium acting like we were ten years old, turning cartwheels and giggling for a couple of hours. After that crazy night I promised myself, once again, that I would never ever smoke again.

But hey, promises are made to be broken. Even though I was trying hard to keep smiling on the outside, inside I had once again been crushed by yet another encounter with Puffy. And, the situation proved to be more than my sober brain could handle.

Tymira Mack

I don't know why I constantly let him get all up in my head? Awww shoot, forget the dumb; fire it up and pass the joint!

ভ ন্ধ

Over the next couple of days I hung out during the daytime at Greg, the son of Satan's, posh suburban Atlanta home while Thunder was at work, and I spent my nights with Thunder. And yes, without the slightest bit of guilt, I did with both of them what I did best; had sex.

Then early Wednesday morning, I got in my car and headed up I-85 on my way to Kentucky. Although Greg and Thunder provided effective diversions for my thoughts over those couple of days; once I was all alone in my car on the six hour drive to Kentucky, I could no longer hide from myself. For probably the first time in my life, I felt truly ashamed of my freaky self and tired of all the games.

How much longer can you continue going through life without feeling any emotions?

ভ ন্ধ

I wasn't scheduled to meet my internship supervisor until Friday, so I spent Thursday finalizing my housing arrangements and exploring the City of Louisville. On Friday, I met my supervisor, completed my employment paperwork and got a tour of the huge manufacturing plant. Afterwards, I was told to report to the Company's Medical Center to complete my physical exam.

My What?

It turns out the company had a policy requiring all new employees to pass a physical exam and a drug test.

Drug Test? Oh my gosh, no way.

If I hadn't already signed a three month apartment lease, I would have just packed up my stuff and headed back to Tallahassee right then, cause there was no way I was going to pass a drug test.

The List.

Fortunately for me, the Company did such a thorough physical that by the time I completed the routine portion of the exam, it was too late to do the drug test. The clinic staff joked about running out of time and commented that it wasn't a big deal because they were sure that I'd pass the drug test anyway.

Yeah, if you only freaking knew, ha-ha-ha.

So I was given an appointment to come back and take the drug test the following Monday morning.

Oh crap. What am I gonna do?

ᘓ ᘔ

As soon as I got back to my apartment I called up Aayden and told her what was going on. And then she rocked my world. "Girl you know what-cha-call-it failed his drug test at XYZ Corporation and now they're talking about kicking him out of the Business School and taking his scholarship."

I was dumbfounded. "When did this happen and why didn't you warn me about this?"

"Oh, girl it happened while you were interning in Miami. Besides, I didn't warn you that a lot of companies had started drug screening interns because you weren't smoking anymore. Remember?"

Dang, I could lose my scholarship and get kicked out of school. Mama is going to kill me.

But Aayden didn't get to be a big time debate champion without being able to think fast on her feet. "Look chill out. Let me make a few phone calls. You remember our freshman summer when we use to hang out at B's house and him and his roommate use to smoke weed all day?" She tried reminding me.

What the hell do those stupid dope-head jocks have to do with the fact that I'm about to get kicked out of school?

Before I could get a word in edgewise, Aayden continued, "well you ever wondered how them Negroes always passed their drug tests before football season?"

Tymira Mack

ᙣ ᙠ

About an hour later, Aayden called me back. "Ok there are these herbal pills that you can buy at the GNC."

"The GNC?" I interrupted.

"Yeah, you know that health pill kinda store where all the body builders and health fanatics go to buy those herbal supplements."

"Say what?" I interrupted again.

"Look just find the mall," she paused, "they do have a mall in that country place don't they?"

"Hey check it, I forgot to tell you, this place ain't country at all," I said all excited. "It's actually a big City. I think it's gonna be cool here."

"Ok focus. If you don't pass the drug test you won't get a chance to see how cool that town is," she quickly reminded me.

"Oh yeah; so what am I supposed to get at the health food store again?"

"It's not a health food story silly. Now see you done made me forget. It's either ginseng or ginkgo-biloba or something like that," she said obviously frustrated with herself for forgetting the name of the stuff. "Just ask the people in the store."

"Oh like, I'm just supposed to go in there and say can you show me your gen-gen-kee-kee-loba-loba pills that help you pass the piss test," I asked her in my silliest voice.

"You are real stupid," she teased.

"Ok so when I get these piss-test fixer-upper pills, what am I supposed to do with them?" I asked getting serious again.

"Well B and 'nem said you have to take the pills for two days straight, and then you should be able to pass the urine test."

"Alright, we'll see." I said hopefully. "Talk to you later."

Even though I didn't believe that the stuff would work, I didn't have any other options. So over the weekend, I crammed down a whole bottle of those darn pills. And in the meantime, I even thought about paying one of the maids at the hotel across the street for a bottle of pee.

Hello? Buy a bottle of pee? What am I thinking? Well I guess desperate times call for desperate measures. After all, what's mama gonna say if your stupid A— gets kicked out of school and lose your scholarship cause you was smoking the ganja?

ଓ ଚ

By Monday, I'd decided that all I could do was roll with the punches. I was geared up for the test and praying that those pills had done the trick. But gosh darn-it, there was yet another obstacle standing in my way. The stupid company required you to sign a statement acknowledging consent for the drug test.

On the form there was a list of different illegal drugs and a set of instructions requiring me to check any of the drugs that I'd used within the past six months. Then at the bottom of the form there was this paragraph which in essence said that "if you knowingly give false information on the form, you would be terminated."

So, here was my dilemma. If I answered yes to any of the questions, then I would get fired that day. But if I lied on the form and my test came back positive, then I'd get fired for lying.

After a painful deliberation, I decided to come clean, tell the truth and hope that they didn't notice that I'd checked yes under marijuana.

No such luck. The freaking plant MD had seen my tiny little check mark and had come out from his office to personally question me, with a look of disgust on his face.

"Well young lady it looks like we've got ourselves a little problem," he said staring at me like I was a villain.

"The question is," he continued "what are we going to do about this?"

Tymira Mack

His face, his voice, his attitude, man everything about old dude, reminded me a lot of the doctor who had brokered my abortion years earlier. And at that point, I just zoned out; had flash backs; and, immediately stopped giving a flip about what would happen to me.

Screw them freaking dream killers and their stupid internship!

But maybe the truth does set you free? To this day, I don't know the results of that drug test; but I do know that I stayed in Kentucky and completed the internship that summer; I never lost my scholarship; and, I never got kicked out of school.

I guess those pills must have done the trick?

22

Army, Navy, Air Force...

A few good men. I can't remember but I believe Aayden was back out on internship the fall that I finally returned to FAMU. I think that's how I ended up living with one of my line sisters who was from up North. She was a really pretty brown girl with gorgeous naturally curly hair, and she was just as kind-hearted as she could be. But sometimes she had the blonde thing going on up in the brains department. And, although we'd pledged together, we didn't really roll in the same circles.

About the most exciting part of living with her was drooling over her "play" brother whenever he came over to visit. He was in the Marines ROTC. He was f–Y–ne, and he had this arrogance and swagger with his fineness that was just so irresistible.

Now I know you're thinking that I was trying to get some. But I'd learned enough from my years of fooling around with Thunder that trying to stay half a step ahead of a totally confident and fine bad boy was hell-a hard work. And besides, he was definitely into the light skinned, petite sistas, anyhow.

So instead I just listened to this brotha and studied the stories that he told about all the girls he was pimping around campus. Unbeknownst to him, I was learning some valuable insider information that would help me to recognize and, more importantly, stay ahead of the game in the future.

Tymira Mack

That first semester back at school, I mostly hung out with a few of my pledge line sisters. Essentially, the six of us partied together; studied together; schemed together; and, even spent quite a bit of time just sitting around being bored together.

I preferred to hang out with them because all six of us tended to have cunningly wicked sides to our personalities; and when you mixed each of our strengths together, we made for a deadly concoction. Aside from wreaking havoc with them, my 'root crew' of choice also helped me to catch up on all the excitement I'd missed during the six months I was away interning.

With 32 line sisters, plus 30 more sorority sisters on campus, it took me a while to update my hook-up notebook. This little mental tool helped me to avoid knowingly kicking it with another soror's ex hook-up. To be honest with you, the hook-up scorecard I was keeping had become so long and polluted, it was quite obvious to me that most of the guys on campus I would have been interested in were no longer fair game for me to pursue.

Oh Bummer!

That was until I bumped into this guy from Atlanta who had been in my freshman Health class. *Oh my, I see a lot has changed since freshman year!*

He had obviously joined the Marines and was a part of ROTC. He had developed these chiseled arms, had gotten a buzz haircut and was in some military fatigues that were wearing the heck out of him. *Dang, a few good men; they sho' weren't lying!*

When he smiled and said hello, I was done. He still had a young, cute, innocent looking face, but his new and improved body was definitely banging. I promise you I can't remember how long after I first saw him again that he ended up kicking at my

134

apartment. I don't know if he'd come over with my roommates play brother or what? I just remember hooking up with Mr. Semper Fi.

We had all been sitting around drinking one evening when I not so innocently asked him to tell me a bedtime story. Semper was a very intelligent Engineering major, and he spun this very alluring tale of a deer, a forest and a bulldozer.

Although the moral of the story was the detriments of innovation, the symbolism and the manner in which he told the story was very sensual. Very sensual indeed! And, well, Semper Fi became the second highly intelligent, phenomenally talented liaison I'd ever had.

This time I'd better not engage homeboy in no deep pillow talk, 'cause I don't think I could take it if his eyes start to glow, too.

23
Shake What-cha Mama Gave Ya

Mama's boy, mind games & milkshakes. A few weeks after my encounter with Semper Fi, I met a tall, but red, young fellow at one of our sorority parties. He'd asked me to dance and we were basically having fun together until a slow jam came on and I decided to bow out politely.

I saw him a couple of more times during the evening and I thought he was kinda cute, for a red guy. So when he asked for my number at the end of the party, a definite no–no, I decided to take his. I figured I'd add his number to my 'When I Ain't Got Nothing Better To Do' pile.

A few nights later around 10:30 pm, when I didn't have nothing better to do, I dialed up the number he'd given me. To my surprise this woman answered the phone.

"Oh I'm sorry I must have the wrong number," I said, swiftly hanging up. Click.

Then I looked at the number and tried dialing it again. Once again a woman answered the phone. Since I knew I dialed the number right the second time, I simply said, "hello may I speak to Mama's Boy."

136

The List.

"Who is this?"

Ok, first of all I'm a grown A- woman; and second of all, besides the Casper & Samantha incident from last summer, I can't remember the last time a female questioned me when I was calling a brotha.

Even though I was a little pissed by homegirl's tone of voice I politely told her, "This is Tammy, is Mama's Boy home?"

"Sweetheart do you realize what time it is?"

Did this chick just call me sweetheart?

"Yes I do and I apologize if I disturbed you," I was saying when she simply cut me off.

"Well you did." Click.

Oh, no she didn't! That rude heifer just hung up on me?

I was actually going to let it go; but, I was pissed 'cause up to that point I had not been disrespectful. So, I just had to call back. You know, it was the principle of the thing. Luckily, Mama's Boy answered the phone and I immediately began to tell him I didn't appreciate how that rude chick had hung up in my face. I thought that maybe she was his sister or maybe even his roommate, since a lot of people in college had roommates of the opposite sex.

Evidentially, homegirl was also on the phone line because the next thing I know, she was telling me "You're the rude one, around here calling my son so late on a school night."

Huh? Her Son? What did she just say?

"A school night?" I repeated out loud this time. "Exactly what school does your son attend?"

"He goes to Rickards High," she said all indignant.

Did you say high school?

"Oh I am sooo sorry m'am," I said feeling real stupid. "I met him at a party on campus so I just assumed that he was in college. I'm truly sorry that I disturbed you. Goodnight!"

Well they didn't have caller ID back in those days, but you could *69 somebody and return the last call. And, that's exactly what Mama's Boy did after his old girl went to bed around 11:30 p.m. As soon as I picked up the phone and realized his butt had the nerve to call me back, I just started going off on him.

Tymira Mack

"Look little BOY, I ain't know you was still in high school. And your mama is a rude heifer too," I snapped.

"I know. I just called to tell you I'm sorry for how she tripped," he said sadly.

"Well that's an understatement," I grumbled.

"She usually trips real hard like that 'cause she doesn't like most of the little girls who call our house," he confided.

"Well tell her I ain't no LITTLE girl," I snapped back.

"I know. I told her that you went to FAM and she kind of chilled out a bit," he said all excited.

Oh yeah, I'm glad you mentioned that because I almost forgot about the whole you're still in high school thing. "So what's the deal, how come you ain't tell me you was still in high school?" I asked, all geared up to hear some game.

Instead he came clean, "cause I knew that you wouldn't even give me a chance if you knew that."

After dealing in the world of deception and dishonesty for so long, his sincerity caught me off guard, and we ended up staying on the phone until 2 am. From our conversations over the next week, I learned that his mom was hard on him because she had real high expectations for him. He was 17 and a senior in high school. He drove a pretty decent little sports car. And, his birthday was three days before mine.

Once I stopped and thought about it, although I was a junior in college, I was still only 19 years old. So I relaxed on the whole high school trip and began to sort of date Mama's Boy. And, before I knew it, his mom had even fallen in like with me. Actually, I think she was more impressed with my educational accomplishments, than with me; but whatever floated her boat was fine, as long as it kept her from being rude to me.

As our friendship blossomed, Mama's Boy remained extremely polite. In fact, lots of times, he seemed over eager to make me happy. *Big mistake. I remember the last brother who was this nice. He didn't last very long.*

The List.

Well you know me. The whole nice guy thing started to get a little boring. I suspected that there was a bad boy in there somewhere, just dying to get out; but, I figured my age may have been intimidating him. So one Saturday morning I suggested that we drive down to this little Island I'd heard about. I was actually hoping to be able to catch a glimpse of his bad boy side while we spent the day together on the beach.

Since I was always up for playing mind games, during the one-hour drive I decided to test Mama's Boy by asking him questions about his sexual desires.

"So tell me mama's little high school boy, are you still a virgin?" I asked while placing my hand on his knee.

I could immediately sense that one move alone had made him uncomfortable, especially since we'd barely even kissed over the past three or four months we'd been hanging out. And, now here I was asking questions about his sex life.

He held up pretty well under round one, assuring me, "nope I'm not a virgin."

But as my questions got more intimate, "You ever done X; or, how about Y & Z?" I could tell by the expressions on his face that when it came to sex he had done a whole lot more window shopping than he'd done buying. One thing was for sure, homeboy was quite adamant that he would never, ever go shopping downtown.

Ooooh, wrong answer! Boy do I love a challenge.

I really wished that he had not used such an absolute term when answering my questions, 'cause it was just like telling an adrenaline junkie that a dare-devil stunt was impossible.

Game is on now.

And well, I just couldn't help myself. With a whole lot of coaxing, teasing and straight up conniving on my part, within a week, I'd convinced baby boy to not only order the combo, but also to super-size the fries, order a milkshake and add a hot apple pie.

Never say never young fella! You're no match for Mother Nature.

24
HYT (Handsome Young Thang)

Na–na–na–na. I guess time really does fly when you're having fun. It had only been three years and a couple of months since I'd graduated from high school, and there I was starting my final semester at FAMU. It was 1988. Life was good. I had a new off campus apartment, all by myself. And, I had a pocket full of internship money.

To top it all off, as an early graduation present, dear old papa had bought me my third new car in less than five years. It was a 1989 sports car. It was sleek. Hot off the assembly line. Candy apple red. Fully-loaded. With a sun roof and dual spoiler kits. It was about as pimped out as could be in the late 1980's.

Pops you truly topped yourself this time. I sure hope mama don't kill you for this one! Yup the ride is a real head turner.

And that's precisely what it did one afternoon while I was parked behind the English building waiting for my Econometrics class to start. I was darn near cross-eyed trying to make sense of the Classic Linear Regression Model, when this voice came through my sun roof and said "nice ride."

Since I'd heard the statement over a million times in the month since I'd gotten the car, I was just going to say thanks without even looking up; but, there was such a sexy quality to this brothers voice that I just couldn't resist checking out the face behind the

The List.

voice. As I gazed up through the sun roof, there stood this dark chocolate, well-dressed, young tenderoni, with a beautiful smile peering in at me. *Ahhhh sookie, sookie, now. Dang, I ain't nev-va seen this sexy brother on campus before.*

Obviously vibing off the attention I was giving him, the brother stayed a while and conver-sated with me. Turns out, he was a freshman, he was at FAM on a baseball scholarship and yes, he was from Hot-lanta.

Mental note to self: After graduation, invest $1 grand in the Metro Atlanta Water Department, 'cause the secret's got to be in the water!

Although the brother was young and fresh around the gills, he was a little too fine for me to throw back.

Yup, I've definitely got to gut this minnow, throw him in the skillet, sprinkle a little hot sauce on him, and slip him between a couple of pieces of light bread.

Hey it's not like I haven't robbed the cradle before. Besides, he's got to be at least 18 and I'm only 20, so it ain't like he's jail bait anyway. Right?

While Tenderoni was writing his number down, 'cause of course he couldn't have mine, a plan was quickly coming together in my head. The way I figured it, Tenderoni lived on campus and he didn't have a car, so there was no way for him to just pop up at a sista's apartment.

Ohhhh I smell the perfect set up. My own personal little boy-toy. I can see him at my discretion and not sacrifice any of my upperclassman options.

ଡ଼ ଫ

Atlanta boys came a close second to my weakness for all things chocolate. So when you mixed the two, well it was a combination that I was simply too weak to resist. I'm sure that's why I wasted no time calling Tenderoni that evening and kicking it on the phone with him for a couple of hours.

I enjoyed talking to him 'cause he had a smart mouth and a smooth tongue. Truth be told, in a lot of ways he put me in the mind of Puffy; except that Tender had this old school Billy D kinda vibe going on.

In no time, Tenderoni began coming home with me from campus every day. We'd hang out, study, watch videos, and munch out until around midnight. This went on for a few weeks. Then one night when I was about to take him back to the dorms, Tender smoothly declared that he was staying the night.

"Look, I don't have a class until 10:00 am, so I'm not getting up early to take your butt back to campus in the morning," I warned him like he was my kid.

"It's cool Chocolate girl, I'm straight," he responded with the utmost confidence.

Oh no he didn't just flip the script and call me Chocolate. And how that Negro gone have extra clothes all up in his backpack tonight?

ÈÊ

That night marked the first of many intimate nights I spent with Tender. But unlike many of my past arrangements, what was developing between he and I was not just all about sex. I was drawn to the fact that even though he was younger than me, he was quite confident. He had these chilled out mannerisms that were superimposed on this GQ, inflated ego kind of persona. Plus, he was sexy and he knew it. In fact, he skillfully worked that quality and his chocolate–ness to his advantage.

The truth of the matter is, because of all the time I spent with Tenderoni, I was actually beginning to fall for him. And, things were going pretty good for us, until his mama found out he was dating a senior. Never mind that technically I was only two years older than him.

Although Tender would never tell me everything, from what I could gather, she warned him to be careful and said it probably wouldn't be long before I broke his heart.

How she gone trip on me and she don't even know me? I ain't even like that. Well at least not anymore. I don't think?

The List.

Somehow I let his mom's comments get all up in my head and I think Tenderoni did too. Although we were still seeing each other every single day, he'd started spending his nights at his cousin's house. So being a proactive type of sister, I figured it was time to deal with the little problem at the source.

Yup, it's time to meet moms.

❧ ☙

I had a pretty good track record of having everybody's mama, besides my own, think that I was such a sweet little angel, so I figured getting in good with Tenderoni's mother would be a piece of cake too. Besides, I was itching to get back to the Land of Milk and Honey.

Yup. It's definitely time to take a road trip, so that weekend, me and Tender and his cousin went to Atlanta.

We got into town around 8:00 at night and were greeted by his mother and his older brother's girlfriend. While his brother was busy giving him dap for "snagging an older chick with a kicking ride," Tender's mom and his sister-in-law seemed to be staring straight through me.

Even though his mom was cordial to me, it was obvious that she was not going to fall for the okie-doke.

Oh no sweat, on to plan B. "Well Tender it's getting late and my girlfriend is expecting me," I told him, because I was just itching to get out of that uncomfortable situation.

"I'll pick you up around 3:00 on Sunday," I confirmed with him. Then I turned to his family, "Well it was nice to meet you all." And I was out.

❧ ☙

Maybe if I'd received a warmer welcome at Tender's house, I might have felt a little guilty about calling Thunder up and asking for directions to his new apartment.

Tymira Mack

"Hey baby, guess who's in town?" I said in my sexiest voice. *Girl you sure do love living on the edge. But oh well, who cares?*

"Oh you've moved by Greenbrier Mall?" I repeated. "Hummm well actually I'm just pulling into town off I-75," I lied, "I can be there in a couple of minutes."

As, it turned out Thunder had moved into a townhouse located less than a half of a mile from Tender's house. So I pulled into the mall parking lot to kill time for a couple of minutes before turning into his apartment complex.

When I pulled up to Thunder's townhouse I was struck by the fact that this place was way better than the last couple of places he'd lived.

Hummm, I guess the stripping and the security gigs have paid off?

His latest roommates seemed cool, but his new pet *Kudjo* the Rottweiler was another story. The way he growled at me; the slimy drool seeping past his huge canine fangs; and the boarded up bay window by the front door should have been my first clues that this was not going to be a typical weekend. *But hey a sista has needs, so I'll take my chances.*

While Thunder and I were preparing to chill and make up for lost time, he got a phone call from three of his homeboys who had come into town unexpectedly; and, of course they wanted him to hang out with them. But I was tired. Besides, I wasn't down for hanging out with four dudes.

"Hey baby why don't you just go hang out with your boys while I get some sleep?" I suggested.

At first, he seemed a little reluctant to go; but once I reassured him I wouldn't snoop through his stuff, he agreed to hang out with his homies.

Yeah right, and I've got a lovely piece of Florida swampland to sell ya stupid. I grinned to myself. But actually I was too tired to snoop. *Awwww, I've got the whole weekend to snoop,* I reminded myself as I changed into one of Thunder's T-shirts and climbed in his bed, hoping that these were fresh sheets?

144

The List.

CR &

Thunder's homies dropped him at home around 2:00 in the morning, and then they headed back out to search for another hot spot. As soon as he came upstairs, I could immediately tell he'd been drinking.

Oh great!

I'd been around Thunder enough to know that excess alcohol really didn't agree with him; so I wasn't thrilled at all. It was bad enough that Thunder was a super-hyped person when he was sober; but, when he got drunk he was boisterous at best and belligerent at worse.

Maybe if I pretend to be asleep he will just come in, lie down and sleep some of the alcohol off.

But he wasn't even in the room five seconds before he was trying to get busy with a sista.

"Look baby why don't you just lay down and chill, I'm really not trying to get with you while you're all drunk-up," I said as I moved away from him and turned to face the wall.

Unfortunately, Thunder wasn't trying to take no for an answer. So I reluctantly just lay there as he did his thing. At some point during his little freak-fest, the telephone rang.

Oh good, please stop and answer the phone!

Unfortunately, Thunder only had one thing on his mind, and it wasn't that three am telephone call. That was until the answering machine turned on.

"Thunder?" the voice yelled.

"Thunder, man answer the phone!" he continued getting louder.

"Man they broke in your car! Man your radio is gone!" His homeboy said in an obvious panic.

The next thing I knew, Thunder had jumped his 6'4", 220 pound, big black naked butt up like the Incredible Hulk and snatched the phone off the hook. After rattling off a bunch of curse words, sprinkled with a few "I'm gonna kick ya'lls blankedy-blanks" he slammed the phone down. Then he yanked the phone cord out of the wall and started pacing around the room like a mad man.

Oh my gosh!

I was truly afraid because I had never seen Thunder in a rage before. And as I sat curled up against the wall in the corner of his bed, I didn't know what to do. I tried calming him down by using soothing words and logic, "chill out baby. It's gonna be ok," I reassured, "it's just a radio."

But my comments just made him angrier. Then as he turned and started to head straight for me, he changed course, spun around and whacked the stand-up oscillating fan with the back of his hand, sending it flying across the room as it broke into pieces.

Whoa, all this for a stolen radio?

Well he must have been reading my mind, "You don't understand, I just got that radio. Man I told them to take the faceplate out whenever they got out of the car. That freaking radio cost me $250 bucks."

And the thought of how much he'd paid for his radio sent him into another rage. The brother punched a hole in the bedroom wall and then ripped the handrail off the stairwell on his way downstairs.

About ten minutes later, I heard his homeboys drive up and come inside. By this time, I had already gotten dressed and was trying to figure out where I could go at 4:00 in the morning, 'cause I had to get out of there.

But I was too afraid to go downstairs and navigate my way through the feud that had jumped off between Thunder and his homies. I knew all of those fellas were from some of the roughest parts of the greater New York / New Jersey area, and it was no telling how they rolled. Besides, I had no idea where Kudjo was either.

146

The List.

About 20 minutes later, Thunder came back up to his room, still naked, and found me fully dressed with my bag packed.

I just know you wasn't down there arguing about a radio while your big black butt was bucket naked. This just about beats all.

"Where are you going?" He asked half surprised and half perturbed.

"I' own know, but I ain't trying to stay up in here with your psychotic A–," I said no longer certain about what this Negro might be capable of.

"Man I'm sorry Tam but you just don't know, I work too hard for my stuff," he insisted as he grabbed a towel off his dresser and tried to drape it around his waist.

"That's the point Thunder, its just stuff; if you're trippin' this hard off a little radio, who knows how you might act in a real difficult situation?" I said, really sad things had gone down like this.

To illustrate my point, I directed this attention to the hole in the wall, "Look at the wall Thunder. Just look at that gaping hole."

"Yeah," he said sitting on the edge of the bed and hanging his head in shame, "you know I don't usually get this mad…but I've been drinking too."

"And that fact is supposed to make it better?" I asked in disbelief.

"Well what do you want me to say?" He snapped.

"Sorry would be a good start," I shot back, insulted by the fact he was still capable of snapping at me after all that had happened.

"You really scared the crap out of me, Thunder. I mean, you were in such a rage, I kinda wondered if you were going to hit me next."

"Tam, come on," he pleaded as he reached out and pulled me down to sit on his leg, "you know I would never hurt you. Never have, never will."

Humph? I' own know about that?

147

Tymira Mack

"Look I'm sorry ok? And I'm tired too. So just put your bag down," he pleaded, "get back in the bed and let's get some sleep. Please?"

Then he added, "I promise I'll make it up to you in the morning."

Oh, I don't think so.

 appendixG

Within minutes, Thunder was fast asleep, snoring off all the drama. I don't know if it was his snoring or my inner voice that was preventing me from sleeping; but I was seriously tripping off the magnitude of his earlier tirade.

I kept telling myself, even if tonight's violent reaction was not typical for him; it's obvious that the excessive drinking was more than typical. Here we were seniors in college and he was still boozing and partying like he was a freshman.

Then I got this awful image of us 10 years down the line —

We'd be married and every day when we'd come home from our corporate jobs, up would pop a gang of his homies and they'd sit around drinking beer and watching football all night.

I'm just not down for living this college lifestyle for the next 20 years. And besides, Thunder and I both have such strong personalities. I can't hardly see how we could make it together, 'cause neither one of us would be willing to compromise on anything.

He'll want to live up North with all those cold and impersonal people who commute to the urban jungle; and, I'll want to live in the slow and friendly south with all the people who still hold tightly to grits and jherri-curls.

He'll want to go to professional football games and sit around drinking beer; and, I'll want to go to plays and sip White Zinfandel.

He'll get angry and break up the house that we'd worked hard to furnish and pay for; and, I'd eventually end up putting six bullets through his forehead.

The List.

Dang, as much as I hate to admit it, there really is no future for me and Thunder. True, the sex is phenomenal, but there is so much more I want out of life.

I don't know how long I stayed up conver-sating with myself. All I know is pretty soon the sun was shining in through Thunder's blinds. I was never so happy to see 7:00 am as I was that day 'cause I wanted to be gone before Thunder woke up.

I knew Thunder's room was at the top of the stairs and the staircase was only steps from the front door. But, I wasn't sure where *Kudjo* slept.

Can I make it to the front door, unlock it and get out before that dog bites a plug outta my A-? I 'own know but I've gotta get out of here!

So I took my chances, crept out of the bedroom and down the stairs. Fate was with me that day because I made it out of there without waking up Thunder or *Kudjo*. Thank goodness I didn't find out until later the reason the front window was boarded up was because *Kudjo* had stuck his head through it trying to get a cat that was sitting outside. Otherwise I'd probably still be sitting up in Thunder's bedroom to this very day.

Anyhow, I spent the rest of the weekend at my homegirl's apartment 'cause I had no intention of seeing Thunder ever again.

Hey–Hey–Hey, Good-bye!

25
Pumps 'n a Bump?

On the DL? By the time I picked Tender up on Sunday for our drive back to FAMU, I had developed a whole new outlook on our relationship. The whole Thunder fiasco convinced me that it was finally time out for games. When I really thought about it, except for his age, I actually liked everything about Tender. So for once in my life, since Mickey had dumped me in high school, I made up my mind to see what it would be like to fully commit myself to one person.

I can do this. I know I can.

And that's exactly what I did. I spent the next two months of the semester 100% committed to Tender. Besides class time, Thanksgiving break and a couple of overnight corporate recruiting plant visits that I went on, Tender and I were together 24/7.

After finishing school in December, I turned down two corporate jobs up north, opting to remain in Tallahassee and take an accounting position with the State. I even left home the day after Christmas and drove to Atlanta to spend time with Tender for the remainder of his school break.

By Christmastime, Tender's people had warmed up to me a little more. Unbelievably, his brother's girlfriend even gave us the keys to her posh Atlanta apartment so that Tender and I could enjoy the weekend alone.

The List.

After Christmas break, I began working for the State and was making enough money to pay my bills, shop and party on the regular. And I'd moved on up to a kicking 2 bedroom, 2 bath condo on the east side of Tallahassee. It had a fireplace and a serene second floor terrace overlooking+- a wooded area.

ભ ૪૦

For the most part things between Tender and I were good. He still spent the night at my house quite a bit, but since my condo was a little farther out from campus and I was working a 9 to 5, the whole transportation thing became an issue. Allowing him to drive my car had never been a big deal for me; but, with him having spring baseball practice, he didn't always pick me up from work on time.

After about the third time he was late picking me up from work, I went off on the brother; especially since he hadn't had baseball practice that particular afternoon. Unfortunately, whenever I got upset with Tender, I had a bad habit of ending my statements by yelling "with your young stupid A-."

Normally Tender would try and stand up to me by telling me to stop disrespecting him. He'd also remind me that when it came to what he could do in the bedroom, I didn't call him young. But, I guess on this particular day he had heard this statement one time too many 'cause when we got to my apartment, he went straight upstairs and began packing up all his stuff.

I was so angry that he had the nerve to play me so close, I started helping him pack his stuff.

Yup Negga, take all your stuff! Because if you wanna leave; then hurry up and get your crap and go!

Since we had a habit of wearing each other's sweatshirts and t-shirts, I was also helping the Negro pack, just to make sure he didn't put anything in his bag that belonged to me. In fact, as he was stomping around the room I noticed he was actually wearing one of my sweatshirts.

Tymira Mack

"Oh and make sure your young A– leave my sweat," I ordered.

"You ain't said nothing but a thang Chocolate girl," he said in his sly ole seductive voice as he slipped the sweatshirt over his head revealing his bear chocolate brown chest.

Be strong. Don't look. Unless he apologizes for being late and disrespecting your car, just let his young A– finish packing his stuff and get the hell out.

Tender was wearing a pair of loose fitting jeans, and as he bent over to drop some more of his things in his bag, I noticed a black waistband underneath his jeans.

I ain't never seen this brother wearing no black shorts, what in the heck... I thought as I pulled the back of his jeans out so that I could get a better view.

"Naw choc' don't try to get in a brotha's pants now. Remember you want my young A– gone?" He said like I was begging him for some stuff or something.

"Negro pl – eeee – ase. I'm trying to see what you're wearing. Oh but hell's no," I hollered as I unzipped his pants. I couldn't believe my freaking eyes. This Negro was wearing a pair of my black bikini underwear.

"What in the F– ?" I screamed while trying to determine if I was imagining things. "Are these my dang-on panties?"

"Yeah." He said matter-of-factly.

"Yeah? What the hell do you mean yeah?"

"I mean what's the big deal. You know I wear briefs."

"Briefs – Negga – briefs, not bikini's," I hollered utterly flabbergasted.

"Look Tam, I didn't have any clean underwear over here this morning, so what's the big deal? I mean it's just like wearing briefs."

"What's the big deal?" I yelled.

"Neg-ga you got your prick all up in my dang-on draws and that's just so nasty. That's what's the freaking big deal!" I screamed at the top of my lungs. "Besides you had my car all day. Why you ain't go home and put your own draws on?"

The List.

"First off, all of my laundry is dirty and I was late because I was getting my stuff together to come over here and wash. Second of all, you're clean; third of all, your underwear were clean," he said as he got louder with each point he was making.

"And, forth of all my prick ain't so nasty when it's all up in you, so why you got a problem with it being all up in your draws?" He concluded boldly.

I was so angry I couldn't even see straight.

"Neg-ga take off my draws and get your trifling little young A– up out of my apartment right freaking now!"

"Tam?" He called after me in a dejected voice.

"What!"

"I need a ride back to campus."

Great. Just great. Before we go, do I need to check your bags to see if you've got any of my pumps or maxi pads too?

"Just get in the car and don't say one word to me," I ordered as I slammed my door and headed towards his cousin's house.

Looking back and knowing what I now know about a lot of Atlanta dudes, Tender could definitely be the type of brother that I'd figure for living on the down low.

I wonder if that brother has come out of the closet, or if he really just didn't have any clean underwear to put on that day?

I might be wrong; but I'd bet my life that the average brother would have just decided not to wear any drawers at all?

153

26
Big Baller

Money, money, money, money, mon-eee. Even after our big blow up about the car and the panties incident, it took a while for me to completely work Tender out of my system. After all, he was the first person, in a really long time, that I'd let my wall down for; and, I was as close as I could possibly come to being in love with him. But even though I tried apologizing to him on more than one occasion, his pride wouldn't let him forgive me for all the ugly things I'd said to him.

Besides, he'd told his mama 'nem that I'd kicked him out of my apartment and they'd bombarded him with a million "I told you so's."

In the end, he claimed he "just didn't trust that I wouldn't do the same thing to him again the next time I got angry."

Now ain't this a blimp. He's the one wearing my draws and I'm the one with the problem? Well no use crying over spilled milk.

છ ર

It was springtime and the Daytona Black Student Beach party was just around the corner. Since I went to the Beach Party every year, it's hard for me to remember exactly who I went down there with in 1989. But I do remember that two of my cousins were

The List.

definitely there because one of my cousin's boyfriends played baseball at Bethune-Cookman.

At a private cookout that weekend, my cousin ended up introducing me to this brother who was footing all the bills for the food, liquor and festivities.

"Tammy this is Kee. Kee this is my cousin Tammy."

While she was introducing us, I found it difficult to focus on the brotha because his bling was just about blinding me.

Oh I'm really not in the mood for another dope boy.

But even though I wasn't feeling Mr. Kee's outward flashiness, I'd be lying if I didn't admit I was a bit intrigued by how freely he was kicking out the cash and paying for stuff. Besides he was tall, slim and chocolate, a deadly combination where I was concerned. So I decided to see if there was any substance to this brother.

"Humph. So is Kee your real name or did you get that nickname 'cause you're in the business of pushing weight?" I asked semi-sarcastically.

"Dang you straight out the box on a brother huh slim?"

"I was just curious. Kee just doesn't seem like the typical name that someone would be given at birth, that's all," I said in my intellectual voice.

"Kee is short for Keewon and no I ain't in the game," he assured me.

"Oh let me guess, you're financing this little shin-dig with the proceeds from your stock portfolio?" *I mean get real brother, you're standing here all blinged out, buying cases of meat and beer left and right; plus by the looks of things, you're riding tight, too. So please cut the crap, 'cause I know you ain't holding down a regular 9 to 5.*

"Oh no baby, I works hard for mine," he responded, seeming somewhat insulted by my attitude and line of questioning.

"Well I give up. What exactly is it that you do to make such a lucrative living Mr. Keewon?"

"I play ball," he said quite confidently.

"Ball? Yeah right. Ok me too," I retorted.

Tymira Mack

Play ball my left tit, I thought as I walked away from the brother to find my cousin and curse her out for introducing me to this clown. *That Negro is way too skinny to play football; and a wee bit too short to play basketball. Cuz better slow up on sippin' the Cisco, 'cause that heifer know I been decided to turn in my I'm Dating a Slanger Card!*

"Girl, what I told you about introducing me to them damn dope boys?"

"Who?" She asked squenching her nose at me and looking all confused.

"Ke-mosabi or whatever his freaking name is," I said in disgust.

"Girl you are so stupid," she giggled. "Keewon ain't no drug dealer girl, he plays for the Braves."

Well I just about choked on my wine cooler. "Girl you know you are lying!"

"Un-Unh, I ain't lying. Well he don't play for the Braves, but he plays for their main minor league team."

"For real?" I was dumbfounded. *Girl now look what you done-did, dismissing Ke-mosabi like he was ya typical hood rat. Dang!*

"Yes, girl. He was sweating me to introduce him to you. Tammy girl I can't believe you just F'– d that up. He is so sweet," she said shaking her head, obviously disappointed I'd slipped like that.

"But he looks like a straight thug," I mumbled, still pissed at myself for letting that one get away.

"Girl he's just perpetrating, he is so softhearted underneath all that mess," she assured me.

"Oh well, I guess this just wasn't my night," I cringed as I moped over to the cooler to get a cold one to try and wash away all thoughts of that lost opportunity. As I was leaning over in the cooler searching for a Cisco, I felt someone tap me on the back. When I looked up, to my surprise it was Keewon.

"Why don't you ride out with me, I've gotta go pick up some more stuff and maybe by the time we come back you won't think that I'm such a bad guy?" He asked sincerely.

The List.

So, I rode with Kee to the grocery store and the liquor store. And he was right, the ride gave me an opportunity to find out that he really was a nice guy. He told me all about his ball career and how he'd just been moved up to the majors when he got a call that his father was very ill. So he walked away from everything to come home and see about his dad.

Wow, how sweet. I can't believe this guy walked away from all that money just to check on his dad. But he said he was heading back to Atlanta at the end of the month before he lost his contract or something like that.

Lose your what? Man I' own know nothing about no baseball.

While we rode, I was alternating between humming to the radio, listening to Kee talk and looking out the window at all the Neg-eros that was up and down the Daytona Strip.

The strip? Wait a minute why are we over on the strip?

"Kee why we way over here beachside? I thought you had to take the stuff back to the party at the apartment," I asked feeling a little unsettled."

"Yeah, I just got to stop by my hotel room to get my wallet," he said nonchalantly.

"Ok I guess I just look stupid? You gotta go get your wallet, huh? Neg-ga you been spending money all day. Besides I don't know anyone stupid enough to leave a wallet in a hotel room."

"Now why I got to lie? And no I'm not stupid, I messed around and forgot it by accident," he said as he parked and got out of the car. "You gone just sit here or would you like to come up?"

Even though I smelled a rat, I was interested in seeing how ballers rolled, so I got out of the car and headed upstairs with him. But, as it turned out his hotel room wasn't spectacular at all.

The crap around his neck is worth more than this rinkey-dinky looking room, I thought as I stepped in and looked around.

In fact the brother must have been reading this very expression all over my face. "What? Not what you expected?" He asked peeping the sour look on my face.

Tymira Mack

"Well considering the mess around your neck is worth a few grand, and your car is pretty tight, I just figured you for a Marriott Marquis type of brother," I mumbled a little snobbishly.

"Yup, well I don't care if you're the President, you can't get a room close up on the strip at the last minute in Daytona during Beach Week. And believe it or not this little room costs $200 a night plus tax and not counting the dang-on $200 security deposit," he groaned as he tossed his medallions up on the dresser and then took off his shirt.

Oh shucks, not the chocolate six-pack.

"Well number one you got robbed. $200 bucks a night? Get real? And, number two, exactly why are you taking off your shirt?"

"Number one you're right; and, number two 'cause I'm tired," he replied as he laid down across the king sized bed and stared at me.

Without all the bling blinding me, I actually noticed the brother had a softer attractiveness thing going on. Even so I politely plopped myself down in the chair by the window, grabbed the remote and clicked the TV on. "Oh I hope the TV won't disturb you while you rest."

Then he gave me some weak line about lying down and resting with him. But I told him I wasn't the typical game playing type of female. "Look, we're both too old for the games. So why not just be a big boy and say exactly what it is you want from me?"

I guess my bluntness completely threw him off his game. So I just kicked my own game into high gear and gave him a taste of what it was really like to play in the major leagues. Too bad homeboy wasn't serving up any homeruns that day.

"I'm ready to go. Can you please take me back to the apartment?" *I sure hope he's got more skills on the baseball field. Otherwise, he'll never make it in the pros!*

ଔ ଯ

The List.

About a week later my cousin called me nearly speechless, "Girrrrrl guess what?"

"What?" I asked all excited because she seemed so excited.

"Guess who got married this weekend?" She asked urging me to think hard.

"I' own know," I admitted, "I give up who?"

"Girrrrrl Keewon!" she said all excited. "Tammy, did you hear me?" She asked obviously surprised by my silence.

"Yeah girl, they had a big A– wedding; and I heard all kinda big time people was up in there."

I managed to squeeze out a simple "Oh," all the while thinking, *home for a couple of weeks to see about your sick daddy huh?*

"I was really tripping when I heard it 'cause I knew how hard he was sweating you last weekend," she insisted. "I didn't even know him and her was still together after all these years," she continued, "I had heard that she might be pregnant, but since Kee was up the road I definitely didn't think she was pregnant by him."

"Oh yeah," I replied simply to keep up my end of the conversation.

"What-cha-ma-call-it 'nem said that's why Kee threw that big ole' party we went to in Daytona. It was supposed to be like a bachelor party for him and his boys. Girl it's a good thing you wasn't feeling that neg-ga after all, 'cause that would have been just plain foul."

"Yup, it woulda been foul all right." *Real damn foul.*

Well Mr. Keewon, I guess you are a true professional playa after all. Just when a sista thought I'd thrown the perfect curve ball and struck you out; at the last second you hit the mutha straight outta the park.

Batter Up!

27
Pusher Man

Slanging, packing & slamming. Not long after Beach Week, FAMU and BCC were scheduled to play a baseball game in Tallahassee. So, that weekend, my cousin came up to see her boyfriend play and to hang out with her sister and me.

Since she didn't want to drive all the way to Tallahassee alone, her boyfriend's cousin rode with her and they all stayed at my condo.

When they first drove up and got out of the car, I could tell from the kitchen window that homeboy's cousin was tall, thin and almost chocolate. But dang-on-it, it wasn't until they had come inside that I realized slim had a gold tooth.

I must be a freaking bling magnet?

It didn't take long for me to figure out this brother was a straight up hustler. And like a true hustler, he spent the whole weekend trying to run this smooth street game on a sister.

Look Neg-ga. Game recognizes game.

I really wasn't down for hooking up with another slanger, let alone one living in Tampa; but, I did kinda like the fact that he wasn't ya typical Ebonics speaking, thugged out, disrespectful type hustler. Nope, he had a real playful and lighthearted personality which took the edge off the fact that he was definitely a project boy who knew how to hold his own on the streets.

160

The List.

∞ ∞

By the end of the weekend we'd hooked up, and thus began our long distance relationship. But time out for the playfulness, 'cause with the quickness this Negro began trying to keep tabs on me from 250 miles away. Although I tried to convince New Jack Nino that I wasn't messing with anyone in Tally; he really wasn't trying to believe me.

Well what do you expect a brotha to believe? Heck didn't he hit the pou-nanny in less than 3 days?

Oh well, it really wasn't a big deal to me because aside from working, I really didn't hang out all that much anymore. So his little attempts to keep tabs on a sista weren't a big deal because I would have normally been home every night at 7:00 and 11:00 pm anyway.

Dang this Negro is acting like a prison guard, making a sister line up for count every 4 hours.

Soon, Nino went from calling me two and three times a day to wanting to see me every weekend. But, by the beginning of the summer, I'd been admitted to graduate school at FSU; and since most of my grad school classes were held at night and on the weekends, squeezing in a weekend trip to Tampa was no easy task.

Between working during the day, going to graduate school three nights a week and studying all in between, how the freak am I supposed to hang out in Tampa on the weekends?

Nevertheless, just to shut him up, I'd go to Tampa once or twice a month.

The first couple of times I went to Tampa, I stayed at my Aunts house; but later on I started staying at Nino's house 'cause it wasn't really like his mama gave a flip. Although Nino's family no longer lived in the projects, the little house they were living in didn't seem a whole lot better to me. It was old and kind of rickety. It had two bedrooms and a less than desirable little bathroom and kitchen.

At the time Nino, his mother and his thirty-something-year-old crack addicted brother lived there. His mother also had custody of his sister's two kids while she was completing a five year prison sentence for assault with a deadly weapon. And then there was their nasty little flee ridden dog and the pet alley cat that I'm told was supposed to help kept the rats away. *Ewwww!*

Each time I went down there to visit, it took every ounce of compassion in me to stay at that house and pretend like I wasn't judging their living conditions. I suppose I should have been thankful that his mother always graciously gave up her bedroom and allowed me and Nino to sleep together while she slept in the recliner in the living room. But I wasn't.

Overall, I tried to make the best of the whole situation. But I drew the line when it came to hanging around his house all day while he went to work.

Nino was a Rec Leader at one of the parks located adjacent to the projects where he grew up, which was such a big joke to me. For the life of me I couldn't figure how this Negro was actually employed at a City Recreation Center.

Am I like the only one who sees the irony of paying the dope-man to supervise the kids?

Now Nino was cool with me hanging out with my cousin at the Rec Center where she worked, since I refused to spend my days at his house. But, he never allowed me to hang out with him at the Center where he worked.

"This area is too rough for you to be up in," he'd tell me every time I'd ask about going out there.

"Yeah, but I'll be with you, ain't nobody gonna mess with me."

"But you know a brother always gotta be on top of his game, you'll just be distracting me."

"What-ever Nino. Oh yeah, some lady named Joanne called you twice and I heard your mama tell her you were at the park. Who is this Joanne?"

"You ask too many questions. She ain't nobody you need to be concerned about," he assured me.

But I wasn't trying to take his word for it, so I asked my cousin if she knew who this Joanne was.

162

The List.

"Yeah girl, she's Nino's supplier's old lady. She handles all the deliveries so her old man can keep his hands clean, since he's still on papers," my cousin told me.

"Oh word. Ok, so he was telling me the truth," I said relieved that I wasn't going to have to deal with more female drama. "Girl Nino will not let me go out to the park with him. And, can you believe he still won't admit to me that he's slanging?"

"I know. He's forever bugging me because he thinks you'll break up with him if you knew what he was doing," my cousin confided in me. "Yeah girl, he be tripping off the fact that you're a college girl and he's all worried you might flip off him being in the game."

"Well do he think I'm that stupid? I know the park ain't keeping his pockets that full. Especially not hell-a full of ones and fives anyway," I said laughing.

ଔ ଛ

That afternoon when he came home from work, Nino and I went to pick up his son who was supposed to spend the weekend with him. Besides Bert, who really was never my man way back in the day, I'd never dated anyone with a kid.

Ok, how is he going to introduce me to this kid? And what's the kid's mama gone say when she sees me all up in the car?

I guess Nino must have been reading my mind. "Relax Tam. Me and his mama been broke up. She got another neg-ga and she's pregnant with his baby right now."

"Oh for real?" I said, feeling one zillion percent better.

"So how often do you have your son?" I asked out of curiosity.

"I have him all the time 'cause his mama's been sick a lot. I guess this new baby is really kicking her A – or something," he said in a semi-concerned voice before getting out of the car and heading up the stairs to his baby mama's, mama's apartment. A few minutes later he emerged with about six little kids following him out the door.

Tymira Mack

What in the?

Then he grabbed the hand of the cutest little deep chocolate fellow, I'd ever seen; told the rest of the kids to get their little bad A–'s back upstairs; came down and got in the car.

Nino, Jr. was about five or six years old and he was absolutely gorgeous. He had long eyelashes and dark wavy hair; but, even though the kid was cute and chocolate, the whole thought of me having to play mama for the weekend really didn't appeal to me!

ର ଛ

I managed to make it through Nino Jr. Weekend and afterwards, I spent just about every other weekend of the summer in Tampa. Toward the end of the summer, I found out I'd been awarded a fellowship under some minority program which would allow me to attend graduate school for free.

Now that's what I'm talking about! But there was one catch, I wouldn't be allowed to work. *Oh heck, now I'm gonna have to move outta my hell-a condo.*

Oh well. I definitely liked the idea of a free education, 'cause paying the tuition myself the first summer was quite expensive. Plus, no work meant I'd really be free to travel back and forth to Tampa.

ର ଛ

I'd spent the last few days of the summer in Tampa, and had returned to school just in time for my week long fellowship orientation. But, within a couple of days of getting back to Tally, I started having problems in the 'privacy' department.

What the?

Fortunately, one of the perks of attending a major white university is that they had a top notch health clinic on campus. Unlike the rinkey-dinky little clinic at FAMU, you could go to the FSU clinic and have just about any medical need attended to. Even though the clinic was staffed by a lot of nursing and pre-med

The List.

students, unlike FAMU, I wasn't worried about my personal business getting out because most of the staff at the Clinic were white people who didn't know me from Eve anyhow.

Boy was I happy to have this campus convenience; especially after having spent countless hours in the waiting room of the Leon County Health Department over the past few years just to get my mandatory six month supply of birth control pills and condoms for free.

I went to the FSU Health Clinic fully expecting to have a little yeast infection or something. But gosh be darn it, I had something called Chlamydia.

How the hell? I always used protection. Well almost always? There was that one time this past weekend when the condom broke, but the pill had me covered.

Even though the HOW–in–the–hell was a bit of a mystery to me, the WHO–in–the–hell was no mystery at all. *Oh my gosh; not a– freakin'–gin. I'm gonna kick Nino's A–!*

I left the Health Clinic with a purse full of antibiotics and a mind set on revenge.

I was so angry that I didn't talk to Nino for a couple of days. I just went to orientation every day and went home. On the third day, I was in such a rush to get to orientation on time that I left the house without eating, and ended up taking one of those antibiotics on an empty stomach. By the time I got to campus, I was puking my brains out.

A couple of my fellow classmates were kind enough to help me to the Health Clinic. Evidently, someone from the orientation staff had also taken it upon themselves to call my parents because as I was sitting in the clinic feeling like my life was about to end, one of the staff informed me, "Your dad is on the phone and he wants to talk to you."

Oh crap. What am I gonna say? Its ok Daddy, I just forgot to take food with my VD Pills, but everything should be cleared up and I'll be just fine in about seven days?

Tymira Mack

I came up with some quick lie to tell my Dad to get him off the phone, and managed to get excused from orientation for the rest of the day. When I finally got home, I was so stinking mad that I refused to wait for Nino to get home from work, and ended up calling him at the park.

My piss-is-i-tude level was already off the chart before I even called him. And then he had the audacity to swear up and down he didn't know what I was talking about, 'cause he wasn't having any privacy area problems.

"Tam I swear to God I ain't got nothing and I ain't been messing with nobody."

"You just wait 'til I get to Tampa on Friday Neg-ga, I'm gonna kick off in your A–" I declared as I slammed the phone down and began pacing around like a mad woman.

Since I was no longer working, I'd moved into a cute little 2-bedroom 1½ bath townhouse with my younger cousin. Unfortunately, the walls in this new apartment were paper thin, so it was a little difficult for me to pretend that all was well with me. So I just decided to fess up, tell her what was going on, and ask her if she would ride with me to Tampa for the weekend.

This was a no brainer. My cousin had a man back home, so of course she was down for riding with me. In the meantime, we put her sister on the job in Tampa to find out what Mr. Nino was really up to.

Later that night when my cousin called me back, she told me that when she popped up over at Nino's, his mama and his sister –who'd just gotten out of prison the week before – were there, but homeboy was MIA.

"Tammy girl, Nino's mama claims that ain't no other females been coming around there to see him."

"Yeah right."

"But that ain't all, you know she the nerve to tell me that 'far as she knew, he ain't had nothing because she do his laundry and she ain't never seen no stains in his drawers'."

The List.

"Cuz I know you lying, right?" I wanted her to be lying cause I was about to go ballistic. When she didn't answer me, I knew she was telling the truth. "Ah hell naw. I c'aint believe this neg-ga told his mama about our personal stuff."

Then she had to go and put the icing on the cake. "Girl when I was driving off, Joanne was pulling up to the house, and Nino was in the car with her."

"What?" I hollered.

"Yup, and she ain't just drop him off either. She was getting out the car and going in the house."

"Thanks cuz. I'll see you in 3 hours."

☙ ❧

True to my word, even though it normally took 3 ½ to 4 hours to get to Tampa from Tallahassee, that Thursday night I made it there in three hours flat. Oh yeah, I almost forgot, I also brought along my roommate cousin, this chick from Jersey who was one of my new graduate school friends and my loaded .22.

Once in town, my first stop was at my cousin's apartment. When we got there, the dude that my roommate cousin was messing with and two of his partners were there. I noticed that both of the other guys were cute, chocolate fellows and one had Marlon Jackson / LL Cool J lips. But they were both a little on the short side. Besides, I was in town to take care of business.

Since it was a Thursday, I knew Nino wouldn't expect me to be in town; and, I was just itching to get over there to see exactly what he was up to. Unfortunately, my cousin didn't have anyone to watch her daughter so she couldn't ride out with me. But since I was already hyped up, I ended up storming out and heading over to Nino's by myself. And, since she really didn't know anyone else at the apartment, my Jersey friend jumped in the car with me, just before I was about to drive off.

When we rolled up on Nino's block, the car my cousin had described as belonging to that Joanne lady was still parked out front. Wanting to maintain the element of surprise, I cut my lights, coasted into their side yard, hopped out of the car, ran up the front steps and headed in the front door without knocking.

Since I knew that his sister had just gotten out of prison for armed assault, I had 'mine' in my purse just in case she wanted some.

Evidentially, my bursting through the front door unannounced must have caught everyone off guard 'cause Nino's eyes were hell-a big and his sister, Ms. Joanne and his mama's mouths were fixed wide open.

I was nervous as hell, but the adrenaline rush and my anger had overcome my better judgment. And, before I realized what I was actually doing, I'd snatched Nino up off the couch, pushed him into his bedroom and locked the door behind me.

From the other side of the door I heard his mama say "Ya'll don't fight."

Then the front door opened again and I heard Nino's sister say "Girl you better go in there and get your cousin before Nino kills her."

"Not hardly Red, ya'll need to just chill and let them handle theirs."

My cousin? Awww sookie - sookie now, I got back-up! Ohhhh, it's really 'bout to be on up in here now!

Feeling confident that my cousin had the situation on the other side of the door under control, I dropped my purse on the bed and commenced to ripping my poster sized bathing suit pictures off Nino's wall and ripping my nugget rope chain from around his neck.

Then the brotha grabbed me and held both of my arms down at my side.

Oh no this neg-ga ain't just put his hands on me?

"Turn me loose Nino," I screamed.

"Calm down girl," he said trying to get me to relax by restraining me.

The List.

"Neg-ga, you got five seconds to get your got damn hands off me before …" I stopped mid-sentence and on impulse opted to literally kick off in Nino's A–.

While still holding my arms, he somehow managed to back up and avoid my kick, before spinning me around and twisting my arms behind me like I was wearing a strait jacket.

I definitely wasn't giving up that easy; so I tried jerking away. But, Nino wasn't letting go.

We ended up falling onto the bed with him landing on my back. Fortunately for me, during the fall he lost control of one of my hands and I reached out, grabbed my purse and unzipped it. That's when Nino caught a glimpse of the barrel of the gun.

"Oh you brought a gun up in here to shoot a neg-ga?" He said half surprised and half pissed?

"A gun?" I heard his sister say from the living room as she started beating on the bedroom door.

"Oh Lawd, what is ya'll doing in there?" His mother said in a grief stricken voice.

"It's all right mama, she ain't gone shoot me," Nino declared in a confident voice.

And well hey he was right; even if I would've shot him, then what? His sister was about 5'10 and 250 pounds. Chances were that if I unloaded all five of my remaining bullets in her big red butt, she still would have had enough strength left to beat me silly. And if the rest of the chicks up in the State Penn were half as big as she was, I definitely didn't want to end up being some big heifer's girlfriend all because I'd shot Nino's trifling behind.

So I got up, collected my broken jewelry, my pictures and my purse, unlocked the bedroom door and left without looking back.

ଔ ଓ

When we all got back to my cousin's apartment, she asked Jersey what jumped off before she had pulled up; and Jersey commenced to giving her and the other guys the play by play.

169

Then I asked my cousin, "how come you came over there, I though you didn't have anyone to watch little Ti-Ti."

"Cause I knew you was mad as hell girl, and I ain't know what you were about to do. Plus," she continued, "I knew that Nino's sister, Big Red, was crazy; and I'm pretty sure that Joanne be packing everywhere she goes since she be transporting."

Then she looked at my friend, "Now no offense to you Jersey, but I don't know you like that and I ain't know if you would have my cousin's back or not. So I had to leave my baby with them and get over there just in case things got outta hand."

"Tammy, please tell me you did not pull a gun on Nino?" She asked me trying to determine whether I'd totally lost my mind.

"Girl the Negro put his hands on me," I said still pissed.

"Oh no he didn't hit you?" She asked while starting to gear up like she was ready to go back over there.

"Naw, man. He was just trying to keep me from hitting his sorry A–."

Right about that time, I remembered that my cousin's friend guy and his partners were still over there. When I looked up all three of those brotha's were looking at me like I was straight crazy.

Then one of the dude's pointed at me, "Saturday Night Special Slim is ya'll's cousin too?" He asked shaking his head. "Ok that settles it," he concluded, "all the females in ya'll family is straight crazy!"

All we could do is laugh 'cause this wasn't the first time we'd heard that statement from some dudes.

Then my cousin introduced me to this neg-ga, the comedian, and I immediately recognized his name as one of her sideline squeezes. And then she introduced me to Mr. Funny's brother, Mr. Sexy Lips.

Dang, I sho' wouldn't mind licking those lips, I thought. *Girl chill out, what is wrong with you?* "Has anybody ever told you that you got some sexy behind lips?" I asked him as I stared at his mouth.

170

The List.

Then as he smiled and answered "Yeah," I saw the gold tooth. *Awwww Darn!*

That dang on gold tooth turned me straight off and snapped me right back into reality. Turning away from Sexy Lips in disgust, I remembered I needed to take Jersey to her homegirl's apartment.

Jersey's homegirl lived way across town and I really didn't know that part of Tampa very well. Since my cousin couldn't leave her daughter again, Sexy Lips volunteered to ride with me.

I was already tired from the drive from Tallahassee; plus, I was drained from all the physical drama that had jumped off at Nino's. So once we got outside, I just threw Sexy Lips the keys and told him "handle thangs."

After we'd dropped Jersey off, we had to take a quick detour to Sexy Lips' house so that he could get his wallet. *Here we go with the wallet trick again. Is that the standard line these Tampa neg-ga's use? Hey wait, if he doesn't have his wallet, then he ain't got no driver license with him either. Oh well, whatever. I'm too damn tired to even care.*

But true to his word, Sexy Lips ran inside, got his wallet and came right back out. Then he took me to get some barbeque at Big John's Alabama B-B-Q Pit. *Ooooh Lawd! I just can't come to Tampa without getting me some Big John's!*

By the time we got back to my cousin's it was almost midnight. My roommate cousin had already left to go home; and, my other cousin was getting ready to hang out with Mr. Funny, Sexy Lip's brother, for a bit. And, since my cousin's daughter was asleep in the only bedroom in the house, I figured that if I stayed over, I might be in the way.

So where am I going to stay tonight, I wondered. It was definitely too late for me to go to my Aunts house, and staying at Nino's house was out of the question. So when Sexy Lips offered to let me go home with him, I took him up on it without even thinking twice. *Shoot, cuz IS dating his brother, so it ain't like he could be a serial killer or nothing. Right?*

Tymira Mack

CR 80

Sexy Lips lived in this little house in West Tampa with his brother and his mom. When we went inside, his mom was sitting up watching TV in the dark living room with a glass of beer or something in her hand. Lips politely introduced me to his mom, and she halfway spoke and halfway nodded to acknowledge me; then he led me through the kitchen to this little storage looking room off the kitchen that I guess served as his bedroom.

He offered me a t-shirt and some shorts to sleep in and politely left the room while I changed. *Whew, thank goodness I don't have to sleep in these tight behind jeans.*

When he came back, he had changed into shorts and a t-shirt himself. "You want something to drink?" he asked while peeping in the frig. "Look like we don't have nothing but beer, water and diet coke."

"No thanks, I'll pass."

"You need to go pee?" He offered.

"No. No thanks, I'm ok," I assured him.

As we both kind of stood there awkwardly, Lips asked "would you feel more comfortable if I slept out in the living room?"

But since I was a bit nervous about being in a strange house in an unfamiliar part of town, I certainly wasn't hyped for sleeping alone. "Naw its cool, you can sleep in here."

I mean he's got a queen sized waterbed so it ain't like we'll be all up under each other. And, besides I'd feel guilty about kicking him out of his bed when he was nice enough to give me somewhere to sleep for the night. What's the big deal? After all he has been the perfect gentleman so far. Right?

Even with all of my attempts at rationalization, I found it very difficult to sleep that night. I was still upset about the whole Nino incident. Plus, I was in a strange house with a strange man. And, I just kept wondering if or when Sexy Lips might try to make a move on me. Somehow I finally gave into the exhaustion and fell asleep, only to wake up a few hours later scared out of my mind.

172

The List.

I'd just rolled over and opened my eyes when I saw Sexy Lips sitting in a chair at the kitchen table. He had his arm propped up on the table and he was injecting himself with a needle.

Oh my Gosh. My cousin done sent me home with a dope fiend. This neg-ga's in here slamming Herrr-ine. How am I gonna get outta here? The front door is thru the kitchen and I don't know where he put my car keys.

Sexy Lips must have felt me staring at him because he looked over and saw that I was awake. "Hey what's the matter you can't sleep?" He asked in what seemed to be a concerned voice.

Hummm. He don't sound like he's high? I thought to myself as I kept staring at the needle hanging out his arm.

He must have followed my gaze and realized I was looking at the needle.

"What's wrong?" He said in a puzzled voice.

"Nothing I was just wondering if you was shooting up heroine or something?" I whispered in the calmest voice I could manage 'cause I'd heard that heroin addicts were unpredictable and I didn't want to do or say anything to upset this brotha before I could figure out where he'd laid my car keys.

All of a sudden, the brother got this big grin on his face; he pulled the needle out of his arm, made a fist and bent his arm against itself. Then he snapped his head back and began laughing like a madman.

Bingo this brother is on that stuff.

And just as quickly as he'd busted out laughing, he got serious. "Relax Tammy, I'm not shooting up."

"Yeah, right. Can you please tell me where you put my keys?" I said as I got up and began putting my own clothes back on.

"It's 5:00 in the morning. Where are you gonna go at this hour? That's why you came over her in the first place, remember?" He reminded me, leaving me feeling real stupid.

"I' own know I'll find an I-Hop or a Denny's or something but I ain't trying to stay here with your doped out self," I said as I fell over trying to hurry up and pull my tight jeans back on.

"Girl I'm not on drugs. This is insulin Tammy. See here look," he said as he held up this little vial.

"Here's the bottle right here," he proclaimed while handing it to me.

Boy do I feel real stupid. But heck, how was I supposed to know he was a freaking diabetic? Shoot I only met him a few hours ago.

I left Tampa that weekend with a new resolve. *No more dope boys, brothers with gold teeth, or project Negro's for me!*

28
Buckwild

Take that, rewind it back. FAMU's Homecoming occurred a few weeks after I broke up with Nino. As was our normal tradition, my cousin had come up from Tampa for the weekend and was staying with me and her sister. That weekend we hung out with a few of my sorority sisters, hit a bunch of the frat parties, and just had a wild time.

At one of the frat parties, we ran into one of my cousin's ex-squeezes, along with his cousin and a couple of his boys. I'd known all these guys for over a year since I use to hang out at my cousins apartment the year she attended school in Tally. In fact, I'd briefly kicked it, without sex, with her ex-squeeze's cousin a while back; and, I also remember how I use to think that all of their friends were tall, chocolate and handsome, too.

During the party, I danced with one of those guys who seemed to be acting uncharacteristically Buckwild. *Humph, must be the alcohol?*

My cousin and her ex-squeeze ended up hanging out together for most of the weekend, consequently Buckwild and I ended up in many of the same social settings too. By Sunday, Buck and I were kind of vibing off each other; and soon after Homecoming we began officially dating.

175

Tymira Mack

At first our dating activities were strictly platonic. But as time went on, we began sleeping together. And of course, as always happens, once we'd mixed friendship with sex, things started to get crazy. All I can say is that what resulted was a very complicated two year relationship.

Our relationship was a combination of the worst aspects of all of my previous relationships put together. The two years we spent together were filled with monogamy and infidelity; pleasure and violence; gifts and thefts; trust and stalking–you name it and it was probably part of our relationship.

About the only area of our relationship which wasn't full of strife was our sexual relations. But in the end, even that had disastrous results.

Looking back now, I realize Buckwild was a very insecure brother at that point in his life. In fact, he told me, on more than one occasion, he felt like our relationship was a constant power struggle. *Power struggle? Neg-ga either you're my man or you're my B–eee-ach? Which is it gonna be?*

Once he even admitted that because of an off-hand comment I'd made, he even felt compelled to assert his dominance in our sex life. *Huh? The brother has always had it going on in the sex department. What could I have possibly said to bruise his ego?*

❦

During the good times, Buckwild spent more nights at my townhouse than at his own apartment. We hung out together. We took regular trips to his hometown on the weekends to visit his family and his church. He came home to South Florida with me and spent a couple of weekends with my family. We even took trips to Six Flags Atlanta, Disney World and the Caribbean. On the whole, about 40 or 50% of our relationship revolved around the good times.

176

The List.

Even though I can't place all the blame for the bad times on Buck; I do know things really started going downhill when he decided to pledge a fraternity.

It probably was wrong of me to be so unimpressed with his desire to join a frat; but, it had been over three years since I'd pledged and all the newness and excitement had worn off for me. Besides, I was now keenly aware of all the games that went on before, during and after the pledge period; so I just wasn't sympathetic to what he was going through.

Needless to say the mental strain of his pledging efforts plus my unsympathetic attitude began to take their toll on our relationship; and, pretty soon, he began to take his anger and frustrations out on me.

Like the night his big brother's had obviously beat the crap out of him and plastered him with all sorts of condiments and other vile waste products. I was soooo pissed that the brother had borrowed one of my white sheets without asking; and, then had the nerve to show up at my house at 4 am with all sorts of indescribable crap all over himself and my sheets.

I was so angry I wouldn't have even gotten out of my bed and gone downstairs to open the door for him, except I got tired of him banging and screaming up at my window like a mad man; cause of course he didn't have a key, that was a definite no-no.

"What took you so got damn long to open the door?" He scowled, immediately jumping down my throat.

"Well first of all, if you had taken your dirty, stinking A– to your own freaking apartment, you would not have had to wait," I grumbled, locking the door behind him and heading back upstairs to my bed.

"Well I didn't have a ride home so I caught a ride with one of my line brothers who lived out this way," he hollered as he followed me to the stairs.

Realizing that this dirty, stank brother was headed up the stairs behind me, I stopped and asked, "Where the freak are you going with your filthy behind?"

Tymira Mack

"I just had the worst night of my whole F'ing life and you don't even care do you?" He growled at me.

"Nope, sure don't," I said matter-of-factly. "Neg-ga you act like you're the only brother who ever had a rough pledge period. Besides them pretty fella's you're trying to join up with probably ain't even bringing no heat. You want to talk about a bad night try pledging a fraternity full-a real neg-ga's," I insisted with as much attitude as I could muster for 4:00 in the morning.

Then I turned and headed the rest of the way up the stairs. When I looked back, he was just standing there at the bottom of the stairs looking at me like he wanted to bash my head in. *Don't even think about it brother, you know the deal.*

The last thing I remember is hearing him go into the kitchen and snatch the phone off the hook on the wall. *Good I hope he can find someone to pick his stank butt up!*

I was awakened, about fifteen minutes later, by a set of headlights shining up in my window and the sound of my front door slamming.

Good Riddance!

‎ଓ ଞ‎

About a week later, Buck was inducted into his fraternity. And remember what I told you about the neophyte tradition: stepping, sexing and sleeping, in that order. Well Buckwild was no exception.

And yup you guessed it, right after that came his flaming stage. But, homeboy was a four alarm blaze. He got the tattoo; he got all the T-shirts and other paraphernalia; he was always stepping and hanging out at the frat house 24/7; and, of course there were also all the women.

Even though I was attending FSU at the time, I kicked it in the FAMU Frat & Sorority scene enough for people to know that Buck and I were a couple. So because of this fact, I was never openly disrespected by any females. But his activities on the low-low were a whole 'nother story altogether!

The List.

As luck would have it, my cousin's best friend was Buckwild's ex-girlfriend's roommate. Thus, through this convoluted connection, I got my first inkling that Buck was back kicking it with homegirl and trying to keep it on the hush.

Although I really wasn't sure, I was smart enough to know that all rumors usually contained at least one thread of fact. And besides, ex's are hard to get over mentally and easy to get with physically. So when Buck started spending more nights at his own apartment than at mine, I knew what the deal was.

This was no biggie to me because I really wasn't feeling Buck during his flaming stage. And, fortunately for him I wasn't looking for payback nor was I into the "DOING the whole frat thing" like a lot of college girls were. Otherwise I definitely would have taken advantage of the fact that Buck had always brought this one particular extra sexy, chocolate, frat brother of his to my house on a regular basis.

Anyhow, the way I figured it, as long as Buck didn't openly disrespect me, who really cared?

ᓚ ᕗ

One afternoon the brother took my nonchalant-ness for granted and tried to straight play me for stupid all up in my face.

Why every time you give a Negro a couple of kernels, he wanna be making popcorn?

He'd been missing in action all evening and was nowhere to be found later on that night. Still I didn't lose any sleep over it, I just figured I'd deal with the brother whenever he decided to pop back up. And sure enough, 24 hours later, he got dropped off on my door step.

"What's up?" He asked, coming in with a big grin on his face like everything was normal.

"Where you been?" I asked cutting straight to the point.

"Huh?" He said obviously trying to stall.

"Where've you been since yesterday?" I repeated, reinforcing the fact the question was quite clear the first time I'd asked it.

"Oh ummm I had to go home," he said nervously.

Now I knew the brother didn't have no car and I was about the only dummy willing to drive the 50 miles to the little one-horse town he was from.

Get real. You've gotta do better than that, I thought to myself. "Go home? For what," I asked just itching to see how far this brother was willing to take his lie.

"Oh, I went to see my uncle, he's in the hospital," he responded obviously becoming more comfortable with the lies he was telling.

"Oh my goodness is everything ok?" I asked, feigning concern.

This obviously made the Negro feel real confident. "Yeah he had a heart attack and he's in critical condition in the intensive care."

Bingo Neg-ga. I knew you'd slip up sooner or later.

"Critical condition?" I asked amazed at how far he was actually willing to take this lie. "You're lying."

"Naw for real he's gonna be ok," he reassured me.

"No Negro, I didn't mean you're lying like 'is he gonna be ok, for real'," I said. "I mean you're lying, lying."

"Huh?" It obviously hadn't dawned on Buck that I was on to him.

"You're lying, because number one if you left here at 6:30 yesterday, it would have put you at home around 7 or 7:30 and I don't know no hospital with visiting hours after 8 pm," I said as I raised my hand toward his face to shut him up before he could even start trying to dispute my logic.

"And number two, Critical Condition my behind, because ya'll ain't got nothing but a stinking medical clinic in that one-horse town of yours. All true medical emergencies are sent to Tallahassee for Intensive Care."

"Ahhhh, just hush," I ordered as he fixed his mouth to lie some more. "Furthermore if he was in such critical condition, how did you figure out in less than 12 hours that he's gonna be ok?"

180

The List.

I was on a roll then.

"And if this uncle is so special to you how come I've never heard of an uncle with a heart condition? And why'd you leave dear old unc' on his death bed to come back to Tallahassee? Huh?" I insisted as I got all up on him and poked him in his chest.

He obviously realized he was in this one way too deep, so he just got pissed and asked me to take him home. When I refused, he grabbed my keys off the kitchen counter and headed out the door.

Oh, it was on then. I ran outside behind him and tried to grab my keys out of his hands. But he held the keys up over his 6'4 head where I couldn't jump up high enough to reach them.

At that point I got pissed and bit the Negro square on his chest, figuring he'd just drop my keys. But, to my surprise, he threw them up on the roof of my townhouse and bit me right back on my freaking jaw.

And there we were outside my townhouse with our teeth clamped into each other when my homegirl Aayden drove up.

Thank God, homegirl to the rescue.

"Take that with ya punk A–," I screamed behind him as he walked off toward his homies townhouse, figuring he was out numbered.

Look at my freaking cheek; I can't believe this Neg-ga bit me back! And how am I gonna get my keys off the roof?

ೞ ಏ

During my second year of graduate school I'd begun interning part-time at another State office in order to fulfill one of my degree requirements. While at my internship one day, an opportunity that was too good to be true presented itself. It seems one of my co-workers' boyfriends had a homie coming into town from Michigan and they were all headed down to Orlando for the weekend.

There were about four couples going on the trip and my co-worker asked me if I wanted to go along so that Michigan wouldn't be by himself. I wasn't too sure about the whole idea, but once I met this fine, but red, Negro and learned that he was paying for everything, I figured *what the heck?*

What are the odds that on the way down to Orlando we would stop at the same gas station as one of Buck's frat brothers? But fortunately I had two things in my favor. Number one, Buck and old dude hated each other since dude was now dating a chick who'd seriously broken Bucks heart. And, two there was about eight of us traveling together, so dude really couldn't tell I was supposed to be chilling with Michigan.

Whew, that was a close call!

The rest of the weekend was truly the bomb. Michigan wined and dined, and dined and wined me. We partied at a hotspot in Eatonville, went out for steak and lobster and basically had a very relaxing weekend. But, even though I was still mad with Buck, I only smooched a little with Michigan; 'cause I still respected my relationship enough not to get busy with dude.

I' own know if I could have exercised that much self-control if the brother had been Chocolate.

C03 80

A few weeks later Buck and I had made up, so I was surprised to wake up around midnight and hear voices coming from downstairs. I figured it was just my cousin and her boyfriend, until I realized Buck wasn't in bed with me any longer.

Humph, he must be downstairs watching videos since we don't have cable upstairs.

But something inside told me to get up and check the situation out for myself.

When I got up and cracked my door open, I could still hear voices downstairs even though the rest of the house was pitch black, except for a tiny bit of light coming from underneath my cousin's bedroom door. Knowing that Buck wasn't dumb enough

The List.

to have anyone in my house, I tiptoed back over to my nightstand and eased the telephone off the hook.

"Did you hear something?" The girl on the line said.

He's talking to a freaking female? Oh no this neg-ga ain't all up in my house, on my phone talking to some female.

"Something like what?" He asked, sounding a bit nervous.

"It sounded like someone picked up the phone. Is your roommate home?"

"Naw he ain't here," Buck said to her lying.

"How would you know if your roommate was home when your black A– is all up in my house on my phone talking to some other trick?" I yelled as I slammed the phone down and took the stairs two by two; determined to kick off in his A –.

"Oh hell here they go again," I heard my cousin say as I raced past her room on my way downstairs.

"Please go get between them before something jumps off down there," she instructed her boyfriend just before he bolted out of her bedroom swift on my heels.

"That's it Buck. That's the last damn straw," I screamed as I got all up on him pointing my index finger in his face.

"Awwww hell," my cousin's boyfriend mumbled as he pulled me back out of Buck's face.

"Thank you man; I ain't never hit no girl before but cuz she's about overdue for an A – whooping," Buck said while opening and closing his fists.

"What? Brang it on neg-ga," I hollered as I tried to get away from my cousin's boyfriend. "Neg-ga you just got outta bed with me and then you gots the nerve to be all up in here disrespecting my house, by being on the phone with some other B; and, now you tripping like you gonna whoop my A–."

"Brang it Neg-ga, Brang it," I screamed like a mad woman, cause in my right mind I knew that there was no way in hell I could have whooped Bucks 6'4 A–.

"Man I ain't got time for this stuff," he huffed as he grabbed his coat off the chair and headed toward the door.

Tymira Mack

"Get the F– out then Neg-ga, and don't come back," I yelled as the door slammed behind him.

That's it!

೮⃝ ೮⃝

What Luck? A couple of days later I ran into Semper Fi and my mind immediately raced back to the last time we'd kicked it together. After the two of us exchanged small talk for a few minutes, I just boldly came out and asked him "Heard any good bedtime stories lately?"

Well the huge grin that broke out on his face spoke volumes. And needless to say I enjoyed several of Semper's bedtime stories that evening, despite my phone ringing off the hook. But something in my gut told me not to let him spend the night.

And, it's a good thing I listened to my instinct because Buck knocked on my door less than three minutes after Semper left.

If I didn't know any better, I'd swear this Negro was watching my house or something?

"How come you haven't been answering your phone all night?" Buck asked as soon as I opened the door.

"Oh, I just got home," I said lying.

"So where you been all night?" He asked suspiciously.

"I was over my 'adopted' sister's house." I replied, a little perturbed by all the questions.

"Ummm, I drove by there but I didn't see your car," he said as he pushed his way past me and entered all up in my apartment.

"Well you see me now Neg-ga," I said pissed he'd just barged into my house and had obviously been around town looking for me. "Now what do you want?"

"I just wanted to apologize for the other night," he offered as he reached out to hug me.

"Ok," I said as I backed out of his reach.

"Ok?" In less than twenty seconds, he'd gone from apologetic to pissed off, simply because I'd refused his weak apology and hug.

184

The List.

"Yes, ok. You've apologized. And now you can leave," I coldly insisted while turning to open the door.

"Why is that neg-ga coming back?" He asked with this look of rage on his face.

"What are you talking about now Buck?" I asked as I wondered whether this brother really had been watching my house or something.

"I thought you said you just got home," he interrogated, while walking up on me.

"I did," I insisted as I began to back up near the drawer where we kept the butcher knives.

"Then why is your car cold and why you got on a damn bathrobe, huh?" He demanded as he snatched open my robe to reveal that I was wearing nothing underneath.

Oh freak, I'm busted. Wait a minute; did he just say my car was cold? But I couldn't dwell on the curious statement for long because I just couldn't stand there and go out like a sucker.

"Have you ever heard of a shower?" I said thinking fast on my feet. "That's just what I was about to do before you knocked."

"Yeah go on upstairs and wash that ROTC neg-ga off your A-," he said as he slammed my front door, jumped in his frat brother's car, spun out backwards, and sped off.

Oh snap, rewind that back? How he know about Semper? This Negro really was watching my house tonight.

185

29
Poison

Coochie, coochie, coochie, coo. A day or two after my last big blow out with Buck, I began having itchy privacy department problems. I figured all the drama I'd been going through with Buck, plus the added stress of trying to complete my graduation thesis paper had caused me to have the mother of all yeast infections. But after a couple of days of receiving absolutely no relief from the usual over the counter yeast infection zapping creams, I knew I had a for real – for real problem.

What in the?

I really wasn't in the mood to go to the clinic at school, but I didn't have any other option, 'cause the itching was unbearable.

I'm sure they'll be able to give me some prescription strength cream that will clear this itching right up, I thought as I signed in and sat down to fill out the 'reason for my visit' paper while I waited for my number to be called.

"Ok, let's see here," I thought out loud as I began filling out the form.

Name, address, phone, social security, sex, race.

Done. Done. Done. Done. Done. Done.

Reason for today's visit?

Hummm, I wonder what they'd say if I put "itchy coochie," I thought giggling to myself and writing "Yeast Infection," instead.

The List.

Date of last menstrual cycle?

Shoot, I' own know. I don't have to keep track of that mess. I wonder what they'd say if I put "two days after I took the last white pill in the pack," I thought making light of the whole situation.

Before I could get to the bottom of the form, they were already calling my number.

Yippee, I'm ready to get this taken care of.

I certainly knew the routine by now. Enter the room; take the paper gown from the nurse; undress from the waist down; sit with your legs dangling off the edge of the exam table; and, squirm around to keep your butt from showing through the opening in the back of the gown while waiting for the physician's assistant.

"So what brings you in to see us today Miss Williams?" The physician's assistant asked as she breezed in, sat down and began skimming over my incomplete Patient Questionnaire form.

"Ummmm, I think I might have a yeast infection," I said modestly.

"Alright," she said standing up, washing her hands and heading over to me. "Lie down and let's just take a look."

After turning on the super-powered, search and destroy looking lamp and shinning it in my private area, she made a couple of incoherent groans and then motioned to the nurse, "Hand me a specimen collection kit, please?"

The nurse handed her this extra-long Q-Tip, a long tongue depressor looking thing with a scooped out edge, and a Petri dish.

What's ALL that for? I wondered. *Usually they just take a peek and confirm right quick that it's just a little yeast.*

Then after she finished collecting the specimen – *SPECIMEN?* – she instructed the nurse, "Do me a favor, set that up for the lab and ask Dr. Something–or–Other to pop his head in please."

"Relax, just a couple of more minutes and you'll be able to get dressed," she told me as she pointed the search and destroy light away from my pie-pie and down toward the floor.

"What's the other doctor coming in for?" I asked getting a little nervous.

Tymira Mack

"Oh it's just a routine procedure, you see some of our diagnosis have to be confirmed by the doctors."

"Oh ok," I said relaxing a bit 'cause her explanation made perfect sense to me.

True to her word, the doctor came right in, and together they shined that bright light back towards my stuff, pointed some, nodded some, washed their hands and then left the room so that I could get dressed.

While I was dressing, the nurse knocked on the door and peeked in, "once you're dressed, take a seat in the waiting area and the Nurse Health Educator will call you when she's ready."

The Nurse Health Educator? Wha? Boy I tell you these fancy white institutions just make up all sort of positions. I bet that's why the tuition is so darn high.

"Miss Williams?" A warm voice called, startling me out of my thoughts.

"Yes," I said getting up and walking toward the lady with the warm voice.

She politely ushered me into an office filled with all sorts of books, pamphlets, posters and plastic models of various body parts. "Please come in."

"Thank you," I mumbled as I took a seat and watched as she sat down and placed my chart on her desk.

"I see you came in today to have a problem looked at?" She asked obviously knowing the answer to her own question since she was holding my chart.

"Un-hum," I whispered having a flash back to the scene back in high school when the Health Department nurse told me that I had the Big G.

Oh Gosh, couldn't be, I prayed silently to myself.

"Well Miss Williams, I'm happy to report that you don't have a yeast infection."

Well hallelujah! I thought, breathing a sigh of relief.

"But," she paused.

But? Did she just say But? Oh my gosh.

The List.

"But," she continued, "I'm afraid I have to inform you that you have contracted genital herpes."

"I did what?" I timidly asked as a lump welled up in my throat.

"When was the last time you had sex?" she asked.

"What?" I said mad that she had just dropped such a huge bomb on me and now she was asking about my sex life?

"I'm sorry Miss Williams but by law, we have to ask you these questions."

"Oh my God, my sex life is a criminal issue now?" I mumbled more to myself than to her, before beginning to cry.

"Oh no, no, no," she said reaching out and grabbing my hand to console me.

"No Miss Williams, by law we have to report the information to the State Health Department, not to law enforcement authorities."

Even though I was relieved by her statement, my head was spinning so fast that I couldn't even respond.

So she asked again, "When was the last time you had sexual intercourse."

"Um, a couple of days ago, I guess," I mumbled.

"Think real hard this is important," she emphasized.

"I can't really remember," I lied because I'd been with Semper Fi just a couple of days before. "I mean why does it matter?" I asked really curious about what the big deal was.

"Well because we know this disease has a 2 to 10 day incubation period—meaning the time between when you came into contact with it and when you begin having symptoms," she informed me.

"Oh," I said as I started calculating the timing of the itchiness. *That would mean it couldn't have been Semper, besides we used condoms anyway. So it had to be Buck.*

"But how could this be? I–I mean we, well we always used condoms." I said softly to myself as I looked down at my hands that had begun to make fists all on their own.

Tymira Mack

The Health Lady must have heard what I'd mumbled because she responded, "unfortunately, condoms don't offer 100% protection in this case, because there are still uncovered areas of both you and your partner's body which could come into contact during intercourse."

I just sat their silently wringing my hands and barely listening to what she was saying.

That dirty dog; um-ma kill that neg-ga, was all that I kept thinking.

Then she continued, "And if either you or your partner has any active lesions on any of those uncovered areas, well then you become susceptible to contracting the disease," she emphasized before continuing. "I can't tell you the number of students who come in here each week, tell me the same sad story, and leave devastated because they trusted in condoms."

"Now don't get me wrong," she switched gears, "I'd be remiss if I didn't tell you that condoms offer just about the best measure of protection out there for sexually active students, I'm just saying –well as you've found out for yourself today–condoms aren't a 100% guarantee."

Right about then, I was so mad and so sad and so confused that I didn't want to hear no freaking condom lecture. All I could do was sit there and cry; snot and all.

After wiping my nose with the tissue the Educator Lady gave me I managed to ask her, "What exactly is genital herpes?"

"It's a viral STD which causes painful blisters in the genital area."

"Oh it's a virus like the flu or something," I said perking up a bit, "so I can just take a shot or some pills and just get rid of it?"

"Yes, while it IS a virus, it's a little different than the flu," she said. "This virus remains in the body for life."

"For life?" I moaned as the tears came streaming down all over again.

"Yes, unfortunately there is no cure for Herpes."

The List.

"So you mean I'm gonna have bumps down there forever?" I asked as I began to realize that my sex life was over.

"Well not exactly," she explained, "herpes lesions occur in sporadic episodes that last for about 5–7 days. Then the virus lays dormant in your body until triggered by such things as your menstrual cycle or stress."

I just sat there with my shoulders slumped over, in a state of utter shock.

What am I gonna do now? I wish I could just die.

"What's wrong," the Nurse Lady asked, "you can share your thoughts with me."

Even though she was trying to be comforting, I was a little perturbed by her question. *What's wrong? You just told me my pie-pie is gonna be poison for life! HELLO?*

Realizing I wasn't really angry with her and since I didn't have anyone else to talk to, I confided, "but I want to get married and have babies and live happily ever after when I grow up." I knew that sounded stupid coming from a 20-and-a-half year old chick, but it's really how I felt right then.

"Listen, you can still do all of those things," the Nurse Educator Lady encouraged.

"Yeah right," I responded.

"No really, Tamara, can I call you Tamara?" she asked.

"Well my name is Tymira, but whatever," I said quite accustomed to people butchering my name over the years.

"Well Tim – ear – a," she said taking her time to pronounce it right, "although there is no cure, herpes has become a manageable disease."

She went on to spend about 15 minutes explaining to me that herpes outbreaks were more frequent at the initial time of infection; the frequency of the outbreaks could be managed or even lessened with medications; and, over time some people had even been known to have fewer than two episodes a year.

"Oh, ok," I said starting to see a little light at the end of the tunnel. "But what about the having kids thing?"

Tymira Mack

"Well that can be tricky, because if you give birth at the time active herpes lesions are present anywhere in your vaginal area, your child could be at risk for a number of birth related defects, including blindness or even death."

That bit of information just made my heart sink and my body slump all over again. But I guess my time was up and the Health Nurse Lady had other stupid college students to educate.

"Here, take these," she encouraged as she handed me a number of pamphlets on herpes. "Read 'em over, and you'll find a lot of good information to help you navigate your way toward managing this disease. There's also a 1-800 number in there for a herpes support group you can call."

Then she said, "although the official confirmation of your diagnosis won't come back for a couple of days, we've seen enough cases like yours to be fairly confident its herpes. Thus," she said handing me two more slips of paper, "the doctor has written you two prescriptions for Zovirax. You can get them filled at the student pharmacy downstairs; and, if taken according to schedule, they should help relieve your symptoms."

"Thanks," I said reaching for the prescriptions and all the pamphlets.

I stuffed all those things way down in my book bag and left her office hoping no one could tell by the distraught look on my face that I had a poison pie-pie.

൦൫ ൬൦

Wouldn't you know the gosh darn university pharmacy had a black female student working the drop-off counter? I was actually tempted to leave 'cause I know how females talk, but my stuff was itching so bad I had to swallow my pride and get those prescriptions filled quick, fast and in a hurry.

Maybe it was my own paranoia, but I noticed how her eyebrows raised and a tiny little smile crossed her lips, as she was reviewing my prescriptions. As I waited for my itchy-coochie

The List.

cream and pills to be ready, I sat there with my legs crossed tightly –to help squelch the itching–feeling like the whole world was staring at me.

"Williams?" The chick called out.

Yes! I'm ready to get out of here! I thought as I hurried to the counter.

"Do you have any questions about your medication today?" She asked pulling the bottle of pills out of the bag with a bit of a smirk on her face.

Even though I did have questions, I declined because there was no way anyone was going to give me instructions for these pills out loud where everyone and their mama could hear. I'd just have to read the information for myself and take my chances.

"Ok then, your total is $55."

"Fifty, who?" *Surely she must be mistaken, the last prescription I got from here only costed $3.*

"Fifty–five," she repeated without blinking.

"Is that the student discount price?" I asked hoping she'd forgotten to include the discount.

"Yup," she said smugly.

"Oh, well ok. Can I please write a check?" I asked 'cause I ain't have that kind of cash on me.

I paid for those expensive behind prescriptions, grabbed the bag and hurried out the door. Once I got in my car, I pulled out the prescription bottle and read the instructions:

Take one pill; FIVE TIMES a day; for FIVE to SEVEN days
EVEN AFTER symptoms disappear?
Oh my God!

30
Kiss & Say Goodbye

Let it burn. Soon after the whole Herpes diagnosis, I learned I'd been selected to receive the first ever award of a new minority Doctoral Studies Fellowship at my particular graduate school. The award meant I would receive 100% funding toward earning a PhD.

This should have been a time of extreme excitement for me. Here I was given the opportunity of a lifetime to earn a Doctorate degree, for FREE, before my 25th birthday; but I didn't even care. I was in such a state of shock over the lifelong impact of my recent diagnosis that I failed to recognize and appreciate the educational gift which had been literally handed to me on a silver platter. So instead of focusing on pursuing the college degree of a lifetime; I just concentrated on coping with a lifetime overshadowed by an incurable STD.

Except for dragging myself to class, I blew off work and stayed locked upstairs in my room, in bed, with my blinds closed tightly for almost a week. I didn't want to see or talk to anyone. Heck, I barely even wanted to eat.

Every so often I would take all those pamphlets the Nurse Health Educator Lady gave me out of my super top secret hiding place, spread them all over my bed, read 'em and just weep.

The List.

What am I gonna do? How could something like this happen to me? I've been so careful lately.

What am I gonna do? I've taken the pill regularly and used condoms faithfully. And, I ain't never messed with no body who was downright nasty.

What am I gonna do? I wish I could just make this go away! It's not fair. Nobody's ever gonna want me again.

What am I going to do? I might as well just die.

"Tammy?" My cousin knocked at my bedroom door and interrupted my thoughts; but, I didn't answer her.

"Tammy, telephone," she urged, "it's for you."

"I' own feel like talking to anybody," I insisted.

"Not even Thunder?" she asked.

Thunder? Wow, it's been over a year since I've heard from him.

"Tammy did you hear me? It's Thunder," she repeated, "What do you want me to tell him?"

"Tell him to hold on a second," I said as I wiped my tears, rushed to gather up all the pamphlets and placed them back in their super top secret hiding place.

"Hello?" I said as I yelled to my cousin, "I got it, you can hang up now."

"What's up?" His sexy chocolate voice boomed through the phone line and instantly made my heart melt.

"Nothing much," I said lying, "what's up with you?"

"Just missing you," he confided in his ultra-sexy voice.

"Where did that come from?" *Why all of a sudden you're missing me and calling me out the blue?* "I mean it's been almost a year since we've seen or even talked to each other COUSIN," I said sharply.

"Oh man, I know you aren't still holding the cousin thing against me?" He jokingly asked. "You put a brotha through hell trying to make up for that one."

"Well you should have schooled your boys better, or showed them a picture of me or something," I said feeling the piss–tivity from that night coming back all over again.

Tymira Mack

"Come on Tammy, I told you, my boy knew I was excited about the fact you were coming into town for the weekend. He just didn't know that you, were you," he said trying to explain all over again.

"Just call me Cousin Tammy from Florida," I teased, referring to what his boy had mistakenly called me when he found Thunder and I talking outside a party at the Frozen Palace in College Park. It seems his friend didn't know I was the *real* Tammy. Instead, he thought I was just some girl Thunder was making moves on; so he walked up to us and asked Thunder, "Hey man, has your cousin Tammy from Florida got to town yet?"

"You know I've kicked myself for how that whole situation went down over a million times," he said apologetically. "But that's not why I called."

"Ok so I'm listening," I said, as I thought *I'm really listening 'cause I've REALLY missed the sensual sound of your voice.*

"I called because I miss you and I was thinking of coming down there to see you."

Say what? In the whole 2 ½ years we've known each other you've never once come to Tally.

"You're what?" I repeated as I couldn't help but think, *geesh, if only you'd called me about 10 days ago maybe none of this would have ever happened in the first place?*

"Yeah, me and some of the boys were thinking of taking a road trip," he said eagerly, "and, well I really wanted to come see you."

Wow, I really want to see you too!

"That is if you want to see me?" he asked expectantly. "I mean I know the last time I talked to you, you'd committed to a relationship with ole' boy."

Oh geesh, why'd you have to go and mention him?

"Are ya'll still together?" He asked.

"I can't really say. . .I mean I' own really know," I stammered; 'cause in reality I was feeling like, *with this diagnosis and all, I don't really have any choice but to settle for being with him right now.*

"So what are you saying?" He pressed.

196

The List.

"I'm just saying that coming here might not be such a good idea right now," I answered from my head and definitely not from my heart.

"So are you saying you just don't want to see me?" He probed.

"No of course not! Truth be told I'd love to see you," I admitted, but I couldn't chance him coming to town and Buck acting a natural fool, especially before I got a chance to deal with him about this whole Herpes thing.

"So what then? When and where can I see you?" he pressed for an answer.

"I 'own know."

"Well I tell you what, why don't you just come to Atlanta then?" He said obviously not willing to take no for an answer.

After a long pause to figure out how to best communicate my desire, "Look, I'll come on one condition."

"What condition is that?" He asked obviously unaccustomed to having any conditions placed on our time together.

"No sex." I blurted out quickly.

"Huh? No sex?" He repeated as if he hadn't heard me correctly.

"Yes. No sex." I reiterated, "I'll come if you can promise you won't pressure me for sex."

"I can't promise you that," he told me straight up.

"I can't believe you," I whined, unfairly unleashing a week's worth of frustrations on him.

"What did I say Tammy?" He asked. "I don't know why you're jumping down my throat all of a sudden."

"I'm upset because it seems like the only reason you want to see me is to have sex," I sighed. The truth of the matter was I wanted him too, but I just couldn't have him like that anymore.

"That's not true, Tammy."

"Well that's what you said Thunder."

"No I said I couldn't promise you I wouldn't want to make love to you," he asserted.

197

"Come on Thunder, you're playing with words now. The answer is either yes you can commit to no sex; or no you can't," I insisted.

"Well if you put it like that, then no I can't," he said straight up.

"You know a year ago, you asked me for a commitment, and I said WE weren't ready for that. And, now here you are proving me right," I sulked.

"What?" He questioned. "I don't get how you're putting those two things together."

"What I'm saying to you is that over the past two or three years we've known each other, we've proven that we're totally compatible in bed," I insisted.

"Yeah," he giggled happily, as if having flashbacks.

"But outside of the fact that we spent almost 75% of what little time we had together in the bed, you and I have no idea if we have any compatibility in other areas of our life," I said nailing the point home.

He remained silent, so I continued, "so what I'm proposing is that we spend three or four days together without so much as touching each other to see if we can start building a friendship on more than just great sex?"

"I hear what you're saying and I'm willing to try," he said.

"Good," I felt relieved.

"But," he continued "I can't make you any promises."

"Oh here we go again," I said beginning to cry as I got frustrated all over again.

"All I'm saying is, as attracted as I am to you, there's no way I can promise you I'll be able to spend four days alone with you and not want to make love to you," he said falling into his sexy voice all over again.

"You're serious?" I mumbled as I licked the tears that were running into the corners of my mouth.

"Dead serious." He replied firmly.

"Then I guess I can't come see you," I concluded sadly.

The List.

By then the tears had started flowing heavily. The thought of the diagnosis; the thought that I couldn't share this problem with Thunder or anyone else; and, the thought that I'd probably just passed up my final opportunity to take my friendship with Thunder to another level, were all more than my brain could handle.

"I gotta go," I said struggling to keep my voice from cracking.

And, then I hung up first 'cause I knew it was probably the last time I'd ever communicate with him again.

 જી જી

I was about as sad as I could possibly be. I'd even contemplated suicide more times than I care to remember; but fortunately I was too chicken to go through with it. Instead, I just moped around until a deep depression set in.

It had been almost exactly two weeks since the diagnosis when Buck showed up at my house. I just happened to once again be in the kitchen, wearing a bathrobe, when he knocked.

"Damn girl you look like hell," he said as I held the door open.

I started to say *'yeah that's 'cause I haven't had a chance to wash that other neg-ga off me yet,'* but instead I opted for an even more hurtful response.

"Your mama," I quipped, knowing full well those were fighting words since his mother had abandoned him as a child and left him for his father and his grandmother to raise.

"Look," he said obviously not appreciating the smart remark I'd just made, "I didn't come here to argue with you."

"Well don't start nothing, won't be nothing," I mumbled while gathering my bag of chips and glass of Coca-Cola, and heading back up to my room.

When I got to the top of the stairs, I noticed he'd taken a seat on the couch and was playing with my pet Chow-Chow Cinnamon.

Tymira Mack

Why are you cavorting with the enemy, Cinny? You need to bite that neg-ga, I thought as I went in my room, plopped on my bed and ate chips while flipping through Tallahassee's five measly noncable TV channels.

About five minutes or so had passed before I heard Buck's footsteps as he climbed up the stairs and peered into my room.

"Dang-on girl, your room looks just as worse as you," he declared in a not-so-nice voice.

"Negro, before you start doling out insults, why don't you first learn the King's English," I replied, obviously in no mood to tolerate him, *with his poison self.*

"What?" he asked all confused.

"It's bad, you moron," I quipped, "My room looks just as bad as me, not just as worse."

"Well whatever heifer," he shot back.

"Look," I said eager to get to the bottom of this little surprise visit, "why the hell are you here?"

"I just came to see what was up," he said as if the last big fight we had never even happened.

"What's up? Buck get real," I sighed, even though I really wanted to say, *'Neg-ga, I've been through hell over the past 10 days. I've had to endure an unbearably itchy coochie for over a week. I've had to have my pie-pie poked, prodded, scraped and evaluated. I had to sit through a Herpes 101 lesson taught by some old white lady. I had to have an expensive A– $55 itchy coochie prescription filled by a sister who I'm sure will remember my face the next time she sees me around campus. I had to try and remember to take 5 itchy coochie pills a day, for seven days. I got my period. And, worse of all, I had to say good-bye to all hopes of ever living happily ever after with the love of my life. Neg-ga, that's what's the F– is up!'*

"Naw man, I mean I ain't seen you around nowhere," he said sounding all concerned. "I went by your job and your friend told me you hadn't been to work all week."

The List.

He continued, "I rode by your sister's house a couple of times and didn't see your car over there. And," he emphasized, "You weren't even at your sorority's party the other night."

Who the F– are you now? Beretta? Kojack? Magnum P.I.? 5'0? The Mafia? The FBI? The CIA? The freakin' KGB? Why are my freaking whereabouts all of a sudden of such great interest to you?

"What's it to you?" I asked a little startled by the revelation that he'd taken such an uncharacteristic interest in my routine activities.

"You feeling all right?" He asked as the conversation took a strange twist in a whole 'nother direction.

"No, the question is are you all right?" I asked while staring out my bedroom window trying to figure out how to get this whole situation out in the open. I really needed some answers to the questions that had been swimming around in my head.

I can't believe it. He's exposed me to this crap and I'm the one dancing around trying to find the best way to address the issue?

Enough is enough, I thought to myself as I decided to quit beating around the bush.

"Buck a couple of weeks ago I was diagnosed with an STD. Over the past 6 months you've done some foul crap to me," (finally admitting it out loud was a real awakening for me) "but I never thought YOU were even capable of being this LOW."

There was this long odd silence between us, as I turned from the window to face him.

I can't believe he's actually being silent for once. So either he's truly shocked to hear I have an STD, or the bastard is guilty as sin.

"Um, hello?" I snapped, "Did you hear what I just told you? You gave me a freaking STD damn-it!" I said angrily. "And not just any old STD; oh no, you had to go and give me a lifetime gift you bastard."

"Wait a minute Tammy," he paused, "who says I gave you anything?"

"The school health clinic, that's who!" I shouted.

"Well you're wrong 'cause I don't have anything," he insisted.

"Well prove it!" I challenged.

"What you want me to do?" He said making like he was unzipping his pants. "Whip my Jimmie out so you can examine it or something?"

"Ha – Ha real funny," I said in no mood for him or his jokes. "Let's see if your black A– is still laughing when the folks at the Health Department prove me right."

○ ○

It took me another week and about five thousand more arguments before Buck allowed me to drag his butt down to the Health Department for testing. If I hadn't been there myself, I wouldn't have believed him; but, they said because it had been more than three weeks since his possible exposure and because, by his own supposed admission, he didn't have any physical symptoms, then they had no way to perform a specimen test.

Instead they advised him to have a blood test to determine if the virus was present in his body.

"Ok well roll up his sleeves, and test away," I insisted.

"I'm sorry but we don't do that here," the lady said. "You'll have to go to your private physician or lab and have the test done."

"Since when the Health Department don't do VD testing?" I asked pissed.

To this day, I don't remember the reason the lady gave us; but, I do remember Buck leaving that place looking real relieved he wasn't being tested.

Not so fast Mr. Poison Pee-Pee, I thought as I spent the next two days calling around to find a doctor who would see and test Buck and his jacked-up Jimmie, ASAP. Luckily I found one, and I didn't waste any time dragging Buck over there to be tested; of course I didn't tell him where we were going until we got there.

The List.

Since Buck didn't have any insurance, the doctor's office required payment up front; and, once again Buck thought he'd found a way out by crying broke.

Oh I don't think so buddy-o.

To resolve this latest roadblock, I begrudgingly coughed up the $35 to pay for the doctor's visit plus another $30 or so dollars for the lab work.

As far as I'm concerned, I don't care if it costs $5 million dollars, I'm determined to prove that your trifling butt ruined my life!

Buck filled out the paperwork and unenthusiastically went through with the exam as I waited in the lobby for him to be done.

"What did they say?" I asked nervously.

"They said they'd mail me the results in a few days."

"Oh, ok. Well, which address did you give them, yours or mine?"

"I gave 'em mine." He said as we got into the car and drove off.

છ ૪૦

Almost two weeks had passed since Buck's test and according to him, the doctor's office still hadn't mailed him any results.

"Well call 'em up," I'd urged on more than on occasion, "and ask for the results."

But each time I'd remind him to call, he'd make up some excuse for not following up. I even tried calling the doctor's office to get the results myself; but they refused to give me any information, citing something or other about doctor–patient confidentiality.

Hell 'um the one who paid for the stinking tests, so technically the results belong to me!

Pretty soon it became evident to me that Buck was taking me on a wild goose chase. And, even though I felt like I was all out of dating options, I still had one sliver of self-respect left. So I made up my mind that I could indeed do bad all by myself.

Tymira Mack

That day I broke up with Buck for good, packed my stuff, and quietly moved to another area of town.

Enough is e– FREAKING – nough!

31
Private Eyes Are Watching

If I can't have you. My new apartment was located a little closer to FAMU. This one had two bedrooms and one bath; and, since my cousin had moved in with her boyfriend, I used the second bedroom as an office/study lounge. The new crib wasn't as fabulous as the last two places, but it was cozy enough; and I was enjoying living all alone again.

Once I'd put Buck behind me, I decided to try and salvage the remaining pieces of my life. So I accepted the PhD fellowship and began to align my remaining master's degree courses with the prerequisite PhD coursework.

Even though I wasn't interning anymore, the reading, research and paper writing requirements for my graduate classes were consuming a great deal of my time. Only on rare occasions would I take time out of my busy schedule to go out. One night my sister and I went out to simply cruise through the parking lots of the main clubs which catered to FAMU students. While stuck in traffic in the parking lot of one of those clubs, I met Man.

Man had boldly stepped up, placed his hands on the lower window frame of my car, leaned in and began speaking to me and my little sister. My first inclination was to go off on the brotha for being so bold, but I was simply awestruck by how much he looked like one of the finest guys on campus; a guy who was so dark and luscious that I'd nicknamed him Black Licorice.

After pulling over on a side road and talking to Man for a while, we exchanged numbers. I guess the STD thing had shaken my confidence when it came to being stingy about giving out my number. Anyway, Man called me around 7:00 the next evening and asked if he could come over to visit me.

"I was just about to wash my hair," I said tying to discourage him from coming.

"So what, I got four sisters and I use to help wash their hair. I can wash yours if you want me too."

"No thanks," I said not even wanting to open up that potential Pandora's Box.

"Well can I just come over and keep you company?" He insisted.

"I guess so," I agreed, giving in to the loneliness. "I'll probably be under the dryer so knock loud."

I hung up with Man and hurried to wash and set my hair because I was determined not to put myself in any awkward situations. I'd just set up my table top hair dryer in my office and was about to get under the dryer when Man knocked on my front door. I got up, let him in and led him through my dark apartment to my office.

Man wasn't in my apartment 5 minutes when my phone rang.

"Hello," I answered with a perky voice since Man's presence had cheered me up.

"Why are you so happy tonight?" Buck asked.

Dang, can you please just get this through your head. You and I are finished.

"I just am," I replied, not in the mood to deal with him. "What do you want Buck?"

"I just called to see how you're doing?" He asked.

"Oh just peachy," I said, sarcastically.

"What-cha doing?" He pressed.

"I washed my hair and I was just about to get under the dryer when you called," I answered cordially.

The List.

"Yeah right!" He screamed through the phone.

"Whatever Buck, I don't have no reason to lie to you. In fact I don't even have no reason to talk to you." Click!

Ten seconds later the phone rang again. Instinctively I knew it was Buck. "What!" I screamed into the phone without even bothering to say hello.

"I thought you was under the hair dryer, so how you heard the phone ringing?" He questioned immediately.

"Negro I would be under the dryer if your butt would stop calling me. Now good-bye."

"I know that neg-ga is over there," he said before I could hang up.

"What are you talking about? What neg-ga?" I asked wondering what the hell was going on.

"That black A– neg-ga, in that white sweat suit, driving that white car," he screamed through the phone. "That's what neg-ga."

"You've really lost it, you know that?" I thought wondering how he knew there was a white car in my driveway, let alone exactly how Man was dressed. "Where are you?"

"Don't you worry about where I am," he warned, "that neg ga just better be gone by the time I get there." Click.

Oh shoot, how could he know all of this, I wondered as I looked out my front window and scanned the parking lot of the high school across the street. Then I remembered that one of his frat brothers lived in the townhouses across the road and down the street a piece.

Maybe he's watching me from there, I thought as I closed my blinds tightly.

"What's wrong?" Man asked as he watched me pace around nervously.

"Nothing," I tried to convince him.

"It's not nothing," he said, "who was on the phone."

"It was my ex –," I said. "Look I think he's either watching my house right now or on his way over here. We need to leave now!"

"It's cool, I ain't worrying about it," Man assured me.

207

"I know but I'm not in the mood for dealing with this tonight," I said nervously.

"Well where are you going and what about your wet hair?" He asked in a concerned voice.

"Maybe I'll stay at my sister's house tonight," I said glad that the idea had come to me. "I can just dry my hair over there."

I put some fresh water in a bowl on the back deck for Cinnamon; grabbed some clothes and my hair dryer; turned on the light in the bathroom; and, headed out the front door with the quickness.

"Look can you please do me a favor?" I asked Man.

"Yeah what's up?"

"Can you please wait a couple of minutes after I pull off and then follow behind me until I get to Monroe Street?" I asked. "I just want to make sure he isn't following me or something."

"Alright."

"Thanks," I said really grateful that he was being so understanding. "I'll call you after I get to my sister's house."

CR SO

I spent the night at my adopted family's house and woke up relieved I hadn't seen or heard from Buck all night. I got up early the next morning expecting to go home, change clothes, feed Cinnamon and get some studying in. But my plans were abruptly altered when I got home and found that my front door was partially open and the door jamb was broken.

Oh my God, I've been robbed, was my first thought. However, from the little bit I could see without going inside, the place didn't looked ransacked at all.

Even though I was pretty certain whoever had been in my apartment wasn't there anymore, I was still afraid to go inside alone. So I went next door to my neighbor's house and called my sister and Man. When Man got there, he told me to stay outside while he looked around.

The List.

"It doesn't look like anything was touched besides the front door," he informed me as he came back out with a puzzled look on his face.

"Check this out." He pointed, taking a closer look at the door. "This looks like a shoe print or something. Like somebody kicked the door."

Immediately my heart sank. "Oh my God, he did it."

"He who? Did what?" Man asked.

"I know it was Buck. I just know it," I thought out loud.

Right about then, my adopted Tallahassee sister drove up and she sat down on the porch while I grabbed the phone to call my daddy and tell him what happened.

"Hello," my dad said as he answered the phone.

"Hey Turkey," I said using my pet nickname for him and straining to hold back the tears.

"Hey Scooter, what's going on?" He seemed happy to hear my voice, as usual.

"Nuh'-thin," I squeaked right before I began balling.

"What's wrong?" He pleaded, sounding alarmed.

"Buck, Buck, he 'um, he kicked in my front door and 'um,"

"He did WHAT," Daddy hollered into the phone before I could finish my sentence.

"Yeah we 'um, we broke up and stuff, and 'um he 'um been watching my house and stuff, and 'um he musta seen my new friend's car over my house last night, and 'um he called here threatening me that I 'um better 'um have that neg-ga out of here before he got here and stuff." I said without taking a breath.

"Say WHAT?" My daddy hollered as he put his hand over the telephone receiver to tell my mother a little bit of the story.

"So then I didn't know what to do, so I went and 'um stayed the night at what-ya-call-it them house and when I got home this morning my door was 'um, it was kicked in and stuff. But ain't nothing stolen or ram-shackled or anything. That's how come I know it was him Daddy."

"Did you call the Police?" He asked.

"Nope cause it don't look like nothing was stolen," I said wondering if I should've called the cops.

"Are you there by yourself?" He asked concerned.

"No, me and my sister and Cinnamon and my friend guy Man are here."

"I forgot about Cinnamon. I told you that darn dog wasn't worth two cents," my dad complained. "Listen look in the phone book and see if you can find a handyman who can come out this morning and repair your door. No better yet, have that young man, you know you're new friend, make the call. They'll probably give him a better price; and, I'm going to the bank to put $250 in your account today to cover the cost of the repairs. Do that now and I'll call you back in about fifteen minutes."

"OK," I said hanging up and feeling much better now since Daddy was on the case.

ଔ ଛ

Daddy called me back about an hour later and I told him we'd found someone who was coming right over to repair my door.

"Good." He said switching to a serious tone of voice. "Listen, I talked to Buck and he admitted he'd kicked in your door."

"What!" I was shocked. "I can't believe he actually admitted it to you."

"Well he and I talked and he told me that I just didn't understand," he paused, "he told me ya'll had been going through a lot in your relationship lately and he was just upset to know that some other guy was at your house."

Oh my God I wonder if he told my Daddy what our "problems" were, I thought as I sat silently listening to all the stuff this fool was brave enough to say to my Dad.

"I told him you told me that ya'll had broken up; and I also told him, even if you hadn't broken up he had no right to be spying on you," he emphasized, "and he definitely had no right to break into your house."

"Well what did he say to that?" I asked curiously.

"He said he'd just talked to you on the phone and told you he was coming over."

"Yeah," I confirmed. "But it's not exactly like I'd invited him to come over Daddy."

"I know, I'm just telling you what he said," my daddy told me laughing.

What the hell is so funny? Huh? This Negro just kicked in my door Daddy. HELLO?

"I can't believe you think this is funny?" I whined.

"No but the young man was just upset," he continued. "At first he claimed that when he got there the front of the house was dark but he could see a light coming from the bedroom; and, when he knocked and knocked you didn't answer the door. So he said he thought you may have been in there having a medical emergency or something worse."

"Ooooh, the lying rat!" I screamed.

"Relax Tam," my Daddy grinned. "You know I didn't buy that and when I told him as much he confessed he'd kicked the door in because he thought you and the other young man might be back there doing something."

"I can't believe he told you all of this," I said shaking my head in disbelief.

"Well you know he and I talk like that," my Dad confessed.

"Talk like what?" I asked totally clueless.

"Well you know I saw a lot of myself in Buck, and I wanted to see him succeed and finish school. So I'd been sending him a little something every month to help him make it through school, plus I wanted him to be able to do things with you without struggling for cash."

"WHAT? Daddy I can't believe this." I was some kind of pissed that he'd been sending money to help support this poison pee-pee Negro without telling me.

Tymira Mack

"Well I'm going to continue sending him something from time to time because I made a commitment to help him," my Dad informed me. "HOWEVER, I did tell him that he is to stay away from you; and, if I hear he's done anything to stalk or otherwise aggravate you, I'd file a police report right after I came up there and pistol whipped his black A double S."

Word, now that's what I'm talking about!

32
Liar, Liar

Kissin' kousins. Daddy's threat caused Buck to back way off just long enough for me to begin exploring my new friendship with Man. So about a week after Buck's pitiful SWAT Team door kicking escapade, Man and I began splitting our spare time between my apartment and the apartment he shared with two white guys and a ferret.

A brotha living with two white guys and a stinking ferret? What's up with that?

Well, it didn't take very long for me to sense there was something that wasn't right about Man, even though I couldn't quite put my finger on it. Man was one of those guys who talked and dreamed real big, but the far off stare in his eyes should have been my first clue somewhere up in homeboys mind, there was a serious disconnect with reality.

After about two weeks of listening to one strange story after another, I slowly began to figure it out. *This neg-ga is a habitual liar.* Problem was, I couldn't decide whether he was a liar on purpose, or if he just plain couldn't help himself. The only thing I was pretty sure of was unlike Buck, on the surface Man's lies didn't seem to be malicious in nature. So despite his obvious problem with telling the truth, I opted to keep him around figuring, *what the heck, kicking it with him will help fill up my idle time.*

ೞ ಹಿ

Tymira Mack

Totally out of the blue one day, Man came by my apartment, brought me a brand new puppy, and then completely disappeared without a trace; only to resurface about a week later.

"Hey Tammy what's up, how's the puppy?" He asked matter-of-factly.

"I had to get rid of him, my neighbor told me he had the mange."

"Oh for real, I was wondering why dude was just giving those puppies away. I'm sorry."

"It's no biggie. So where you been?" I asked only half caring.

"Remember I told you I was going home to see my mama?" He reminded me.

"Oh yeah, that's right." I'd forgotten he'd mentioned something about running home to visit his family way down on the outskirts of town.

"Yeah but I thought you were just going to slide by there. So what happened, you decided to stay a while?" I asked.

"Naw man, I got picked up," he said sadly.

"Picked up?" I repeated confused.

"Yeah, when they stopped me they said I had an outstanding bench warrant."

"When WHO stopped you for WHAT?" I asked. "And what exactly is a bench warrant?"

"Oh I was driving Julie's car and her tail light was out," he advised.

"Oh for real?" I asked as I thought about the fact that although Man didn't have a car, in the three or four weeks we'd known each other, he was always driving a car that belonged to some cousin of his named Julie. Although I'd never seen Julie, I had followed him over to her house a couple of times and waited right outside the front door while he went in and dropped off her keys.

"Yeah and 'um," he continued, "when the police stopped me and ran my license, THEY said I had an outstanding warrant TALKING ABOUT I violated."

214

The List.

Say Wha?

Then Man, the resident habitual liar, began giving me a more detailed account of what led to his arrest, "SEE a few months ago, I was locked up on this felony drug charge they HAD GAVE me…"

"Wait did you just say you were in jail for a FELONY DRUG CHARGE?"

"Yeah, but SEE I got RAIL-ROADED on THAT charge…any way a couple-a months ago, when Chocolate Pudding Pop got stopped, he musta used my driver license number…"

"Wait did you say Chocolate Pudding Pop?" I asked as I wondered if it was the same Chocolate Pudding Pop I'd kicked it with. *I' own know no other dudes by that name in Tallahassee.*

"Yeah, why you know him?"

"I think I heard my play-play sister call that name before," I half-way admitted, "anyway, what were you saying?"

"Yeah, well 'um see, he MUST OF HAD used my information when he got stopped, and SO THEN his charges got stacked onto mine. BUT since 'um still on papers, my PO musta had to violate me. BUT, I ain't even know it – RIGHT? SO anyway, when I went home, some bustas MUSTA messed with Julie's tail lights and then snitched me out."

"Stacked charges? Bustas? Snitching?" I repeated. "Man what in the hell are you talking about? What does any of this have to do with why your black A– is locked up?"

As if the doubt that was all up in my voice hadn't even registered in his head, Man continued right on with his unbelievably sorry conspiracy theory, "SEE when the bustas snitched me out, they musta gave the police a description of Julie's car. SO THEN, the police just used that as their excuse to pull me over. And SO NOW all because of that broken tail light and that lie Pudding had told way back when he first got stopped, NOW me and Julie's car is both locked up."

"Huh? Julie's car is in jail too?" I asked puzzled.

"Yeah, they impounded it."

215

"Oh," I responded, but by then I'd already stopped listening to Man's version of the story and begun thinking, *in jail because of a broken tail light my booty? Neg-ga you's a lie. You in jail because you violated your probation, you freaking criminal.*

Then my mind immediately flashed back to the couple of times me and him had gone out to eat in my car and I'd let him drive. *What if I'd been in the car with that neg-ga when he got stopped? Oh geez! I tried to tell ya something wasn't right with that brotha.*

"Tammy?" He called out. "Tammy you still there?"

"Oh, ummmm, I gotta get to class," I said as I snapped out of my trance and hung up the phone. Click!

☙ ❧

Over the next few days, Man tried calling me collect from the local jail several times, but I refused to accept the calls. Then he started calling straight through.

"Oh you back out?" I asked when his voice wasn't proceeded by the warning that 'this is a collect call from an inmate at the Tallahassee Leon County Jail, will you accept the charges?'

"Naw, I'm still locked up," He told me.

"Then how you calling me?" I asked curiously.

"Oh, Julie called you on the three-way for me."

"Oh," I said feeling a little uneasy that this heifer, cousin or not, may have been listening in on our call.

"You gonna come see me?" He asked.

"Say what?" I snapped, wondering if he'd totally lost his mind.

"Saturday's are visiting day," he told me as if it wasn't anything strange. "If you wanna come, I'll put you on my visitation list."

"Naw, I pass, I ain't down for visiting no jail." I advised him.

"Oh, ok."

"So how are you?" I asked genuinely concerned.

The List.

"I'm alright. Julie brought me some boxers and some t-shirts and hooked me up with a little change in my commissary," he said sounding pretty happy.

"Commissary?" I repeated. "What's that?"

"Oh that's like our jail bank account. See we can't have money up in here, but our family can put money on our account and we can buy snacks and other stuff we need," he schooled me.

"Snacks, don't they feed ya'll up in there?" I asked truly confused.

"Yeah, but I ain't trying to eat the crap they give you up in here," he said sounding disgusted. "Ain't nobody trying to eat no green baloney sandwiches."

Ewww green baloney, I thought wondering whether or not the lunchmeat was really green or simply another one of Man's exaggerations.

By the time our brief conversation ended, I felt sorry enough for Man that I agreed to visit him in jail that next week.

ʘ €

I honestly can't remember all of the restrictions and hoops I had to jump through in order to get into the jail. But, I do remember I had to leave my purse and other personal effects in my car; and, I had to show my driver license at the front entrance. Then I had to stand there spread eagle as they scanned me with an electronic metal detector wand thingie, before patting me down by hand also. As if that wasn't bad enough, the truly embarrassing part happened once I reached the sign-in desk and advised the attendant I was visiting Man, using the last name I knew him by.

Unfortunately, the Leon County Jail had no record of an inmate by that last name. And, since there were lots of other stupid females waiting to see their felony squeezes, the attendant didn't have time to look up a guy who I obviously didn't even know by name.

Tymira Mack

CR SO

"Hello?"

"Hello, what happened?" Man asked. "I thought you was coming to see me today?"

"Neg-ga I did come up there; but unfortunately, them people didn't have no record of a Man XYZ," I yelled. "So you ready to tell me why in the hell you gave me the wrong freaking name all this time?"

"I didn't give you the wrong name, MAN is my real name," he insisted.

"Well not according to the jail people," I replied through gritted teeth.

"That's 'cause they got me under my prison name."

"What?"

"Yeah, see they pulled me up by my fingerprints and they got me down by the name they have on the FDLE records," he said matter-of-factly.

Florida Department of Law Enforcement records? Prison? I could hardly believe my ears, as I imagined the blank look he probably had in his eyes while he was telling me this new pack of lies.

"So what's your prison name?" I asked cutting straight to the chase.

"La'MAN-ley ABC," he told me.

"Ok so the first name I know you by is obviously an abbreviated version of your real name, but your last name..."

But before I could say the last name I knew him by, he cut me off. "It's cool, just ask for La'Manley ABC, when you come next week. OK?"

Come to see you next week? Neg-ga is you stupid or just plain dumb?
"Yeah. Right. Ahhh-ha. Ok." I said, totally determined to blow him off. Click!

CR SO

218

The List.

The next week, I got through security pretty fast since I already knew the routine, plus I had the right name this time. The sign–in attendant advised me that Man was housed on the third floor, and directed me to the stairs and up to the cellblock floor.

What happened to the little room with the two telephones separated by the glass window like on TV, I wondered as the guard at the entrance to the cellblock told me how to reach the cell Man was in.

The cellblock was laid out in a square and I followed the hall around past several cells with about ten guys in each of them, until I came to Man's cell. It had a huge iron door with about an 8-inch square window opening that was filled with iron bars and then covered in Plexiglas material with these microscopic little holes in it for you to talk through.

When I got to his cell, there was already a chick standing at the little window visiting someone I couldn't see; but, she was nice enough to back up so I could have a turn.

"Thanks," I told her as she stepped back about four feet and leaned against the wall.

When I got close to the little window I was relieved I was able to spot Man quickly, and he seemed genuinely surprised to see me.

Feeling totally uncomfortable with my surroundings, I just starting making idle chit-chat to block out the thought that I was up on a prison cellblock floor visiting a felonious drug dealer who I only knew by a criminal alias.

"Surprise, I changed my mind," I said trying to be cheery. "So how are you?"

"I'm cool," he answered rather nonchalantly.

"Oh," I said searching for more words. "I didn't know it would be like this, I ain't know they let you come up here."

"Yeah."

"Oh, um so when do you go to court?"

"I' own know, my public defender 'spose to be trying to catch up with my PO, so he ain't even been back to see me yet."

"Oh, so they gone let you out on bail?"

219

"I won't know 'til probably sometime next week," he said sounding like he was resigned to the fact he might be staying in there for a while.

"Oh, well, what ever happened to your cousin Julie's car?" I asked, trying to change the subject. "Did they ever give it back?"

"Yeah but she had to pay $350," he hesitantly told me.

"Dang, that's messed up," I smirked as I noticed the girl who'd moved aside earlier had begun to fold her arms tightly across her chest and was coming back up to the window like she was getting impatient.

"Oh I'm sorry, I won't be here much longer," I told her since I was more than ready to get out of that creepy place. "I don't want to hold you up from visiting your man."

As I turned back to Man, I noticed his eyes were as big as grapefruits.

"Hey I'm about to take off, 'cause I think that girl wants to finish visiting her boyfriend," I explained, briefly peering over my shoulder at her.

"Hey which one of them dudes is her man?" I asked trying to whisper.

"Man is," the girl spoke up, answering for him.

"Huh?" I asked as I scrunched up my nose and looked back and forth between Man and the chick.

"Ummmm Ta....mmy this is Ju....lie; Ahhhh, Ju...lie this is Ta.....mmy," Man stuttered as he introduced us.

"Oh snap" I shrieked as I turned and stared at this very pretty but way cross-eyed red chick. "I thought you were his cousin."

"Oops, my bad," I concluded before turning and heading off the cellblock, leaving Cousin Julie to deal with La'Manley ABCDEFG, or whatever his freaking real name was.

Thank goodness I never slept with him.

Or did I? Hummm?

PART 3:
Tumultuous Twenties

|||| |||| |||| |||| |||| |||| |||| ||||

ର ଊ

For where envy and self-seeking exist,
confusion and every evil thing are there.
James 3:16 NKJV

33
International Lovers

Buju & Zulu. When I was stressed out, my favorite place to unwind was the A-T-L and fortunately for me a couple of my friends were headed up there for the weekend. Truthfully, I'm not really sure why I was going since it had been over two months since I'd last spoken to Thunder, and technically I was still mourning the loss of 'the one'.

Nonetheless if the past was any indication, I was certain that as long as I was going to be kicking it with my homegirl Maria, then I was pretty much guaranteed to have a good time.

ॐ ജ

While just sitting upstairs in her apartment on my second or third afternoon in town, one of my homegirl's little brother's friends came by to visit.

Good–google–e–goo. This young buck is some kinda fine, I thought as I quickly scanned from his smile, to his muscles, to his tight tushy, and back up again, simply out of sheer habit.

After thoroughly taking all of him in, I could only manage to mumble "Dang" softly under my breath.

"Tammy he fine ain't he?" My homegirl quizzed me.

"Hell yeah! He's thick," I said eagerly.

"He's almost as thick as Thunder ain't he?" She mentioned off the top of her head without thinking.

Oh phooey, why'd you have to go and mention Thunder?

"But he looks kinda young," I said halfway wondering about dude's age and halfway thinking about Thunder all over again.

"Yeah he's kinda young, but I think he's Jamaican," she giggled, "and you know how they be drinking coconut milk and sucking down all them rice and peas and beef patties. Yup, that's probably how come he's so thick."

"Yeah well he got just about the best pair of beef patties I've seen on a dude in a long A– time!" I mumbled as I snapped out of my daydream and began staring intently at homeboy's hell-a tight behind. "How old you say he was?"

"He's about 18 or 19," she said as she strained to remember his age.

"Nope, no more minnows for me!" I thought out loud as I silently reminded myself, *you're pushing 23 now homegirl, it's time out for jail bait. Nope, can't be going down that road no more! Just wipe homie clean off the radar screen. RIGHT NOW!*

"So you wanna go to Club 112 tonight?" My homegirl asked, switching gears.

"Most definitely," I sang. "You know I ain't come up here to sit in no apartment all weekend."

രു ഇ

The Club was packed that night with all sorts of eye candy. While I was doing my normal, chilling and drinking amaretto sours in order to build up my courage to get on the dance floor, Maria was busy using her uncommon knack for peeping out the dudes in the club who were vibing off of us.

"Girl see the tall dark skinned dude over there?" She asked while pointing at this brother with very defined afro-centric features.

"Yeah, why?" I asked curiously.

The List.

"He's checking you out," she informed me.

"Ok. And?" I asked wondering where she was going with all of this.

"Look at him, don't he look West African?" She quizzed.

"Ok, West African, South African, what's your point about Shaka-Zulu?" I asked getting tired of playing 20 questions with her.

"Well you know they have money," she said matter-of-factly.

"Big deal, they also have AIDS," I said still partially subscribing to the early 80's myth that Africans who slept with monkey's were responsible for the dreaded disease. *Girl are you for real?*

Well score one more for my homegirl's intuition because before I could get those words out good, Shaka was all up in my face.

"Check out the London Fog overcoat and his shoes," my homegirl stealthily whispered to me. "He definitely ain't pocketing no chump change."

Although his clothes were a pretty good indication of his financial status, once he began speaking to me, it became obvious he was also very well educated; despite his thick African accent. *Then again, how smart could he really be? After all, he is wearing an overcoat inside a club.*

"Hello beautiful lady," he complimented while reaching out to grab my hand.

"Hi," I said as I politely snatched my hand back from him and continued scoping out the club.

"Would that I could buy you a drink?" He asked.

Would that I could? I smirked to myself. *Let me guess you took the Dr. Seuss learn English in 30 days or less class?*

"Ahhhh, no thanks," I replied hoping that Shaka would just vanish.

"Oh come, please let me do this for you," he pleaded, reaching for my arm and pointing me toward the bar.

"No, I'm fine really," I insisted as I polished off my drink and looked for a table to set the empty glass on.

In one smooth move, Shaka took the empty glass out of my hand, set it on a table and motioned for a waitress to come over.

"Please make sure this beautiful lady's glass never runs dry," he instructed the waitress as I peered astonishingly at him through one open eye.

Before I could protest, the waitress had already headed over to the bar to fulfill his generous order, no doubt counting her lucky stars for what would probably add up to quite a healthy tip by the end of the night.

Meanwhile, I graciously thanked Shaka, "Umm, thanks; but, you really didn't have to do that. Besides, I really don't drink all that much."

"That's what I and my wallet were counting on," he said laughing.

I and my wallet? Oh, he got jokes? Who knew they had comedians in Africa?

Two drinks and three songs worth of dancing later, I was finally able to shake Shaka from all up in my space. Thank goodness for slow jams and my hard and fast rule not to be nowhere in public winding and grinding all up on strange Negros.

How ironic? You won't do it in public, but you sure as hell do it in private.

"Wait, where are you going?" He asked while struggling to grab my waist and pull me close up on him.

"Sorry, I don't slow dance with strangers," I said as I wiggled out of his grasp.

"But are we not yet acquainted?" He asked me with all seriousness.

"We are not!" I responded as I hurried off the dance floor and disappeared into the crowd.

I managed to avoid Shaka Zulu for the rest of the evening as my girls and I partied until the club was about to close down. But just like the bubonic plague, he reappeared as we were standing out front trying to decide where to go for breakfast.

The List.

"Beautiful lady, would that I could take you to breakfast?" He insisted.

Would that I could? Geez, here we go again.

"Ahhhh, no thanks I'm not hungry," I lied.

"Oh, Ooo-K, Allll-right then," he said walking off toward the parking lot.

A few moments later, Shaka emerged driving a top of the line Mazda 929 with all the bells and whistles.

"Tammy check him out," Maria told me as she nudged me in the direction of his approaching car.

"Yeah, and what?" I asked, not real impressed by the vehicle.

"Girl that brotha's really got money," she insisted. "Trust me on this one."

"Oh here we go again," I sighed, rolling my eyes just as Mr. Zulu pulled up next to me.

"Beautiful lady, my heart is breaking because you will not join me for food."

I couldn't help but smile at both his accent and his odd choice of words.

"Go-on girl," my homegirl said as she just about pushed me into the side of his car.

"Go where?" I asked her as I tried to maintain my balance. "I' own even know this dude, he may be the Hillside Strangler or something."

I guess my comment was a little too loud because I was startled when I heard Shaka laugh.

"I assure you, I am no strangler," he said as he held out his business card and motioned toward my homegirl. "Here, here is all of my information. You can even take down the number of my tag, if you like."

"We was just going to Denny's to get some breakfast," Maria informed him as she reached in the car and grabbed his business card.

Tymira Mack

After peeping out Shaka's card, she opened the passenger door of his car and all but pushed me inside, instructing him "why don't ya'll just meet us up at Denny's?"

At this point I was seriously beginning to get embarrassed cause we were holding up traffic in front of the club, and it seemed as if all eyes were on us. So I just decided to go with the flow and ride with Shaka Zulu to Denny's. All the while I was praying that homie wasn't from one of those cannibalistic tribes.

ᑫ ᔕ

True to his word, Shaka took me straight to Denny's where we sat and enjoyed a very relaxing breakfast alone. Over breakfast, I learned that he was indeed from Africa; but I can't exactly remember which country he was from. I also learned that he'd come to the states four years earlier to study either architecture or engineering at Georgia Tech.

After a quaint breakfast filled with stimulating conversation; just as I was preparing to part company with him, Shaka asked, "would that I could come by and take you out later this afternoon?"

"Would that you could?" I giggled. "Sorry but I'm leaving this afternoon."

"Leaving?" He repeated.

"Yes, I don't live in Atlanta, I'm only visiting," I informed him.

"No do not tell me this," he said sadly. "Where is it you reside?"

"I live in Tallahassee."

"Where is this Tallahassee?"

"It's in Florida. But I'm not from there; I'm just there attending graduate school."

"Oh. Well must you leave today?" He asked sincerely.

"Yeah, my girlfriends have to get back to school and I'm riding with them," I explained.

The List.

"Well what if I made arrangements to get you home, would you stay and spend at least one more day with me?" He asked with pleading eyes.

"Say what?" I asked as my body tensed, my eyebrows raised and my neck snapped instinctively out of disbelief.

"I said what if I made arrangements..." he began repeating.

"No, 'um I didn't mean 'say what?' like repeat what you just said," I tried explaining. "It was more like an expression of disbelief, 'cause I don't even believe that you'd drive me way down to Tallahassee."

"No, I wouldn't drive," he quickly replied.

"Exactly," I said, knowing all along my intuition was right. "So I'd be left with no way to get back to school."

"No, no beautiful lady. I wouldn't not drive you, I'll fly you," he stated.

"Oh so you're a pilot? No, No let me guess you've got your own private jet?" I asked sarcastically.

"Oh no," he laughed. "I'll just buy you a plane ticket."

His response really caught me off guard. *He'll just buy me a plane ticket? Ok this is too good to be true. Stuff like this doesn't actually happen in real life. Especially not my life!*

"No offense, but you don't know what you're offering." I suggested. "Tallahassee is not a major market, so the plane ticket won't be cheap. Plus, once you add in the fact that it's not a 7–day advance ticket, you 're really talking some serious cash."

"It is ok. I have a travel broker. I am certain he must provide me with a good price. That is if you would like to stay?"

"Hold on, I need to go and speak with my friends for a second please," I blurted out, to buy myself some time.

"Oh, ok. Take your time. I'll just wait here for you to return," he said as he motioned for the waitress to bring our bill.

ര ൌ

Tymira Mack

"Ok, ya'll ready for this?" I asked my girlfriends. "He just offered to buy me a plane ticket back to Tally if I would stay and kick it with him this afternoon and perhaps tomorrow."

"Girl you lying," one of my friends squealed.

"Didn't I tell you he was loaded," Maria reiterated, obviously pleased that her instinct had once again proven correct. "So I know you told him yes. Right?"

"What if I stay and he's just making this all up, then I'll be left with no way to get back to Tally?"

"Well your girls ain't leaving until later this afternoon and by that time the travel agency will be open and you can make sure you have a ticket before they leave," Maria schooled me. "I really don't see what the problem is?"

"Yeah, I guess that might work," I thought out loud. "Would ya'll be mad if I didn't ride back with you."

"Naw girl, you better gone get yours," my friends encouraged.

ଓ ଜୀ

"So what shall it be beautiful lady?" Shaka asked as soon as I returned to his table.

"Um, I guess I'll stay," I stammered, still hardly believing he was actually planning to buy me a plane ticket. "I just need for you to purchase the ticket first thing in the morning before my friends leave."

"Go-od, Go-od," he smiled. "So since you are leaving tomorrow, I want to keep you with me now."

"Say what?" I halfway hollered starting to believe it was just as I'd figured. *I knew this was too good to be true.*

"No I mean, why should you not stay with me now? After all it is now 4 o'clock in the am," he reminded me. "Come home with me and have rest, then I can go about making the purchase of your ticket first thing."

"Oh, wow, well 'um, gee, I don't know if I'm comfortable with that. . . you know just meeting you and all," I stuttered.

The List.

"I assure you all shall be well for you; I shall not harm you," he insisted.

After pow-wowing with my home-girls one more time, I decided to get all his vital stats – you know his name, home address, phone number, and yes even his driver license number– for my homegirls to keep, and then I agreed to go home with Shaka.

What the heck, he IS buying me a plane ticket. Right?

ଓ ଓ

Shaka lived up in Marietta, so during the 20 minute ride back to his house, I learned a lot about him.

"Your car is nice, it seems to have everything," I complimented, attempting to make small talk.

"Yes it's a limited edition, but it's not what I really prefer," he informed me.

"Oh no?"

"No, but I have just completed the research on my preferred car and it is on order."

"On order?" I asked never having heard of such a thing.

"Yes, it is much cheaper to order directly from the factory. And I can also get it made exactly to my preferences," he schooled me.

"Ohhhh so what did you order?" I asked out of curiosity.

Shaka went on to fully describe some impressive BMW or Mercedes I'd never heard of because its number was well above a 2 series. And then he proceeded to tell me about his family and his educational and business aspirations. *Wow. Impressive. Impressive indeed!*

At this point, my mind was moving from '*this guy is too good to be true*', to '*ok maybe I've truly gotten lucky this time.*' But there was still one last test I had to get out of the way before I could honestly decide if Shaka had a rat's chance in hell.

While I was sort of afraid that asking the question which had been rattling around in my head might show my ignorance, I

Tymira Mack

knew I had to get it out because I'd gotten burned in the past whenever I simply took things for granted.

Well here goes. "Hey Shaka, 'um, this may sound kind of crazy, but I was just wondering; um, in your country do ya'll 'um believe in God?" I asked timidly.

"Oh yes, in my country we have many gods," he responded seriously.

Oh crap. I knew it was too good to be true.

Sensing my uneasiness, he quickly added, "but I and my family are born again Christians."

"Oh, thank goodness" I sighed in relief while Shaka laughed heartily at his little jokie-joke.

ભ ૭૦

Shaka's apartment complex was simply breathtaking. From its elegantly lit, gated entrance, with the spectacular water feature; to the well-manicured common areas; to the stateliness of the buildings; I was simply awestruck. And once we got inside, I found Shaka's apartment to be no less impressive. Although sparsely furnished – by design, not by circumstance – the furnishings were most definitely quality pieces that were very tasteful.

Between all the drinks at the Club, the long ride to his house and the late hour, I was totally pooped and eagerly welcomed Shaka's invitation to retire to his bedroom. Thankfully he was the perfect gentleman, and didn't so much as touch me while we both rested comfortably for several hours.

When I awoke, Shaka directed me to his master bathroom where I found a brand new toothbrush neatly wrapped in a plush face towel. After washing up, I headed into his living room where he'd made two place settings complete with some kind of quiche thing-a-ma-jig and spritzers made with freshly squeezed and chilled orange juice.

Ok pinch me, 'cause I don't think I can take any more!

The List.

"Good Morning, beautiful lady," he greeted me with a hearty smile.

"Stop telling stories," I insisted, knowing I looked toe-down since I hadn't showered and all my make-up, including my fake eyebrows, had been wiped off as I slept.

"Would that you rested comfortably?" He asked gallantly.

"Oh most definitely," I purred.

"I hope you prefer quiche?" He asked.

"Yeah it's ok." Although it wasn't on the top of my preferred foods list, I certainly didn't want to offend Shaka.

"Well I've contacted my travel agent, and your ticket should be delivered shortly," he informed me.

"My who, what, what?" I questioned, astonished that he was totally on his P's and Q's.

"But how did you know what name to put it in?" I asked looking around and wondering if he had been snooping through my purse, that is until I remembered I never carried a purse when I went out clubbing.

"No, No, you told me your name last night," he reminded me.

"Oh yeah." I was surprised he'd even remembered. *But hey why not? I asked myself, after all I remember his name, as strange as it may be.*

As we sat there eating in an awkward silence, I couldn't help but wonder, *ok so when is the Turd Fairy going to show up and poop all over my parade?*

Luckily, Shaka interrupted those dismal thoughts as he politely excused himself to answer the telephone.

"Tam-mee," Shaka called out as he returned to the living room and handed me the phone. "Your brother is on the line."

"Brother?" I repeated puzzled. "I don't have a brother."

"Hello who is this?" I demanded wondering what the heck was going on.

"So what a young neg-ga gotta do to get you to spend the night with me? Stick a bone through my nose and move to the motherland?"

"What?" I asked as I strained to place the vaguely familiar voice. "Who is this?"

"This Clive, but you can just call me Beef Patty," he grinned as he was joined in laughter by my homegirl who was also on the line.

"Oh ya'll are tripping," I smirked.

"We was just calling to make sure Shaka ain't eat you. Oh but you may have liked something like that," Maria teased before getting serious. "You straight?"

"Yeah, I'm alright," I reassured her. "He just made me brunch and he's bringing me by there in about an hour so I can shower and get my stuff."

"Ummmm, so I guess you got the ticket then?" She asked.

"Yeah it was delivered about 15 minutes ago. Oh, you can tell my girls they can go ahead and hit the road cause, I'm straight."

"Dang, if I'd known he was rolling like that, I might have kept Kunta Kente for myself," my homegirl giggled.

"But you ain't answer my question yet, what a young neg-ga gotta do to get wit' you?" Clive interrupted.

"Grow up baby-boy," I laughed. "You still got a couple more mango seasons," I swiftly informed him, with his young, sexy-behind self.

"I got your mangos hanging low," Clive slyly retorted.

"Boy get your behind off the phone," my girl yelled just before Beef Patty hung up.

"I'll be over there in a few."

"Ok, Later."

ଔ ଓ

"So?" He asked with both hands palms up and pointing at me.

"Sooooo, what?" I repeated having not the faintest clue what he was talking about.

"Who is this brother, no brother?" Shaka asked.

"Oh you must have mis-understood," I replied thinking quickly on my feet. "That was my girlfriend and her little brother.

The List.

You know my friend from the Club and the restaurant. They were just calling to make sure I was ok."

"Oh, O-K."

ೞ ಔ

    Although I enjoyed every second of the next 24 hours that I spent with Shaka, I was eager to get back to my real life before I turned back into a pumpkin. I don't know if it was a combination of the prejudice/ignorance I had about Africans; or my inner belief that I wasn't really deserving of all of the stellar treatment he wanted to lavish on me; or the fact that Beef Patty was also blowing up my phone; but, over the next month or so, I began to dread receiving Shaka's frequent telephone calls. And, eventually I just asked him to stop calling me all together.

    Who am I fooling? There's no such thing as fairy tales.......at least not for girls like me.

34
I've Come This Far By Fate

Bling—bling & black ties? I really wish that things could have gone better; but, unfortunately, Tallahassee was a small City and pretty soon avoiding Buck had once again become next to impossible. At 23 years old it was hard enough to manage a social life around PhD coursework; but, when you piled the stress of the Herpes diagnosis and my efforts to avoid being in the same places as Buck into the equation, well I began to buckle under all the pressure.

Well so much for stress relief.

Around the same time, two things occurred that worked in my favor. First I saw an advertisement for a management internship with Miami-Dade County government; and, second FSU began offering weekend intensive courses in my degree field.

If fate is on my side, I can snag this internship and just drive or fly up to Tally one weekend each month for classes.

At the time, I guess the fate goddess was on my side because I snagged the coveted Management Intern position with Miami-Dade County; I keep my fellowship award by simply enrolling in FSU's weekend intensive classes; and best of all, I was finally able to get away from Buck. The deal got even sweeter when my father offered to vacate one of his rental units and fix it up just for me.

The List.

With all of this good luck on my side, I had my stuff all packed and ready to go in no time. I'd even managed to convince this nice, but soooo not my type, fella who had a crush on me, to help me load up and drive my U-Haul truck to South Florida. And just to show you how dirty I was, while Mr. Nice Guy retired to my parent's house to rest from driving my stuff all the way to Lauderdale, I spent the night in my new apartment with Beef Patty, who'd temporarily moved back to South Florida for a couple of months.

☙ ❧

I could hardly believe how excited I was about moving back home, considering the fact that less than five years earlier I'd vowed never return to South Florida to live again. And, even though the front door to my new apartment was located less than four feet away from my childhood bedroom window, it didn't even matter 'cause I had my own crib; and, best of all it was rent free!

Fate just seemed to keep working in my favor because my girl Aayden had snagged a pretty tight corporate sales job and had already moved back home a few months earlier. So once again, it wasn't long before her ying and my yang were hitting the Miami party scene hard.

As far as I was concerned, I was happier than a sissy in a wee-wee orchard. I had an awesome job, phenomenal mentors, my own apartment, money in my bank account, a car and a best friend. I had everything a warm blooded twenty-something African American girl could want, except a man.

☙ ❧

I have no idea how Mickey and I happened to run into each other, but seeing him again was like a breath of fresh air. *Humph, the old goddess of fate is working overtime on my behalf!*

237

Tymira Mack

I noticed immediately from the way Mickey was dressed, that joining the military and traveling the country and the world had definitely expanded his horizons.

He was no longer a classic South Florida looking fella, all clad in lumber jacks, wife beaters and the like. Instead, he looked more like the guys I'd encountered while in college and hanging out in Atlanta. And, the new look really suited him well.

Pretty soon, Mickey and I began dating again, and right off the bat, I was impressed with the man he'd become. He seemed to have solid goals for his life. He'd invested in the duplex where he was living; he was working full time; and, he was in school pursuing a professional license in a business that was very lucrative in South Florida.

By all accounts, things between us were really going well. We'd picked up right where we'd left off more than five years earlier. But this time we were both more mature and more focused. This fact was reflected in every aspect of our growing relationship, including our sex–yes our sex–life.

I should have known from my past, when things seemed to be going too well, watch out; 'cause the old fate goddess giveth and the temperamental hussy also taketh away.

Mickey had already told me about his two year old daughter, and heck I couldn't hold it against him, since after all I'd accumulated a lifetime burden of my own. Besides he'd gone to the military and done what so many young guys who are away from home and stationed on military bases in little one-horse towns do. He'd hooked up with a local hoochie desperate for a GI with military benefits; and, made a baby.

Even though I kinda selfishly thought about the fact this kid might cramp our style; in the end I wound up supporting his decision to bring his daughter to Florida to live with him, because her mother was strung out on drugs. In fact, I was rather impressed by his sense of responsibility.

But when the news of long lost baby number two came up, well it was more than I was willing to accept.

The List.

"Hey baby what's up?" I'd asked him as I opened the door and gave him a hug.

"I had a wild day today," he admitted, looking a bit lost in his thoughts.

"What school kick your butt today?" I asked curiously.

"Naw man, I got some wild information today," he sighed, shaking his head in disbelief.

"Well what happened? What kind of information?" I asked getting concerned.

"You remember so-and-so?" He asked, bringing up the bitter memory of the heifer who'd moved in with him back when we were still in high school.

"Yeah," I said begrudgingly, because I didn't like where it felt like this conversation was heading.

"Well I found out today I have a daughter."

Not wanting to accept what I'd heard, "duh, isn't she coming to live with you at the end of the month?"

"No, I mean I have another daughter."

"You what?" I said, immediately realizing I wasn't down for kicking it with a brother whose whole paycheck would be going to support two outside children.

"I'm not understanding," I admitted.

"Well from what I can tell, she was pregnant when she moved up the road," he explained.

"Ok, but how come you just now knowing about this?" I asked wondering if he'd been playing me.

"Cause she ain't never tell me."

"So how come she's just up and telling you outta the blue now?" I exploded, pissed off about the whole situation.

"I' own really know," he admitted.

"So what are you going to do?" I demanded.

"Well um-ma take care of her I guess," he explained.

"Mickey," I said pleading with him to use some common sense, "how do you even know if this little girl is yours?"

He just shrugged his shoulders.

"I mean, she just rolls back up in your life after five and a half years and gives you some weak A– line about being pregnant when she moved away; and oh by the way, now all of a sudden I want you to know you have a daughter," I said sarcastically trying to make a point.

"For all you know, this could be someone else's kid that she's trying to pin on you," I selfishly insisted.

"I' own know," was all he could respond.

"You' own know?" I questioned realizing that somewhere deep down inside, this brother may have been wishing this child was his too.

It was all a bit too much for me to handle. I was already hesitant because I had a black tie affair coming up at work and I wasn't sure if I could invite Mickey and his two gold teeth to accompany me. I mean he was intelligent and all, but would my co-workers see past his appearance and into his heart like I had?

And now with all of this extra drama. How am I supposed to introduce this Negro to my bosses who were Assistant County Managers, County Commissioners and Department Directors?

Good evening, Mr. Big Shot Dignitary, I'd like you to meet my boyfriend Mickey. He's studying to be a licensed XYZ professional. Yeah, yeah, I know he has two gold teeth and two babies, but he's really a smart guy and I'm confident he is going to be successful in life despite those two little faux-pas.

Annnnnk, WRONG ANSWER. The Turd Fairy rides again.

35
On Tha' Chain Gang

I ain't scared. Once again, my memory is real fuzzy about how this brotha and I came to be in contact with each other after more than five years. Just like Mickey, Rock was definitely a dude from my past. But, although he and I vibed off each other in high school, one of my friends had already laid claim to him; and so even though he clearly was not interested in her, back then I'd respected her claim and stayed totally clear of Rock in a relationship kind of way.

 জ ঞ

One of my most vivid memories of Rock from back in the day was the evening he and my friend, and me and this other dude drove my car down off 62nd Street in Miami to buy some blow. Like I told you before, I didn't intentionally mess with the powder, so I was just along for the ride.

That night we headed south to the City, pulled off I-95, made a couple of rights and a few left turns, rolled up on a set of run down looking apartments, approached some dudes on the corner, scored a small package, and got the hell outta dodge.

As criminally inept as I am, I was blessed the whole cocaine buy situation went off without a hitch. Even so I was way too stupid to know any number of things could have gone terribly wrong.

We could have gotten robbed by those dealers or someone else in that neighborhood. Or worse yet, we could have bought from some undercover narcotics agents who would have taken our black butts straight to jail; and then confiscated and later sold my car for being involved in the commission of a crime.

But that night, not one of those negative consequences had so much as crossed my mind. So after scoring the coke, we headed back to Broward County, slid by a little convenience store on 6th street that sold to minors, picked up some wine coolers, and headed to the beach.

We spent the next few hours illegally trespassing up on a lifeguard tower; the guys snorted their coke and me and my girl drank our wine coolers. The stars were out; the ocean breeze was cool and relaxing; and, it didn't seem like we had a care in the world.

Cஐ ஐ

By happenstance, Rock and I ended up communicating again through a mutual friend. Only, the catch this time was that Rock was incarcerated. Well actually he was somewhere between jail and a work release transition center.

But even though he was locked up, I didn't mind communicating with him because he'd somehow worked out a system with his relatives where he could call me without having it affect my telephone bill.

Oh what the heck. Why not talk to an old friend? Besides, it ain't like I got anything better to do.

When I first heard that Rock was in prison, I was surprised. Although he was hell-a silly when we were in school, he also had a mama who didn't play the radio. She was real strict on him and didn't let him hang out and run the streets like so many other dudes in our area.

"So what happened?" I asked him one night.

The List.

"What-chu mean?" He responded.

"I mean how you end up in prison? The last thing I knew your mama was riding your tail and keeping a tight leash on you," I reminisced while wondering how he had fallen so far from point A to point Z.

"Well you know a brother wasn't all brains like you. And, well I got caught up in the hustle."

"Well what did you do to end up in prison?"

"I ain't do nothing," he told me in his signature slick but still silly voice.

"Ok you're one of a million other Negro's up in prison wrongly convicted because you're innocent, right?" I asked a wee bit ticked this brother was playing the innocent black man card with me.

"Listen slim, these phones stay hot, and I'll finish my time, just like I started it," he paused, "not admitting to a damn thang."

Oh ok, I get it, I thought, realizing he was schooling me to the fact that the phones they used were being monitored.

"Well I' own know what you're wrongly accused of my brotha," I joked, " but I do know I just can't picture you as no murderer, or no thief, or nothing violent like that."

"Oh no doubt a brother ain't with that program," he reassured me.

"Well what exactly did the white man wrongly convict you of Malcolm?" I joked.

"Well they say that when they stopped me on I-10 between Tallahassee and Pensacola they found a substantial amount of powder in the car we'd rented."

"Oh is that what they said?"

"Yup, but I maintain I don't know where thet stuff came from. For all I know it belonged to the last person who rented the car."

"Oh word, I feel ya, my brotha."

ɞ ʚ

Tymira Mack

It turns out that Rock was fortunate; if anything about being locked up is fortunate. He'd spent over 14 months in the Tallahassee/Leon County jail awaiting trial, and because he'd had the funds to hire a top notch lawyer, he was eventually convicted on a much lesser charge. By the time all was said and done, at sentencing he had less than 12 months left to do once they figured in time served and gain time. So basically it meant that Rock could serve out the rest of his sentence in the County jail instead of being shipped off to prison with the big boys.

Although Rock had claimed not to be so intelligent, through our nightly conversations, I learned that before his little unfortunate run in with the Florida Highway Patrol, he'd been a successful legitimate business man with a thriving landscaping business. He'd even purchased and renovated a home which was being cared for by his mom while he was incarcerated.

I was quite impressed. *A businessman and homeowner at age 23? Humph, I' own know many brothers that can claim those accomplishments. Alright, maybe there's something here I can work with after all.*

I was even more impressed once he asked his mom to give me a full tour of his home. The furnishings were the bomb. Plus, his mom was a phenomenal seamstress and she'd made custom bedding, blinds, drapes and all sorts of other accessories for every room in the house.

Wow, this neg-ga wasn't just blowing hot air, he really has got it going on.

CR SO

A few weeks after we began communicating, Rock was transferred to a local work release center to complete the final phase of his sentence. Since this place was local, he would usually call me two or three times a night. Sometimes I'd hold on during the time it took for him to line up for inmate count; other times he'd just call me back.

244

The List.

Although, I'd gotten comfortable with this routine, some days I'd find myself thinking, *you never could have paid me to believe I'd have two college degrees and a kick butt job and be hooked up with a neg-ga in jail who has to stop talking to me every hour on the hour so the guards can make sure him and his buddies haven't escaped. Girl, what's going on? HELLO?*

Things really got strange once Rock began earning privileges. Once a week, they were allowed to go to the local Wal-Mart for 45 minutes to shop for personal supplies. The only catch was the days and times for the shopping trip were always changed up without notice, so the inmates couldn't plan anything devious.

So every week, I'd sit by my phone and wait for Rock to call me and tell me "Ok baby, we're headed to Wal-Mart in five minutes, can you come?"

"You ain't scared you gone get caught?" I'd ask.

"Baby I ain't get to prison by being scared," he'd always respond.

"Alright then. Um-ma try to get out there," I'd say uneasy about the whole thing.

"Just hurry, ok?" He'd beg.

And then I'd rush out the door, make the normal twenty minute drive to Wal-Mart in about twelve minutes and still have about twenty minutes to kick it with Rock in the Shoe Department at the rear of the store.

Ummmm, HELLO? Now you're dating neg-ga's up in the Wal-Mart shoe isle? HELLO?

But I only did this twice cause I felt real silly rushing across town to get to Wal-Mart and see a neg-ga who's in prison. It just seemed so Springer.

Then one afternoon Rock called me.

"Guess what slim?"

"What?" I asked curiously.

"I got a job," he said all excited.

"Oh good," I said all happy since he was obviously happy. "Whatcha gonna be doing?"

"Landscaping."

"Landscaping?" I repeated, very unimpressed by the nature of his employment.

"Yup," he stated proudly.

"And you're excited about that?" I asked a wee bit snobbishly.

"You don't get it do you?" He asked like I was dumb or something. "The sooner I get a job and show I can be a constructive member of society, the sooner I can blow this joint. I took it because it came up first and besides, I got plenty of experience in this area."

"Oh, Ok." I said happy he was getting closer to his goal of getting released. "So who you gonna be working for?"

"This big landscaping company," he advised. "Yeah, the guy said they needed guys with experience because they got a big contract to landscape the new mall way out Hollywood Boulevard."

"Oh, my mama told me they were building a new mall, but I ain't know where it was."

"Man, its way out there in the middle of nowhere. I really can't figure who they think is gonna be going way out there to shop. But hey anyway it's a job."

"Well good for you," I encouraged.

ः ॐ ॐ

After about two weeks on the job, Rock called me and asked me to meet him at Wal-mart; but I declined.

About fifteen minutes later, he called me up and hit me with a strange request, "how about you pick a neg-ga up tomorrow?"

"Oh you getting a furlough pass to come home?" I asked remembering he told me he'd be eligible to start getting those passes soon. "But I thought furloughs were only on the weekends? Tomorrow is Wednesday."

"Yeah, furloughs are only on weekends," he confirmed.

The List.

"Well what do you mean pick you up tomorrow?" I asked really confused.

"I want you to come and get me from the job," he boldly suggested.

"Are you crazy? Are them people listening to you?" I asked really nervous that he was possibly implicating me in jail break.

"Relax baby, I'm calling you from the pay phone at Wal-Mart."

"Oh ok," I said breathing a sigh of relief.

"So what's really happening," he asked, "you down or what?"

"Ain't that illegal? Won't that be like you going AWOL or something?"

"Naw, check this out. Ok, Wednesday's is payday out on the job."

"Yeah and?"

"And," he continued, "the big man comes by around 6:30 am and passes out the paychecks. Then he heads out to the other job sites to deliver pay checks."

"Ummm, hummm," I mumbled wondering where in the heck he was going with all of this.

"Well he don't come back on our job site until about 9:30," he continued.

"O-----K?" I mumbled.

"Here's the deal, you can come pick me up, we can ride out for a minute and you can just bring me back," he said all matter-of-factly.

"Pick you up from where and ride out where, to do what?"

"Look Tam, I ain't smelled, let alone touched, a woman in over two years, and all this talking to you back and forth over the phone has really been messing a neg-ga up."

"Well you're at Wal-Mart right?"

"Yeah, why?" He asked all puzzled.

"Might I suggest you go inside and invest in a little KY jelly, that way you can resolve your little problem all by yourself and not risk an escape charge?" I said giggling.

"Oh you got jokes. Look here, although it was a lot of neg-ga's who took that route up in the joint, I ain't even go out like that," he reassured me.

"I ain't even touch my own self, let alone some other neg-ga," he insisted with much attitude.

"Relax playa, I was just making a little jokie-joke."

"Naw a neg-ga don't get down like that, so don't even joke like that," he insisted, obviously still a little salty.

"Ok, ok, I'm sorry."

"Anyway, like I was saying you could just come by and scoop me up," he explained as he began laying out his plan. "I saw these other stores they are building across the street, we can go over there and just chill out together for a while. Then you can just drop me back off before the big man gets back."

"Um–hum?" I groaned. "Well there's two little problems with your plan."

"What's that?"

"Number one, even if the Big Man is gone, the other workers will see you leave," I reminded him. "What you gone do if they call the work release center and turn you in?"

"Like I told you before, I ain't get to prison by being scared," he reminded me. "Number one, I'm the only work release neg-ga working on the job now cause they let the other dude go. Plus, the rest of the workers is all Mexicans, they don't even speak no English. They fresh off the boat and ain't even got no green card, so I ain't worrying 'bout them turning nobody in."

"Fresh off the boat?" I laughed. "Did you take geography? Since when you have to take a boat from Mexico to get to Florida?"

"You know what I mean. Anyway, damn the Mexican's. Are you down for picking me up?"

"Well you didn't hear me out. Number two, I gotta go to work tomorrow," I reminded him.

"Dang, can't you just go in late? I really want to see you," he pleaded.

The List.

"Damn, they loading up the van, look I'll try to call you tonight. But if I can't call you, please just get in your car tomorrow and drive west out Hollywood Boulevard until it ends. You can't help but see the big A– mall. A neg-ga really need to see you girl!"

ରେ ଞ

Against what should have been my better judgment, I woke up at 5:30 am the next morning, showered and got dressed in nothing but a silk jacket that zipped down in the front and a very short cotton mini-skirt. Then I got in my car and headed out west for yet another of my 'doing dumb things for a man' adventures. Truth is, I was curious to find out whether or not my decision to keep my hands off Rock all those years ago, was a smart decision or not. But in the back of my mind, I also reminded myself of the disastrous results I faced the last time I'd made the decision to back track with Lloyd out of curiosity.

Curiosity didn't kill my cat the last time, but it sure left her feeling all itchy! Are you sure you really want to go through with seeing Rock? What if the whole thing goes bad and he gets caught with you?

It took me a good thirty-five to forty minutes to drive way out there, giving me plenty of time to change my mind, turn around and go home. Instead, I ignored my conscious and busied my mind by focusing on all of the new development going on out there in the middle of nowhere. And then, low and behold, there was the mall.

Wow this place is gonna be huge. Now where in the world am I gonna find Rock? Oh there's some landscaper guys, maybe he's over there.

"Hey I wasn't sure you was coming," he confided as he peeked into the window of the car.

"Hurry up and get in please," I said scared out of my mind.

"Why you all scared?" He teased. "Just relax and drive around this way," he said pointing west.

He calmly gave me instructions leading to the rear of this other strip mall that was under construction. As we pulled around back,

Tymira Mack

I felt really nervous about getting caught and being sentenced as an accessory. But as soon as we parked and he kissed me, all those fears melted straight into lust. After all, it had been over two years for him and at least two months for me.

In the middle of our awkward wrestle fest in the front seat of my little sports car, a police car pulled up.

"Oh God," I shrieked, obviously making Rock feel like he had it going on.

"No stupid, there's a police car behind us," I whispered, motioning toward the back of the car.

The thought of the police rolling up on us quickly brought 'Mr. I Ain't Scared' crashing back to reality as he struggled to raise himself up enough to look in the direction I was nodding. "Dang girl, that's just a security guard, see the yellow light?"

"Huh? Oh, well how the hell was I supposed to know?" I asked as I struggled to pull down my skirt and zip up my jacket before the security guard man walked up on us.

"Hello sir," Rock said as he cracked the window a bit.

"Do you realize this is private property and you're trespassing?" The guard asked barely able to keep a straight face.

"Um, no sir we didn't realize that," Rock lied, "but we were just leaving."

"Alright then," the guard responded as he tried to sneak a quick peak before turning to leave.

ଓ ଛ

I've never been so embarrassed in my whole life, I thought as I rushed to drop Rock back off at his worksite.

"I'll call you to...." Rock was attempting to say as I sped off like a bat outta hell wearing gasoline drawers.

I' own even have no words for you homegirl. Have you lost your ever-loving mind? Was your dignity really worth that temporary feeling of pleasure? Are you willing to risk going to jail just to get a not-so-free piece?

36

Smile, Pause, Wave, Get It On

Seven year itch. A few months after I'd cut Mickey loose for what I vowed would be the final time; and not too long after my parking lot escapade with Rock, I decided it was time to get myself together. Figuring I had a serious problem that only divine intervention could fix, I half-heartedly decided to start going back to church.

Right around the same time I'd starting going back to church, I began noticing another handsome smile from my past. Almost every Sunday morning while I stood outside waiting for eleven o'clock service to begin, I would see Mr. Smiley as he rode past, heading for his own church.

Soon Mr. Smiley began waving as he passed; and then one day, he paused at the stop sign just long enough to say a simple innocent "Hello."

"Hello." I chirped, returning the cordial greeting, while trying to place a name with the familiar face.

Before long, the smile, pause, wave and simple greeting became a regular Sunday morning occurrence I was actually starting to look forward to each week. Not long after, the pause lengthened into a deliberate stop and the simple greeting grew into a few lines of polite exchange.

"How've you been?"

"This is the first time I've see you in a long time."

"So whatcha up to now?"

You know cordial "how's the weather" kind of chit-chat. Over time, I began to wonder whether these seemingly innocent exchanges were becoming more deliberate, 'cause I was starting to notice Smiley riding by my apartment some weekday evenings. Granted, my apartment was smack dab in the middle of a main route through our hood; but still, I'd never noticed him pass my house before in the past few months I'd been back home.

ca so

Although my apartment had a front door, it was a lot more convenient for me to enter through the back door because it faced the alleyway where I often parked my car. One evening as I was removing some packages from my car and heading up to my back door, I noticed Smiley's car as it made its way around the curve. To my surprise, instead of passing by, Mr. Smiley slowed down, turned into the alley and pulled up beside me.

Out of natural instinct, I approached his car and spoke to him, "what's up?"

"Nothing, I was just passing by and I saw you, and decided to stop and say hey, that's all," he said innocently.

"Ohhhh, ok, well hey to you too," I grinned before turning to head up the hill toward my back door.

"Ummmm, I was wondering if maybe I could call you sometime?" His question caught me off guard, causing me to stop dead in my tracks.

"Well I guess so, as long as you don't have a girlfriend or anything."

The List.

"Nope, I definitely don't have a girlfriend," he confirmed, smiling from ear to ear and handing me a pen and a piece of paper.

"Good, cause I'm really not up for no female drama," I admitted as I wrote my number down and handed the pen and paper back to him.

"Alright then, I'll call you soon," he promised as he quickly disappeared down the alley.

You do that, 'cause I'm about overdue for some male companionship. Besides I'm a sucker for a chocolate neg-ga with a pretty smile, I thought as I unlocked my door and headed inside.

ᔆ ᔐ

Soon Smiley began calling me on the regular; and after only a couple of brief conversations, I began to remember where I knew him from. Smiley was about six years older than me; but I remembered him because his brother was around my age and was well known in our neighborhood.

"Ain't whatcha-call-it, your little brother?" I asked just to make small talk and to confirm my memory.

"Yeah."

"Oh, is he um still messing with that girl that use to stay over there? Oh what was her name?" I thought out loud.

"Yeah, they're still married."

"Married, oh word? I didn't know they were married."

"Yup they been married about four or five years," he confirmed.

"Dang five years? They must have gotten married right out of high school huh?" I asked, shocked that anyone would be ready for marriage at age 17 or 18.

After an uncomfortable silence, I moved on and decided to grill Mr. Smiley about his own love life a bit.

"So what about you?" I asked.

"What about me what?" He replied sounding confused.

"So who's the lucky lady that stole your heart?" I teased.

"What you mean?"

"Oh come on now, I know you ain't trying to tell me that you ain't got no girl." But then I remembered our prior conversation, "oh that's right, you told me the other day you didn't have a girlfriend, Right?"

"Nope, no girlfriend," he confirmed.

"Hummm, well you don't seem like the type to be gay, so what's the deal, huh? You just taking a break from the ladies?" I asked out of growing curiosity.

"Naw, ummmm, not really," he replied keeping his answers short and sweet.

Wake up homegirl, something ain't right with this picture. This brother is attractive, yet he claims he ain't got no woman, what's really happening?

Not in the mood for games, I just straight up asked him, "So what is it that you're purposely not telling me?"

I guess my candor caught him off guard, because I could sense the tension in his nervous laughter.

"What? Did I say something funny?" I quizzed.

"Naw, you just got a hard edge to you that comes at a brother from outta nowhere."

"Yeah, whatever. You ain't the first brother to tell me that. But you still haven't answered my question yet," I reminded him. "So now what's up for real?"

After a bit more silence, he started "do you remember Fran?"

"Fran, Fran? The name sounds familiar, but I can't place her face," I admitted while straining to remember this chick, and wondering what she had to do with our conversation. "Well anyway, what about her?"

"Well um, you know we use to go together," he paused.

"Oh yeah, I do remember that girl. She was real quiet. I use to know her from church." I said remembering her. "I forgot ya'll use to go together."

The List.

"Well um, me and her have been married for about seven years," he admitted.

"Married seven years?" I repeated confused. I don't know what threw me off the most, the fact he was married, or the fact his wife was my age and if they'd been married seven years, that would mean they'd gotten married when she was 16 or 17.

"Married, seven years?" I repeated again louder as I realized I was indeed pissed he'd lied to me about having a woman.

"Yeah, but we're separated now," he quickly responded.

"But you told me you didn't have a girl."

"But, I don't have a girlfriend," he reiterated.

"Neg-ga, now you're playing with words. You knew damn well what I meant when I asked you that question weeks ago." *Oh, but you wanna play me for Boo-Boo the fool? Aright buddy-o, I got your number!*

"But my point was we're separated, and we've been separated for some months now, so I don't consider myself as having anyone," he pleaded for understanding.

"Look, I don't mess with married men," I stated emphatically, "point blank."

"I understand," he said sounding dejected.

"Good!" I responded just before hanging up. Click!

ଓ ଛ

But I hadn't heard the last of Mr. Smiley. Soon his drive-by's and phone calls became more frequent. And it was always the same thing.

"How've you been?" He'd ask.

"Fine?" I'd reply coldly.

"Where you headed?" or "What you up to today?" He'd ask.

"Nowhere" or "Nothing," I'd reply, before abruptly walking off or hanging up.

But he just kept coming at me with his smiling chocolate self.

255

Tymira Mack

So I decided, *I know the perfect way to get rid of him, I'll just start picking that neg-ga's pockets and it won't be long before he'll hurry up and go away.*

Well what do you know, here comes Mr. "I Do" right now.

"What's up?" He started.

"Nothing."

"How've you been?"

"Fine."

"Where you headed?"

"To get my nails done. Why, you wanna pay for um?" I asked sarcastically as I put my little plan to the test.

"Well how much it costs?" He asked.

"Thirty-five bucks," I lied, intentionally inflating the price.

"Thirty-five dollars? My wife only," he paused realizing he'd screwed up but it was too late to take it back, "um, well she only pays $15 dollars when she gets hers done."

"But I ain't ya wife neg-ga. So don't trip on me just because I appreciate the finer things in life," I replied with much attitude. "After all, that's precisely why you keep sweating me anyway right?"

All homie could do was smile and cough up two twenties.

"I 'pre-ciate it," I said as I snatched the two bills out of his hands and headed for my car without saying good-bye.

"I presume I can keep the change?" I half asked as I started my engine, threw my hand up, waved, and cold drove off.

Un-hum, I bet your A– ain't smiling so hard right now. Bet you won't halla 'bout yo' dang-on wife to me no mo, 'cause I'm not that sista!

ᙣ ᙤ

Eventually, Smiley and his wallet eased their way back into my lonely life on a regular basis. And although he and his wife were supposedly separated, he'd call me every evening from her house where he was over visiting and watching the kids until she came home from work or school; so he claimed. And then he'd

The List.

ride by and briefly visit with me in the alley almost every evening like clockwork.

This arrangement was cool with me. I figured since he was separated; and, since he wasn't visiting me all up in my house; and, since the two of us weren't going places together; I rationalized that "technically" I wasn't kicking it with a married man.

But besides all those perfectly good reasons, I'd pretty much decided I didn't care whether or not he was married anyway. For one thing, even though I'd never told him, I had remembered exactly who his wife was. And sadly, I was still harboring hatred for her because back in junior high school she'd kicked my butt over this ghetto-fabulous Negro while we were away from home at a church convention. So in some small sick way I enjoyed toying with her husband, because it was my payback of sorts.

But when you seek to harm others you often end up hurting yourself. And, that's exactly what happened when I allowed Mr. Smiley to visit me one morning before we both went to work. That particular morning, Mr. Smiley and I engaged in sexual relations and once again I was left feeling like I'd sold yet another piece of my soul to the devil.

I don't know if it was the fact the sex wasn't that great or I didn't feel that great about engaging in the sex; but, I immediately realized I'd sunk to an all-time low.

Well you've finally done it haven't you? It just doesn't get much lower than sleeping with a married man.

Whatever the case, I made up in my mind that day to cut all ties with Mr. Smiley and stop all my reckless sexual behavior with the quickness. Because I reminded myself that if I didn't know anything else, I did knows *what goes around, does come back around; and, God's word is always true…. eventually you will reap what you sow!*

Oh Lord, please have mercy on me!

Part 4:
Amazing Grace

ଔ ଓ

But because God was so gracious, so very generous, here I am. and I am not about to let his grace go to waste
I Corinthians 15:10 MSG

37
Regulate Your Periods

You'll eliminate some dirty laundry. *Wow,* that was one heck of a ride huh? Well just imagine living it! Ten years ago when I first began the journey of detailing my sexual past, I was completely overwhelmed by the 'what if's.' What if I reveal too much and embarrass my husband, my children and my parents? What if my friends, neighbors, co-workers, and church family read this simply to feast on the juicy details? Or worse, what if only a few people read it? What if episodes from my immoral past come back to haunt me and to tempt me back into a life of reckless indifference?

Thankfully, in the midst of all of the 'what if's' I was reassured by HIM who first instructed me to write the book. And, although my family found some aspects of the book difficult to read, I was not ashamed because the truth had indeed made me free! (John 8:32 KJV) *FINALLY!!!* Nor did I fear the judgments of my friends, neighbors, co-workers, church family or strangers because all the while I wrote, I remained encouraged by the words of my beloved Pastor, Rev. Michael K. Anderson, "we are all X-somethings."

While it's rather obvious that my compulsion was the outward power, control and recreational value I attributed to having sex and the low value I'd internally placed on myself; as you read the sordid details of my past, I hope you paused often and asked

Tymira Mack

yourself, *"What constantly compels or tempts me to compromise my own values?"* For, therein lies YOUR List.

ଓ ☙

Hummm, my spirit tells me that many of you probably didn't have to give much thought toward composing your own List which so desperately needs laundering. The good news is you have the power to control the placement of the period that will punctuate the final item on your laundry list.

- ✓ The last time you will allow yourself to be sexually exploited – **period**.
- ✓ The last time you will settle for being the other woman– **period**.
- ✓ The last time you will allow yourself to remain in a physically or emotionally harmful relationship–**period**.
- ✓ The last time you will snort cocaine; take ecstasy; pop pain pills or mollies; or smoke marijuana, crack or meth – **period**.
- ✓ The last time you will over indulge in alcoholic drinks– **period**.
- ✓ The last time you will intentionally lie to your family and friends, or to yourself, in order to continue living in your current state of madness–**period**.
- ✓ The last time you will beat yourself up over a past you cannot erase or change, no matter how hard you try– **period**.

ଓ ☙

So how do you prepare yourself to effectively place your period and eliminate the possibility of adding new entries on your laundry list?

The List.

First you've got to be brave enough to **ACKNOWLEDGE** that your list even exists. So right now, take a deep breath, be courageous and admit it to yourself out loud (*probably for the first time*); and, then write it down on paper.

Having trouble? Well just to give you an idea, here's a snippet from my laundry list.

<u>Sexual Promiscuity</u> – addicted to the power, control, self-gratification and recreation

- ✓ Bert
- ✓ Chubby
- ✓ Puffy
- ✓ Mickey
- ✓ Shorty
- ✓ Twin
- ✓ Lloyd...

Ok now, you try.

Now there, it's out and surprise, you didn't even disappear in a mystical cloud of smoke, now did you?

ભ ૹ

Next, you've got to **ANALYZE** your list. This may take a few minutes, a few days, a few months, or for some (like me) a few years, even. But one thing is for certain, before you can ever effectively place the period that will signify the end of your list, you're gonna have to face it!

263

As you begin to face your list, take note of such things as:

- ✓ The most surprising revelations.
- ✓ The distinguishable patterns, behaviors or categories that are immediately noticeable.
- ✓ The length of your list.
- ✓ The period of time your list covers.
- ✓ How your list makes you feel deep down inside. Etc . . .

Take my case for example,

Most surprising revelations – acknowledging that my behavior was indeed whorish; and, realizing that the just be-causes far outnumbered the thugs and sort-of-loves

Noticeable categories – types of guys: thugs, scrubs, sort-of-loves and just be-causes

Length of the list – 40 past sexual partners

Period of time covered by the list – 10 years

How my list makes me feel – dirty and deeply ashamed

So you've admitted it, both orally and in writing, and you've begun to analyze it, now what?

ℭ ℬ

Next you must **ABSOLVE** yourself of it. In order to successfully punctuate your list with a period, you must forgive the people, places and things that the list represents; for forgiveness represents power and mastery over the effect that these things have/had on your life.

Since there is no such thing as a magic time machine that would allow you to go back and erase or even rewrite portions of

The List.

your list, why keep kicking yourself for a past that you are absolutely powerless to change?

It is only when you become brave, strong and wise enough to forgive what the contents on the list have represented in your life, that you will be able to forgive yourself for accumulating the list.

The one and only effective means that I found for forgiving myself and absolving myself of the guilt, anger and shame that I harbored concerning my list, was recognizing God's amazing grace.

But because God was so gracious, so very generous, here I am. And I am not about to let his grace go to waste....
I Corinthians 15:10 msg

ର ଛ

And so I encourage you to **ACKNOWLEDGE** your List, **ANALYZE** it, and **ABSOLVE** yourself of the burden of carrying that laundry list by embracing the grace of God, and resolving in your heart not to let his grace go to waste another single day!

Love and the Affair Preview

Turn the page for a peek at

Tymira Mack's

next exciting book

♥ ♥ ♥

*I*n addition to all the love and encouragement I've received from so many of the beautiful people who journeyed with me through THE LIST, I've also been bombarded with two questions: "so how'd you finally turn your life around?" and, "how come you didn't talk about your husband in the book?"

I'll tackle the latter question first since it's the easiest to answer. In actuality, the original title of the book was to be Forty Fakers and A Jewel; with the last chapter focusing on the discovery of my earthly jewel. However, while writing THE LIST, God took me on a journey of self-discovery that surprisingly revealed FAR MORE ugly truths about my sexual past than even I had EXPECTED. By the time I'd made it through the chapters detailing my college years, I knew there was no way I could adequately capture, in one chapter, the complexity of the journey which has yielded the ultimate beauty of the relationship I've found with my husband. To cram all the wonderful, yet sometimes painful, discoveries about myself, marriage and the love I've experienced with him into a few hurried pages – simply for the sake of a happy ending – seemed offensive to me.

Now for the second, and perhaps more difficult question, "How'd I turn my life around?" The truth of the matter is The List ended at a pivotal point in my life because the last sexual relationship I described in the book, my brief adulterous relationship with Mr. Smiley, was the third time in my life I could actually remember being deeply ashamed of my behavior.

Even more than the guilt I felt about being so promiscuous, I felt I had hit rock bottom once I'd allowed myself to sleep with a married man. The tryst literally left me trembling in my boots, because up until then, I'd rationalized that my decision to be a fornicator wasn't anyone else's business...*after all, I wasn't hurting anybody;* except, of course, myself.

Love and the Affair

But even an old MVP hoochie like myself, had just enough Vacation Bible School in me to know dabbling in adultery was a BIG sin. Not counting the fact that like most women, I still dreamed of a day when I would get married; and, I feared if I didn't wake up and gain control over the spirits which were controlling me, there was a real chance that someday I might indeed reap the fruit of the bad seeds I had so carelessly sown!

♥ ♥ ♥

*F*alse pretender, practice what you preach. Mr. Smiley was yet another entry on an ever lengthening list of chocolate brothas who I'd kicked it with over the years in an effort to temporarily fill a void; or teach a Negro a lesson; or both. I don't know which category I got the greatest satisfaction from, category #1, the brothas who gave me a temporary high when fond–*ok lustful*– thoughts of them filled my head and my heart; or category #2 the brothas who afforded me the perverse pleasure of screwing with their heads and occasionally their hearts?

Although my original intent was for Mr. Smiley to fill a void, once I found out the scoundrel had conveniently misled me about being married, he swiftly got booted past category #2 and into a brand new category (for me anyway); category #3 p*ick-a-neg-ga's-pockets.*

I was well on my way to thoroughly enjoying screwing with Mr. Smiley's head and his pockets when I reaped the unexpected bonus pleasure of satisfying a decade's old score; sticking it to his wife as well. *Wow, imagine that, two birds with one stone….Im'ma bad girl!*

At least that's what I tried really hard to convince myself, until the morning I slipped and actually gave Mr. Smiley something to smile about. And, even though I'd been an unrepentant fornicator for over ten years, I had just enough religion in me for my little adulterous liaison with Mr. Smiley to screw with my own head and literally leave me trembling in my boots.

Oh snap, did I just get caught in my own deceitful snare?

Ahhhh hello? Girl you really did it this time! How in the heck can you justify getting down with another sista's husband? You crossed the line for real, for real this time!

How in the world could you let yourself get down with Mr. Smiley like that? After all, it was supposed to be JUST another game. Teach 'em a lesson and pick his pockets for lying about being married. REMEMBER? Him pickin' the pu'nanny was definitely not part of the game plan!

Damn-It! You just officially graduated from being a fornicator to becoming a card-carrying adulterer! Damn, Damn, Damn!

Ok but technically, he's the one that's married. So he's the one who committed adultery....I just had sex, right? So I'm still just a fornicator; HE's the adulterer.

Ugggh, this did not just happen. Violation of another one of the big 10; and for what, 'cause the sex wasn't even that damn good...!?!?

Lorrrrd whhhhhy can't I just resist???

♥ ♥ ♥

Although in my past I've more often than not ignored my inner voice, this time even I couldn't deny how right it was about the situation with Mr. Smiley. And when I finally accepted the fact I wasn't strong enough to kick the habit on my own, I once again decided to devote myself to getting good religion.

I'm still not totally sure whether my new resolve to become religious back then was because I was truly repentant about my tryst with Mr. Smiley, or rather the fact I was about to lose Aayden, my best friend, hanging partner, and original sister in crime.

Love and the Affair

I c'aint believe she done up and decided to get married on me. And got the nerve to let Mr. Johnny Come Lately drag her halfway across the country? I really hate her, no him, no both of them!

Fortunately, my brief period of player hating Ayden's pending nuptials was cut short when the church I'd grown up in decided to oust the pastor we'd had for umpteen years. Considering the fact that Black Baptist churches had been perpetrating such travesties for years, this ousting wasn't really front page news, until the Deacon Board, in all their infinite wisdom, decided to bring in an un-married, thirty-something, young preacher to lead our flock.

Now I know what you're thinking. *Hummmm, that situation is right up her freaky alley.* But, I had enough religion in me to know sleeping with a married man, if only once, was a one-way ticket straight to hell; so even in my Hoochie Hay Day I had just enough scruples not to set my freaky sights on the man of God!

Instead, what really excited me about the new preacher man was I figured… *if he can be young and unmarried and still live a chaste life, then gosh darn it, there's still hope for me.*

So clinging to that tiny ray of hope, I thrust myself 100% toward giving the whole religion and celibacy lifestyle a chance. In fact, I'd become so gung-ho about walking the straight and narrow, that in addition to regular church attendance, I even began going back to Sunday School; something I hadn't done since high school when I'd shamefully allowed myself to get knocked up while serving as the Sunday School's Junior Superintendent.

Fortunately for me, Sunday School had changed a lot. No longer was it being taught by the old sisters who had one foot in the grave; and, either had no clue about the temptations us young people faced on a daily basis, or rather forgot about the times when they were young and use to drop it like it was hot.

Much to my pleasant surprise, the new pastor had reinvigorated our Sunday School and had even chosen to teach

271

the young adult, age 18 – 30ish, class himself. The first Sunday I attended, I remember being surprised at just how many young adult women were all up in Sunday School. *Hummmm I really must have been AWOL for a while. Since when did all these twenty-somethin's join our little church?* Ahhhh hello? That should have been my first clue.

One would think I would have found comfort in the fact there were lots of other young ladies in my age category who were also seeking the Lord. But never being one for getting along with multiple females; the truth is I wasn't real excited about hanging out with a bunch of strange women, whether we were all up in the church or not.

Thankfully, the Sunday School class wasn't dull, which made it a lot easier for me to grin and bear the initial uneasiness of being surrounded by a bunch of females. Plus, our young pastor was really humorous, in a dry, old-fashioned sort of way; and, he always tried to relate each lesson to the contemporary issues that us twenty and thirty–something's were facing. So even though I hadn't become brave enough to ask questions about the issues I was struggling with, I was still learning a lot.

Hummmm, this religion thing may not be that bad after all. Hopefully he'll get around to addressing the sex stuff sooner or later. 'Cause if I bring up the subject first, then everybody will know that Mrs. Ophelia–Sunday School Superintendent, Prayer Warrior, School Teacher, Upstanding Citizen Extraordinaire's–baby daughter ain't been living right. Dang hommie......when are we gonna talk about sexual sin? Man a sista ain't got but so much will power!

♥ ♥ ♥

Then one day, I got an unexpected benefit from attending Sunday School; I actually began to make friends with a group of girls in the class. The three girls had grown up in the Bahamas and had recently come to the States to go to school. They were really cool; all of them were extremely friendly; and, one was especially quick witted. But perhaps the strongest trait I sensed about them was their incredible work ethic.

I don't know if it was the fact I was lonely for female friendship, since Aayden had gotten married and moved away, or the fact my new Bahamian friends had vivacious spirits that were simply infectious; but, for the first time since my college sorority days, I actually started hanging out with a group of females again. And, even though we all had busy work schedules, we spent what little off time we had in common hanging out and partying hard.

Up until that point in my life I thought Aayden and I had the inside scoop on all the South Florida Hot Spots, but after hanging with my Bahamian buddies for a couple of weeks, I realized when it came to partying in Miami, I only knew half the story. It wasn't until they introduced me to the world of Caribbean clubs and hole in the wall neighborhood bars, that I really learned what it was to get my party on. Unbelievably, even my rhythm challenged self couldn't help but get caught up in the heat, haze and carefree vibe of such clubs as the Golden Rocks somewhere near Northwest 119th Street.

Besides the masses of people, the alcohol and the infectious dance music, what I really liked most about those clubs was the total anonymity I enjoyed while I was there. Up in those clubs no one knew, or even cared, that in less than one month, I'd be completing my 1-year management internship program; that I was slated to begin a coveted Jr. Budget Analyst position with the largest Metropolitan Local Government in Florida; or, that I'd just inherited 1-point-something billion dollars' worth of budgetary responsibility for multiple capital projects throughout Miami-Dade County.

Nope, up in those clubs I could lose my 9-to-5 persona and be totally free to let my hair down, hike up my miniskirts, and party, rub-a-dub and wind-n-grind with all sorts of strangers until the clubs closed at 5 am.

Unfortunately, what started out as innocent fun, began leading me right back down the path I was so hell-bent on leaving behind. *But let's face it, how many weekends can you spend wearing revealing clothing and dancing suggestively to explicit music before you compromise your values?*

Although I had done a whole lot of dirty dancing over the couple of months I'd started hanging out in the Caribbean clubs, I hadn't yet given into the temptation of sex...until I got some news that turned my world completely upside down.

♥ ♥ ♥

On one of the rare Saturday afternoons one of my girls had a day off, I ended up over her house fully expecting to plan which club we'd be hitting later on that night. But when I got there I could immediately sense something wasn't right. To this day, I almost wish I hadn't pushed her into opening up, 'cause the story that unfolded sent me straight back to square one.

My friend started out by telling me, "Pastor stop' by here today."

"For real?" He was always checking on the members of our church, so it didn't seem strange to me. "So what? Was he just checking up on ya'll?"

"I guess, but I was home by myself. What-cha-call-it was still at work."

"Oh," I mumbled still wondering why she just didn't seem to be herself.

"Ummmm, you know Pastor tried to ummmm…" she hesitated as she focused intently on picking the cuticles around her fingernails.

I knew something was wrong because I'd never seen my friend be so sullen. After a few minutes of silence and some reassurance from me, my friend went on to tell me our Pastor had tried to hit on her.

"No girl! Stop lying," I insisted, but I could tell by the distraught look on her normally jovial face that she wasn't kidding.

"I'm lost," I admitted. "So what did you do?" I asked out of curiosity.

She went on to tell me a long story about how she'd rejected his advances, and how our normally mild mannered and dry-humored pastor had left her house in an angry rage. At this point I was just about speechless.

"I'm really tripping," I mumbled.

"Yeah girl, but I'm not the first he's tried to get fresh with."

"Say whaaaat?" I squealed with my mouth gapped open.

"No girl, make it so bad, he's already been sleeping with about four or five of the girls in our Sunday School Class."

"Come again?" I asked.

She then went on to name a list of young women who, as I began to think about it, had each slowly, but surely begun to disappear from our church.

"Say what? You're lying girl," I insisted, because my mind just wasn't ready to process the news.

I was totally devastated by this revelation. After all, I'd allowed this man to baptize me, I'd submitted myself under his leadership and authority, and in essence, I'd basically put all my faith and trust in following this professed man of God.

Well I'll be damned; I should have known it was too good to be true, I began telling myself over and over.

Shucks, if the preacher-man don't have enough will power to keep IT in his pants and he's all tied up in the Word, then surely there's no hope for a struggling ex-hoochie like me!

275

About the Author

Once an extreme introvert, South Florida native Tymira Mack began writing short stories in elementary school and penned her first play while still a middle schooler. Having discovered her powerfully relevant voice as a young adult, Tymira's books, teachings and inspiring seminars have allowed her to penetrate the hurts, hearts and hopes of several generations. In her signature bold, transparent, honest and witty style, Tymira has excitedly accepted the call to teach teens to value their bodies; to encourage women to forgive themselves for past indiscretions; and, to inspire people to find wholeness through faith in God. Tymira continues to write, serve and inspire through her commitment to Positive Choices Community Empowerment Corporation, a non-profit organization she founded in 2003. She is also a blessed wife and the mother of three.

℘ ♥ ℘

Word-of-mouth is crucial for any author to succeed! If you enjoyed The List, please leave a review on Amazon, post it on Facebook, Tweet a blurb or Instagram a pic of the cover.

A review of a simple sentence or two on Amazon, an IG pic, a Facebook share, a Tweet or a Snapchat would make all the difference in the world... and would be very much appreciated.

Blessings & thanks for your support!

— Tymira Mack